THE SURVIVOR

THE SURVIVOR

Families of Honor, Book Three

S<small>HELLEY</small> S<small>HEPARD</small> G<small>RAY</small>

A<small>VON</small>

INSPIRE

An Imprint of HarperCollins*Publishers*

If you're a survivor, this book is for you.

THE SURVIVOR. Copyright © 2011 by Shelley Shepard Gray. Excerpt from *Christmas in Sugarcreek* © 2011 by Shelley Shepard Gray. All rights reserved. Printed in the United States of America. No part of this book may be used or reproduced in any manner whatsoever without written permission except in the case of brief quotations embodied in critical articles and reviews. For information address HarperCollins Publishers, 10 East 53rd Street, New York, NY 10022.

HarperCollins books may be purchased for educational, business, or sales promotional use. For information please write: Special Markets Department, HarperCollins Publishers, 10 East 53rd Street, New York, NY 10022.

FIRST EDITION

Library of Congress Cataloging-in-Publication Data has been applied for.

ISBN 978-0-06-202063-5

11 12 13 14 15   OV/RRD   10 9 8 7 6 5 4 3 2 1

I'm afraid that maybe when I come that you will be different from the way I want you to be, and that I'll be different from the way you want me to be. I'm afraid that there might be fighting, obsession, losing your temper, competitive opposition, back-stabbing, gossip, conceit, and disorderly conduct.

~2 Corinthians 12:20

We value the light more fully after we've come through the darkness.

Amish Proverb

Chapter 1

Finally, Mattie Lapp had Graham Weaver trapped. For most of their visit to the hospital, she'd been trying to speak privately with him. But every time she'd found her nerve, something would happen. Either she would get called away for one more blood test, or Graham would be busy chatting with one of the *Englischers* in the waiting room.

As the hours passed, she'd bite her tongue and bide her time. Not very patiently, however. She'd always secretly thought patience was somewhat overvalued.

Now was her chance.

At the moment, she and Graham were the only two people on the elevator at the Geauga County Hospital. As the elevator doors closed, Mattie knew she had only mere seconds before they would reach the ground level. Only seconds to speak her mind.

Clearing her throat to get his attention, she said, "Graham, wouldja do something for me?"

Though he'd been standing in front of the doors and watching the numbers blink overhead, Graham turned to her with his usual understanding smile. "Of course. Anything."

Nervously, she glanced at the blinking number. Nine.

The elevator stopped. The doors opened. Her breath caught. This had been the very worst of ideas!

Maybe she'd get a reprieve?

Nee. No one entered. The Lord was obviously telling her it was now or never. As the doors closed with a whoosh, she blurted, "Graham, it's like this. I need you to help me find a husband."

In a flash, his kind expression turned dark and stormy. "Mattie, the things you think of. Why in the world would I want to do that?"

Ach! This was a terribly bad idea. But now that she'd said it, she had to follow through. "I don't want to be alone anymore. I want a man of my own," she said in desperation. Felt herself blush at her poor explanation. Honestly, it sounded as if she wanted a puppy, not a husband.

Graham leaned against the wall. Crossed his well-built arms over his terribly solid chest. "Why?" he asked. His voice was hard now.

The elevator stopped at the third floor. "I'll explain later. Another time," she blurted as she stepped backward and waited for the elevator doors to open and allow people inside.

Except they did not.

The doors didn't open, that was.

Instead, the overhead light started blinking, blanketing them in pitch-blackness every other second. Without thinking, she stepped closer to Graham. Comforted by his presence, she searched his face. Looking for answers.

For a moment, true worry appeared in his eyes before he stood straighter and gently reached out and clasped her shoulder. "S'okay, Mattie," he murmured. "I'm sure this is just a temporary thing."

Of course, his first thought was to reassure her. He'd always been that type of friend.

"I wonder what is going on?" What was she asking, really? Was she concerned about the doors not opening . . . or what was finally happening between them?

"I don't know," he murmured, this time in Pennsylvania Dutch. That was the only sign that maybe he wasn't as calm about their situation as he wanted her to believe.

Mattie pivoted and glared at the stark metal doors. Though it had only been a few seconds, already their enclosure felt confining. So much like the MRI machine that the technicians used to look for cancer. The air felt thick. Too thick.

"I hope the doors open soon," she said. "I don't know what we'll do if they don't."

Behind her, he reached out and raised his other hand to her shoulder, gently squeezing. Reassuring. "They will. You just need patience. A bit more patience in everything," he murmured under his breath.

But she still heard it. Turning again, she faced him. "What's that supposed to mean?"

"You just asked me to help you find a man," he pointed out, none too kindly. "Like . . . like I was some kind of courting service for Amish women."

"That's not fair. I only asked because you work at the garage door factory now. And there's lots of Amish men there . . ."

"Who I would want to start trying to match you with?" His voice was condescending. And . . . a bit hurt?

Well, she was hurt, too. And confused. As the lights continued to flash, she watched him jab at the glowing buttons. "Graham, why are you so upset with me? Is it because I want to find someone? Because I want to get married one day soon? Because I want to have a life like the rest of our friends?" As she said the last words, Mattie heard the whine in her voice and mentally winced. She didn't want to sound so pitiful. But at the moment, she also couldn't help how desperate she was feeling.

With a jerk, Graham turned from the button panel. "I'm not upset about your dreams."

Dreams. Yes, that was one way of putting it, wasn't it? She had dreams that might never amount to anything. Ruthlessly, she pushed the bitter thoughts away.

Fingering her black apron covering her violet dress, she said, "If you're not upset . . . would you? . . . Would you help me?"

"Not now." He turned from her and started punching buttons. Again. As if the doors would suddenly open because of his fingertip on the right button!

Though she wanted to talk more, she found herself hoping his efforts would be fruitful.

But of course they were not.

Why would they?

These days, it seemed as if nothing was ever easy. After all, hadn't she been diagnosed with cancer at twenty-one and not only endured a mastectomy, but lost all her hair and a good portion of her weight, too . . . all while her friends were going about their lives? Finding love and planning weddings?

Eager to get out of their prison, she pointed to a red knob to the right of the doors. "Should I pull this? Pull the alarm?"

"Pull it, if you want."

His voice was still cool. Unused to that tone, she reached out to him again. "Graham, please don't be upset with me. After all, you have Jenna."

"You know things with Jenna and I didn't work out."

"Well, I'd like a chance for a relationship. All I want is for you to talk to some of the men you are working with and see if you think one of them would be a *gut* match for me. It makes perfect sense."

"Mattie, I'm not meant to be your personal dating service."

Oh, but Graham always knew the perfect sarcastic quip to make her feel ridiculous. Beyond discouraged, Mattie shrank from his glare. Pulled at her collar. Though she was sure it was only her imagination, already the confines of the elevator felt warmer. Too warm.

After a long look, he stepped closer. Wrapped an arm around her shoulders and pulled her close. Just like he had when she was so, so sick from the chemotherapy drugs. Leaning toward him, she rested her cheek on his shoulder.

He cuddled her closer. Just like he usually did when she was ill. But no, this felt different. There was more tension between them.

More energy.

"Graham?" she whispered, moving so she could see his eyes under the brim of his straw hat.

He was staring at her. His lips were slightly parted, as if all his words were frozen inside of him. Just like hers suddenly were.

Slowly his head lowered. Realizing what was about to happen, her pulse quickened. She raised her chin. Suddenly, everything felt all right.

Was this what she'd been wanting, but hadn't even realized?

Ding!

They sprang apart. Dropped their hands just as the elevator door opened with a cloying jerk.

Air rushed forward, cooling Mattie's cheeks.

"You two all right?" asked a man in a light blue cotton shirt with the name Tom embroidered on the pocket. Holding the metal door open, he waited for them to exit. "We've been worried."

"We are fine," Graham answered. "What happened?"

Tom shrugged his shoulders. "Who knows? Everything around here runs like clockwork for days, then suddenly it all falls apart!" He rolled his eyes as Mattie stepped out of the elevator.

Weakly, she smiled. "It's been one of those days for me, too."

Beside her, Graham grunted. "You ready, Mattie? We should probably make sure Charlie is still outside waiting for us."

"Of course," she replied, slowly realizing that nothing was going to ever be the same between them again.

She didn't know whether to be happy or cry. She settled for silent.

It had taken them double the usual time to get back to Jacob's Crossing and Graham wasn't happy about it.

"You know how the traffic is this time of day—bad and worse!" Charlie, their English driver, called out good-naturedly from the front seat. "Nothing we can do about it."

Back in the hospital elevator, it had taken everything Graham had not to lash out at Mattie, to tell her that he had no intention of finding her a man. Most especially when he was standing right there practically, pathetically, volunteering for the job!

But she hadn't seen that. No. Impatient, strong, passionate Mattie had only seen what she wanted to see: Her best friend.

It was a label he had never wanted, nor asked for.

Over the past year, he'd gone from waiting for her to return his feelings to coming to terms with the fact that she was in no hurry for love or relationships. Discouraged, he'd courted Jenna for a bit, but it had never felt right.

Jenna, for all her sparkle and beauty, was no Mattie.

After the fourth or fifth time they'd gone out, it had been obvious to them both that nothing romantic was going to happen between them.

He'd resigned himself to waiting a few more years for Mattie to get back to the person she was. To one day be ready for love again.

But instead of looking at him, she was eager for someone new.

With haste, he got out of Charlie's van and strode inside. He would change clothes, then go straight out to the barn and see how he could help Calvin.

Graham was so tense, he was half hoping Calvin would set him to work chopping wood. Yes, chopping for an hour or two—or *four*—would suit him fine.

Grabbing the banister, he circled the wood and strode up the first two steps.

"Graham?" his mother called out. Her voice was high-pitched and strained. "Could you come in here for a moment?"

Abruptly, he turned around and walked to the kitchen. "Mamm, can this wait? I'm hoping to join Calvin—" He skidded to a stop as he saw that his mother wasn't alone. "Jenna?"

"Hello, Graham." She sniffed. Her face was splotchy. Obviously she'd been crying. She met his gaze, then looked hastily away.

For a split second, his heart softened, remembering how much he'd wanted to like her. "What are you doing here?" he asked gently. Perhaps her mother was sick? Or one of her brothers or sisters? She did have a mighty large family.

"Is everything all right?"

Jenna shook her head.

Next to Jenna, his sister-in-law Lucy sent him a glare bristling with contempt. "It seems she got tired of waiting for you to pay her a call."

"What?" He hadn't called on Jenna in more than a month. He looked to his mother for clarification. Surely she would give him an answer? "Jenna, what is all this about? And if you came to visit with me, why are you crying here with my mother?"

At the mention of her name, his mother met his gaze. But instead of giving him a sign that all was fine, she looked wary. "Perhaps you should sit down, Graham," she said after a pause. "It seems we have a lot to talk about."

He took a ladderback chair, but his already strained patience was waning fast. After thinking about Mattie with a new man for the last hour, he felt ready to break something. "Can we make this quick? I really do need to go out to the fields and help Calvin."

Lucy shook her head in dismay. "Honestly, Graham, where is your heart?"

Tired of being the one person in the room who was in the dark, he looked directly at their guest. "Jenna, why are you here? What has you so upset . . . and why does it concern me?"

After taking a deep breath, she finally answered. "I'm here because I'm pregnant."

Stunned, he stared at her in wonder. He had thought he had been the only one to court her lately. She'd seemed so eager for his attentions, too. So eager, that he'd actually felt terrible when he'd told her that it was obvious they didn't suit.

Boy, had he been fooled!

However, he still didn't understand why the three of them were looking at him with such varying degrees of discomfort and dismay.

"Why does that concern me?"

Jenna finally raised her head. "Because the babe is yours, of course."

Graham stilled, then abruptly got to his feet. *"Nee—"*

His mother held up a hand. "Graham, you sit back down. Right this minute." When he complied, she said, "Now, tell me. How could you dishonor her like that?"

"I haven't *dishonored* anyone." Too angry and confused to sit on the sofa like an obedient child, he got to his feet again, shaking off his mother's restraining hand. "What have you been telling them?"

Jenna bit her lip. Darted a glance his way, then looked directly at the floor. "Everything."

"Obviously not." Still feeling his sister-in-law's piercing gaze and his mother's confused expression, he turned from all of them and paced. "Jenna, I don't know who you were keeping company with, but we both know that the babe you're carrying is certainly not mine."

"There's been no one else," Jenna said, her eyes wide. Too wide. "There's been no one but you."

Her words were so outlandish, and so very *wrong*, he felt his world tilt. Reaching for the back of the couch, he gripped the soft cushion for support. "You know that's a lie."

But instead of replying, twin tears rolled down Jenna's cheeks. Making her look even more delicate.

Lucy reached over and took Jenna's hand and squeezed gently.

Next to him, his mother stiffened. "Graham?" she whispered. "Graham, sometimes it's necessary to face our problems—"

"*Jah* . . . but this ain't my problem."

Jenna flinched at his tone and hid her head against Lucy's shoulder.

Lucy wrapped her arms around Jenna and glared at him. "You need to make this right, Graham."

Graham backed away, feeling like he'd walked into the wrong house. Into the wrong life.

Because he and the Lord knew the truth. He had never lain with Jenna. He'd never even kissed her! Moreover, he'd never lain with any woman—had never desired anyone except for Mattie.

But as Jenna started crying harder, as Lucy looked at him with bitter contempt, and as his mother gazed at him with pure disappointment, Graham knew the awful truth: At the moment, what he knew to be true didn't really matter at all.

Chapter Two

John Weaver was finding out fast that some decisions only made life more complicated. Take the last six months, for example. Just half a year ago, he'd been living in Indianapolis and working at a tire distributor. For twenty years, he'd been reasonably happy and had a large circle of friends.

If, at times, he thought about his family, and how much he missed being a part of their lives, he pushed those worries away. After all, he'd known when he turned from his faith and became English that that would happen.

But then last spring his nephew Calvin had come to visit, with his little sister Katie in tow.

And everything had changed.

After one sleepless night, he'd made an impulsive decision to move back to Jacob's Crossing and reconnect with his family. And that step forward had slowly snowballed into a whole new life. At thirty-eight years old!

At first, he hadn't intended to do more than visit for a while. Then he met Amos at the Kaffi Haus and became a part owner. He moved in above the place and bought a secondhand set of dishes and pots and pans.

Before long, he'd started going to dinner at his sister-in-law's house once a week. Though he'd always loved his brother Jacob's family, he soon got to know them as individuals. Little by little he became intertwined in their lives.

All the roots he'd thought he'd severed sprang to life again, digging in with an enthusiasm that took even him off guard. After twenty years, he suddenly felt like he belonged. Maybe he belonged now more than he ever had.

Yes, so much had happened—all just from that first, sudden decision. God had been very busy with him, that was for sure.

All of these things he might have seen coming. Finding a new occupation didn't surprise him. Loving his brother's children didn't, either.

But falling in love had taken him completely by surprise. For a time, he'd been attracted to two women. Jayne Donovan, the librarian. She was vibrant and lovely and joyous. And then there was Mary. Mary, who was Amish and a widow and was struggling to raise her son Abel by herself.

Before he knew it, after much soul-searching, John had made another choice. Against everything he had imagined, he chose Mary. Now he was on his way to finally becoming baptized and embracing his faith, all while working toward developing a stronger bond with both Mary and Abel.

She'd taken to visiting him every morning after Abel went to school, usually sometime around nine or nine thirty. John would be waiting on customers, cleaning tables, making coffee, washing cups and saucers. And then, he'd look up and there she would be. Making his heart warm.

Just like today. She entered the restaurant precisely at nine fifteen, looking as lovely and nearly untouchable as ever. He sought to welcome her with a smile. "You're here early."

Her pale green eyes warmed, looking the color of stormy waters on Lake Superior for a moment before she blinked. "For some reason, Abel wanted to go to school early today."

He chuckled. Already he was starting to realize that Abel was not the type of boy to ever want to spend more hours studying than necessary. "Perhaps there was a test or a project due?"

She shrugged, revealing the dimple that had stolen his heart. "We can always hope, *jah*?" Her eyes twinkled. "Or perhaps there was a girl. That seems far more likely."

At twelve? He'd been a restless teen, but even he hadn't been chafing at the restrictions in his life at age twelve. "He's a bit young for that, don't you think?"

"I don't know. He's twelve in years, but sometimes I think he's far older in experiences. Losing his father made him grow up faster than others."

"I know." He poured her a cup of coffee and carried

it out to her usual spot. Mary liked to sit on the farthest stool at the counter. Close to him, yet out of the way of the other customers.

She took the cup with a grateful smile, circling her hands around the circumference for warmth.

"So, can I bring you a treat? What would you like?"

"*Nee.* I've decided to put myself on a donut diet." When he looked at her in confusion, she grinned. "John, a woman can certainly have too many glazed donuts! If I don't stop eating them, I'll most likely turn as round as one."

John looked her over, not even attempting to hide his appreciation. "I don't think you have to worry about the calories none."

"I will if I'm not careful." She sipped her coffee.

He thought he heard maybe a hint of something new in her voice. Was it wariness? Trepidation?

To his surprise, he felt a knot of fear form inside him. Here, for months, he'd been debating about a future with Mary. With the Amish community. Trying to determine where his future lay, where he fit in. But perhaps she'd already made that choice?

"Does this mean you aren't going to stop by anymore?" he asked, hating the stress he heard in his voice.

"All it means is that I won't be eating as many donuts, John." Tilting her head down, she smiled. "But I think we both know the treats aren't the reason I come here, anyway."

"Oh. Are we being honest now?" Because they were the only two in the restaurant, he took the stool next to her and leaned his elbows on the Formica counter.

She swiveled to face him. "Perhaps it's time, *jah?*"

"I would miss you if you never came back." Suddenly feeling like he'd admitted too much, he added, "I'd miss Abel, too."

"I would miss you, too. And so would Abel."

Eyeing her again, John realized how much she'd come to mean to him. He'd begun to hope he could ease the faint lines of worry around her eyes. Imagined cradling her in his arms, holding her close. Comforting her. Loving her.

"Mary, you tempt me to join the church," he blurted. Her eyes widened. Though he regretted the timing and place of his declaration, with some surprise, John realized he wasn't sorry about his words.

"You would really do that? Without regrets?" she asked.

That was the crux of it, wasn't it? Making decisions without regrets was something he struggled with.

He paused, not wanting to say the wrong thing. "If I thought I had a chance with you."

"And a chance with me is what you want?"

"Yes. I mean, I think so," he amended. He felt bad that his words weren't more flowery. But perhaps the two of them were beyond pretty words. If she wanted honesty, he could be very honest. Heartbreakingly honest.

Her eyes widened as a flicker of suspicion entered her gaze. Good. Now she knew how it felt to lay out a heart and still not be sure how you stood. "When do you think you will know?"

"When I get to know you better."

She sipped her coffee again, gazed at him, then finally

spoke. "Would you care to have supper with Abel and me on Monday evening?"

"I would." He dug into his pockets and then handed her a scrap sheet of paper and pushed it her way. "Write down your address and I'll be there."

Without looking at him, she carefully wrote down her address and passed it back to him. "We eat at six. Is that acceptable?"

"Six is fine. *Danke.*"

Moments later, she left. Bemused, John picked up her mug and carried it to the sink, replaying their conversation. Well, he'd certainly bared his heart to Mary, that was true.

As he turned on the faucet, he realized something else. While he'd been admitting all his feelings, she hadn't revealed any of her own.

An hour before supper, Calvin entered Graham's room without pausing to knock. "What is this about Jenna and a baby?"

Graham, comfortably sprawled across his mattress, opened one eye. "That was yesterday's news. I'm surprised you didn't rush over here as soon as you heard, the bishop in tow."

Calvin paused. "I thought I'd give you some time to figure out things before I planned the wedding."

"Big of you." Calvin was always making plans and rushing forward. Embracing his role as the eldest brother. As the caretaker of them all.

"When I spoke to Lucy, she said everyone was pretty upset when Jenna left."

"That's one way of putting it, I suppose," he replied, recalling the way they'd all parted. Jenna had been moving like she was asleep on her feet, Lucy had been full of condemnation and anger, and his mother's movements had been so stiff, she'd looked like she was about to snap in two.

It had also been obvious that not a one of them had believed him.

Still weary, Graham closed that eye again. His head was pounding and he'd already been questioned enough by their mother and Lucy. He was in no hurry for another interrogation.

"Graham, sit up and talk to me. We need to figure things out."

"Not much to figure out, *bruder*."

Calvin stepped forward and closed the door behind him. "Lying in bed with your eyes closed makes no sense as well. You should be doing something to resolve this matter."

Because Graham knew that Calvin wouldn't leave him alone until he had his say, he sat up and moved to the edge of the bed. "This matter?" he repeated softly. "That is one way to describe the bed of lies Jenna has sown. There's not much I can do to resolve this *matter* when she is lying. I know the truth, Calvin."

"*Mudder* is awfully upset."

Graham winced. He hated that his mother was suffering because of the scene in their kitchen. But even more, he hated his brother's belligerent, holier-than-thou tone.

"I'm sorry Mamm is upset, but I'm not the cause of her grief. Calvin, I haven't done anything wrong."

"Graham, why would Jenna make up such a story if she didn't believe it to be true?"

"That's the point, Calvin," he retorted as he faced his eldest brother. "I don't have any idea of why Jenna would say any of it. I hardly knew her."

Tired of talking in circles—and of defending himself—Graham stood and began to pace. "You must believe me, Calvin. I never even kissed her. If Jenna is indeed with child, it most definitely isn't mine."

Calvin eyed him thoughtfully. "You're speaking the truth, aren't you? You really are taken by surprise."

"Of course." Hurt and ill at ease, he said, "What kind of man do you think I am? How could you even think that I would have that kind of relationship with Jenna Yoder, out of wedlock, without even love?"

Calvin looked away. "People rush . . ."

"People *who are in love* rush," Graham interrupted. "But that wasn't Jenna and me. We only spent some time together."

Calvin relaxed. Pulling out Graham's heavy oak chair from his desk, he sat. "All right, then."

But now that he was all spun up, Graham went on the offensive. Crossing his arms in front of his chest, he looked down at his brother. "How could you accuse me of such things, anyway? I thought you believed in me. I thought you knew what kind of person I am."

"I guess I thought you were the kind of man who was human. Who made mistakes."

Graham was finally realizing that Calvin hadn't been upset about his actions, only about the lies he'd assumed Graham had spoken.

That made him feel a little better, and encouraged him to soften his tone and try to get him to understand. "Calvin, I've made plenty of mistakes in my life. But not like that . . ." Sharing a look with his brother, he added, "And definitely not with Jenna."

Calvin propped one boot on his opposite knee. "All right, all right . . . I believe you. Completely. But I wonder how I can convince Lucy of your words. She is awfully worried about Jenna."

"Why would you have to convince her of anything? I'm family. Jenna certainly isn't."

"That is true, but she doesn't always see things that way." Looking off into the distance, he added, "See, Lucy doesn't think the best of men. She worries about things that happen behind closed doors. Things no one will talk about . . ." His voice drifted off before looking at Graham again. "But you know that, of course." With a sigh, he got to his feet. "Don't worry, I'll think of something."

Graham decided not to comment. After all, there was nothing he could do to change Lucy's opinion of him. Not if she would think the worst and not listen to his side.

"I hope Jenna will stop blaming me. Do you think she will?"

"I don't know. If she is making up lies about you, hoping that you'll reach out to her, then she must be terribly desperate."

What Calvin didn't say but what Graham understood

was that they both feared that this was merely the beginning—not the end—of things. "I don't know what I'm
going to do if she starts telling other people these lies."

Calvin swallowed. "People will judge you."

"I know."

After another pause, Calvin stood up. "Mamm said
supper will be ready soon."

"I'll be right down," Graham promised, though he didn't
fancy the idea of sharing a meal with his family across a
tension-filled table.

And when Calvin left, he lay back on his mattress again
and closed his eyes, trying to relax. But then his head started
to pound as a very dark thought filtered through him.

What if Mattie heard of Jenna's rumor? What if she
heard and didn't believe him? What would become of the
two of them, then? Would they be driven apart before
they'd really ever had a chance to begin?

Chapter Three

"Abel, do be careful of the cars," Mary warned. "Some of the drivers don't pay enough attention to the road, they're so busy with their coffee cups and telephones."

"I am careful," he muttered under his breath as he continued to dart forward on the side of the road, barely walking with her at all. Hardly acknowledging her at all.

Mary bit her lip and prayed for God to give her direction. Here they were, walking together like they'd always done for years, but everything felt different. And she couldn't foist the complete blame on Abel's growing pains, neither.

Much of the confusion stemmed from herself.

Yes, more than ever, she felt like she was at a crossroads in her life, and she was completely at a loss.

Of course, it would've been better if she knew what she

wanted for her future. Or if she knew what John Weaver wanted.

Taken off guard by the direction of her thoughts, she swallowed a lump in her throat. When had she begun to care so much about John's feelings for her?

When had you not? a small, secret voice whispered in her ear, reminding her of the things she hoped and dreamed about in the middle of the night.

After all, everything that had been happening was her doing. She'd been the one who had been visiting John Weaver at the Kaffi Haus. She'd been the one who had asked him to spend time with Abel, and to help give him some guidance.

And now she was the one who had invited him to supper on Monday night.

Now it seemed so foolish. Oh, why had she asked him over, anyway? What would everyone say? Even if John was almost a part of the community, he wasn't. Not really.

Looking at her boy, now striding a good five paces in front of her, his back so straight and slim and proud, she bit her lip. What if Abel wasn't happy about this upcoming dinner? What would she do then?

"Abel . . ." she began, knowing that she needed to talk to him about John, and about his feelings for the man. The last thing in the world she wanted was for him to feel slighted or neglected.

"I'm fine walking on the road, Mother."

"Oh, I know that. It's just . . . Well, I was wondering—"

He turned around, interrupting both her thoughts and

her sluggish tongue. "Mamm, do we still have to visit with Aunt Frieda and Uncle Benjamin tonight?"

Glad he was finally looking at her instead of pretending she didn't exist, and glad for the reprieve from her thoughts, she nodded. "Of course. We always go over there once a week."

"Why?"

She didn't know why, exactly. Frieda and Benjamin were Paul's aunt and uncle. She'd clung to the habit after her husband had died because it was all she knew. But now that it was eight years after William's death, she had to admit it did seem a little bit strange. Though Abel liked the older couple well enough, it was becoming obvious that the three of them hadn't developed the close relationship that Mary had once envisioned they would.

And though the couple was terribly kind to her, it had been obvious for some time that they never expected Mary to ever remarry. No, they obviously hoped that she would simply grow older and be reasonably content as her husband's memory faded just a bit more with each passing year.

"Abel, I suppose we keep going because it's a habit," she said at last. "Are you trying to tell me that you'd rather not have supper with them every week?"

"Maybe." Abel kicked a rock, sending it skittering in front of him, kicking up dust. She watched it roll jaggedly, careening this way and that.

Kind of like her life at the moment.

Finally, she caught up with it. Mary paused for a second, debating whether to kick at it, or step over it. A part of her yearned to kick it with the toe of her boot. Kick it hard, just for the simple joy of watching it fly up into the air and land far ahead of Abel.

But most likely he wouldn't know what to think about that. Most likely he wouldn't see her enthusiasm. Only wonder why she was acting childishly.

She left the rock where it was. "I thought you enjoyed being with Aunt Frieda and *Onkle* William. I know you enjoy their dog Skip."

"I like Skip fine."

Well, there was her answer. Making a decision, she said, "I will tell Frieda that we're only going to visit there one Wednesday evening a month. How does that sound?"

"Better." After kicking another rock, Abel added, "I just wish sometimes we did something different."

Now was her chance. "Well, son, soon we will be doing something different." Inserting false merriment in her voice, she added, "We're going to have a guest for supper on Monday evening."

"This coming Monday?"

"*Jah.*"

"Who?" he asked over his shoulder.

"John Weaver."

He stopped. "John from the donut shop?"

"Yes. I, uh, thought it would be nice to have him over. The two of you seemed to enjoy spending time together."

"But he's English."

"I know." Of course she also knew that he was considering adopting their ways. Or, perhaps, reacquainting himself with their ways?

"Why is he coming?" he asked, his voice full of suspicion.

"Because, child, I asked him to. That is reason enough." Now that they were side by side again, she patted his arm.

"Why? Is it because of me?" Distrust flared in his eyes, hot and suspicious. "Are you still worried about me? That's why you had me work with him some, isn't it?"

Her invitation had had nothing to do with Abel, she realized. In her own way, she'd been yearning for something different, too. "It is because John has become a gut friend and I am tired of eating donuts."

"Like that makes sense," Abel muttered. But as they began walking again, Mary noticed that he continued to look at her curiously. As if he didn't quite trust her, as if he wasn't quite sure what to think about this new development. Or how to react.

Well, that was okay with her. She wasn't sure about her relationship with John Weaver, either. And she certainly didn't know how to react around him.

Not at all.

"Have you heard the news?" Corrine asked Mattie after they'd gotten their Trail bologna sandwiches and were sitting side by side at a table eating lunch after church services at the Millers.

Mattie took a listless bite of her sandwich. Even though she was done with her chemotherapy treatments, nothing tasted all that appetizing. She ate now to try and gain weight and to keep her health. Hardly ever did she find enjoyment in the meals.

At the moment, though, even the silly worries of her

community grated on her nerves. Sometimes she was so tired of people talking about each other and making predictions about their futures.

"What news is that? The news about Abraham's new horse or the Lunds' naughty four-year-old?" she said drily.

Corrine leaned closer. "I'm talking about Jenna Yoder's news, of course."

Feeling a twinge of unease, Mattie put her sandwich back on her plate. Though Graham had told her things were over between him and Jenna, perhaps he'd only been telling her that to spare her feelings.

Resolutely, she prepared herself to hear more wonderful-*gut* news about Graham's past infatuation. "What about her?"

"She's expecting."

Her mouth suddenly feeling dry, she coughed. "Truly?"

"Oh, *jah*. And she has no sweetheart to speak of, you know."

No sweetheart besides Graham. Confusion waged war inside her head as she sought to keep her voice and manner only mildly interested. "Well, I imagine her parents are mighty upset."

"Well, of course they are."

Mattie took another bite of her sandwich, simply to gain another moment or two to coax her emotions back in line. "Who is the father? I haven't heard of her seeing anyone other than Graham."

"People are saying it's Graham," Corrine murmured. "Some are saying that they've been meeting in private, without anyone knowing."

"That hardly makes sense."

"I know. But from what I understand, she's told people the babe is his."

Mattie's hands shook as she tried to process that information. "We're talking about my Graham, right?" When Corrine's eyes widened, Mattie rephrased the question. "I mean, my, uh, neighbor."

"Of course I'm speaking of Graham Weaver." Corrine picked up her sandwich and took a big bite. "The news surprised me, too, it did. I have to tell ya, I've always thought there was something special between you and Graham. I thought one day you two would see past your jokes and friendship and turn things into something more."

Once upon a time, back when she'd been small, Mattie had hoped things between them would turn romantic.

But as the years passed, she'd been more grateful for his friendship. Though sometimes she'd had an uncomfortable stinging sensation when he'd talked about Jenna, she'd pushed that feeling away. After all, she wanted him to be happy; he certainly deserved that.

And then there was that moment in the elevator . . . She pushed the thought aside. Yes, what she needed to do was concentrate on Graham's happiness. And given this news, she needed to get accustomed to the idea that Jenna and Graham would be announcing their intentions to marry soon.

When they married, all of their fun, easygoing time together would be in the past. As they'd both assumed it would.

But she wasn't ready to share all that with Corrine.

And, to her surprise, she also wasn't ready to picture Graham and Jenna together forever. "Perhaps the rumor isn't true," she said quickly. "You know how people like to talk."

"People do talk. But this news is true. Jenna is with child."

"No. I mean, it's not possible that her sweetheart is Graham."

"I know that might make you upset, but you can't deny the facts. Graham did see Jenna for a while."

Mattie hated that here again gossip and innuendo were taking center stage. "That may be true, but Graham wouldn't . . . I mean, he didn't . . ." Oh, but she was so flustered! Too flustered to even contemplate that he'd been intimate with Jenna. "He's just not like that. And believe me, I know Graham well."

Corrine's eyebrows rose as she picked up a celery stalk and crunched. "You might be right," she said slowly. "After all, I did hear that he said it wasn't his. But why would Jenna make up such a thing?"

"I don't know." After all, there was no reason. In fact, Mattie had never heard of anyone outright lying about their circumstances. In their community, each person took care to be the type of man or woman to be proud of. And though no one was perfect, Mattie and her friends had always tried to act in a respectable manner.

"So you really hadn't heard about the babe?"

"Of course not."

"I just thought, you and Graham are such *gut* friends . . ."

"We are friends, but he's never said a word to me about Jenna except that he wasn't seeing her anymore."

Of course, that might have been because he'd known Mattie was a tiny bit jealous of the woman.

Corrine nodded. "Well, most likely Graham didn't wish to upset you."

Mattie grimaced. That could be true. But either way, she was definitely upset. Scanning the area, she attempted to find the girl they were speaking of. But no matter how hard she looked, she didn't see Jenna's usual navy-colored dress. "Where is Jenna, anyway?"

"Not here." Lowering her voice, Corrine said, "I heard that her parents were so upset with her, they made her move out of their home."

"What?"

"*Jah!* I heard they're terribly upset with her for being so foolish, and at Graham because he hasn't married her yet."

Mattie looked around. She sighed when she finally spotted Graham sitting at a long table with his whole family. But instead of talking a mile a minute like usual, he was sitting morosely. A line had formed between his brows, and he was glaring at his parents.

And with that line, a thin strand of worry began to snake through her. Maybe it was true. Maybe he hadn't been honest with her or about his feelings for Jenna?

"Oh, my. I wonder what Graham is thinking." Shifting her chair, she contemplated getting up and walking over to him. But even from her angle, Mattie could see that he was the focus of everyone's attention. If she walked over, even more tongues would start wagging.

Corrine leaned closer. "I feel sorry for him. Jenna is headstrong. They are going to have a rocky life together."

Yes. He and Jenna were not a good match. "Perhaps they won't marry," she said slowly.

Vegetables done, Corrine picked up a peanut butter cookie. "Of course they have to marry. If they didn't, what would happen to Jenna? She doesn't really have a choice, you know."

No choice. Mattie hated that idea. When she was small, she always thought being older meant a person got to make more decisions.

Now it seemed the opposite was true. Time and again, responsibility and duty necessitated choices. She glanced at the Weaver family once more, but to her surprise, Graham was gone.

And then she sensed his presence near her. Looking to her right, she saw him approach, a determined expression on his face. "Mattie, may we talk for a bit?"

Beside her, Corrine almost choked on her cookie. Everyone else surrounding them stopped talking and eagerly listened for her response. Waiting for more fodder for the gossip mill.

And that was something she wasn't eager to deal with. "I don't think so."

Hurt flashed in his blue eyes. "Why not?"

She felt guilty about hurting his feelings, but she couldn't help herself. Though she'd defended his reputation to Corrine, Mattie wasn't completely sure that he was the innocent party in Jenna's drama. There had to be a grain of truth to her story.

With that in mind, she kept her tone cool and quiet. "I'm not who you should be seen with, Graham."

He crossed his arms over his chest. "You're not, huh?" His voice cooled. "And who do you think I should be seeing instead?"

"Jenna."

"She's not here."

"Perhaps you should go looking for her, then."

The fire in his eyes settled into the dim light of contempt. "So you believe the stories?"

"They are hard to ignore." Feeling like their whole community was still staring at them and soaking up every word like a sponge, Mattie picked up a corner of her sandwich. "I really need to eat," she said.

Looking at her like she was a stranger, Graham stared, then with a shake of his head, wandered off.

"I'm proud of you," Corrine murmured.

"It had to be done," Mattie said with a shrug. Resolutely, she took another bite of her sandwich.

And tried not to gag.

Chapter Four

Now Graham knew his worst fears were realized. Mattie didn't believe him. Even worse, she said she didn't trust him, either. After everything they'd been through, she had the nerve to tell him such things.

Graham felt so hurt and betrayed, he hardly knew where to turn. Not that there were plenty of choices. Everywhere he looked, other people—people he'd known all his life—were watching him without a bit of shame.

Their pointed interest and disregard made him feel like something of an embarrassment. And that was a terribly unfamiliar and unwanted feeling.

Seeking solace, Graham raised his chin and looked across the room, to where his brothers sat. He met Loyal's gaze. Loyal was staring at him stoically, not betraying an inch of what he might be feeling. But all the same, Graham knew.

It was obvious his brother was just as dismayed as he was about the situation he was in, and the lack of support he was receiving from those who knew him best.

When Loyal raised an eyebrow, silently asking if Graham needed him, Graham shook his head in silent reply then walked out the door into the frigid air.

Luckily, no one was congregating around the area. From there, it was only a few quick steps until he got to Beauty and walked her to the street. And then, because she was hooked up to a courting buggy, he clicked the reins and motioned Beauty to increase her pace.

With the wind whipping on his cheeks, he let his anger and frustration fly. "I'll admit it, Lord," he said to the empty sky. "Right now I'm mad at Jenna, at my family, at my community, and at Mattie."

Even just thinking about Mattie made him ache. After everything he'd done for her, after every time he'd dropped everything in order to be by her side, he'd never imagined she would turn on him.

"Why? Why is this happening?" he called out, so loud that Beauty started a bit. Lowering his voice, he continued. "I've tried to be as good as possible. I've tried to be the good brother, the good son, the good friend." He shook his head in wonder. "I've even started working at the factory so as not to interfere with Calvin so much."

To his embarrassment, two tears fell. With a fist, he brushed them off. "But that's not enough, is it? Maybe it's never enough."

Beauty neighed. Bringing him back to the present, and

to the other vehicles on the street. Just in time, he stopped the buggy at the stop sign, and took a deep breath.

All his life, he'd prided himself on shaking off bad things. On never letting uncomfortable situations get to him. But he was beginning to realize that until now his faith and his honor had never really been tested. He'd lived most of his life being sheltered by his older brothers and feeling his parents' unconditional love. Even his father's death hadn't shaken the belief that he was strong enough to bear any burden.

Now Graham realized that he'd been reveling in a false sense of security. When his father passed, his brother Calvin had immediately stepped in to offer comfort and guidance.

Even Mattie's illness had been relatively easy to handle, because all he'd felt he had to do was be strong for her. Now his confidence embarrassed him. Of course it was easy to tell others to be strong when you weren't worried about dying.

It had been easy to hold Mattie and coax her to eat and sleep when he'd never had more than a day's worth of sickness.

Two miles later, his heart still heavy but his resolve stronger, Graham turned right and headed home. "I'm now ready to hold my burdens, Lord," he said. "Even if they hurt. Even if they make me feel weaker than I've ever felt."

And as he said the words, Graham felt the strong hand of the Lord resting on his shoulder. Reassuring him that all would be fine. That one day he would understand why he was going through this dilemma.

"I hope so," he said bitterly. "I hope I hear very soon."

"Jenna, this here is your bedroom. I, uh, hope it will suit you?" Mary rocked back on her feet, staying in the hall but motioning Jenna in.

After a pause, Jenna walked through the doorway. Inside was a twin bed covered with a raspberry-colored quilt. Beside it stood a fine-looking oak bedside table. A rectangular rag rug covered the floor. In the corner stood a wicker rocking chair and an oak table.

It was lovely and Spartan and immaculately clean.

It was also the first room Jenna had ever had to herself. The idea of having so much privacy was a bit disconcerting. Until now, her whole life had been about sharing.

Mary nervously rolled the bottom of her black apron between two fingers. "I hope it will suffice."

"Oh, *jah*." Jenna forced herself to smile. Her awkwardness surely had nothing to do with Mary's hospitality. "This is a lovely room. It is terribly kind of you to allow me to stay here."

"We have the space, and you need a place to stay."

Mary's words were exactly right. But still, Jenna was thankful. "I'm so grateful. *Danke*."

Some of the lines around Mary's mouth smoothed. "I'm glad you like it. I know it's not like your home. But, per-haps—"

"It's *wunderbaar*," Jenna interrupted. Actually, it was far nicer than she was used to. Being the oldest of nine children meant a lifetime of hand-me-downs from relatives. And for making due with mismatched things.

Though it had never really bothered her—she'd never known any different—she could admit to daydreaming about having a room of her very own. If even for a little while.

"Do you want this in here, Mamm?" Abel asked as he came around the corner, lugging in Jenna's suitcase.

Mary straightened a bit. "*Jah.* Set it on the bed."

With a strained expression, Abel scooted by his mother and lumbered past Jenna, then with a heft, he plunked the filled-to-the-brim suitcase on the bed.

In answer, the twin bed squeaked a bit in protest.

"Abel, you should be more careful," Mary chided.

"It was heavy, Mamm." With a scornful expression, Abel looked Jenna over. "What did you have in there, bricks?"

"Abel! Don't be so rude."

His cheeks flushed. But his grumpiness just made Jenna smile. She had five younger brothers, four of whom were in their teenage years. "I'm surprised you caught on to my secret so quickly," she said playfully. "Yes, Abel, I packed my suitcase full of bricks just so you'd complain about carrying it around."

His eyes widened a split second before a grudging smile appeared. "It was no trouble." He flexed one arm. "I'm plenty strong."

"Yes, you are. I appreciate you bringing it in. *Danke.*"

He nodded his welcome before brushing past his mother as he exited the room.

Jenna watched Mary look after Abel with a burst of

fierce longing. With a shake of her head, Mary turned back to Jenna. "I'll let you have some time to get settled, Jenna. If you think of anything you need, please let me know."

"I won't need anything else. I promise. Mary, I just want you to know . . . I'm very grateful to you. I don't know what I would have done if you hadn't offered me a place to stay."

"Now, let's not mention it again. After all, everyone needs a place to live, dear. I'm glad I could help." Gripping her apron again, she paused at the door. "Jenna, are you sure your parents don't want you to stay at home?"

Remembering her father's fierce scowl, his hurtful tone when he commanded her to leave before the end of the week, Jenna shook her head. "I'm certain. I'm no longer welcome at home." She raised her chin. "I've shamed them, you see."

Mary's eyes softened in sympathy. "People say things all the time they wish they could take back. Perhaps when things settle down, they'll reconsider."

Mary's words were sweet, but Jenna knew better. Her parents were good people, but they had ideas that couldn't be changed and rules that they insisted be followed.

She'd known the moment she told them about her pregnancy that there would be no hugs or soft words. "I don't think so. I'm the oldest child, with three younger sisters and five brothers, too. All my life, I've been told that it's my duty to be a role model to them. Unfortunately, I've failed at that."

"We all fail from time to time. It's a difficult thing, to

be an example, I think. It's not hardly fair for you or your siblings, either."

Jenna had never heard anything different, though she did appreciate Mary saying such things. After all, it would be nice to imagine having room for mistakes.

But there was nothing to say, anyway. What was done was done.

Mary fingered the edge of her apron again. "When you're ready, come downstairs. I've made some hot chocolate and homemade marshmallows."

The fake smiles were becoming easier. "That sounds delicious. I'll be downstairs soon."

After Mary left, Jenna closed the door, the sound echoing through the room, making her isolation seem even more pronounced. Almost afraid, she leaned back against the door and looked around the room. So pristine. So big.

"I should count my blessings," she told herself. "I am healthy and I have a bed to sleep in. That's more than I probably deserve."

No, it was *far* more than what she deserved.

The awful truth of what she'd done hit her hard. As memories surged forward, Jenna felt her skin flush with embarrassment. Oh, but she'd done so much wrong.

Almost against her will, memories scattered forward. Tiny snippets of the past six months. Remembering seeing *him* for the very first time. Remembering how tingly she'd gotten just from a simple smile.

Remembering one night when the air was thick and hot and she'd let a few kisses become so much more . . .

Feeling her face heat, Jenna shook her head and forced herself to start thinking of the future instead of the past.

"Jesus, do you think I'll ever be able to atone? Will you, at least, forgive my sins?" she asked the empty room.

Without pausing for an answer, Jenna forced herself to go to the bed and unzip her suitcase. The moment she lifted the top, smells of home surrounded her. Lavender and dust. On the very top was her well-worn chenille robe. Her mother had given it to her two years ago for Christmas. Almost her favorite possession.

Jenna had treasured the store-bought robe. It was so clean and perfect. For a time, it had symbolized everything she'd thought she'd wanted. Hope and choices.

Now it just symbolized everything she'd lost.

Tears pricked her eyes as she carefully hung the robe on one of the hooks by the door. Then, with a determination she'd pulled from deep inside her, Jenna strode back to her suitcase. She needed to unpack and go join Mary downstairs.

But right under the robe was an envelope, stopping her in her tracks. Fingering the envelope, Jenna gulped. The sloppy, crooked penmanship was unmistakable. Only her sister Ruth could never master how to make a cursive *J*.

Sitting on the bed, Jenna opened the envelope, then felt her throat constrict as she read Ruth's words.

Jenna,

I can't believe you're gone. That you've left us! Everyone here is depressed, especially Mamm and Daed, though they are right now acting as if you never existed at all.

I can't believe Graham Weaver is lying to everyone, too, and not even getting into trouble. Two girls I know who've talked to Ella Weaver, Loyal Weaver's wife, say even she is sticking up for him.

It just don't make sense!

Jenna, we have to think of a way to convince Graham to do the right thing and stop shaming you. As soon as he does that, why, no one will even care that you've got a baby on the way!

Then we'd be planning your wedding instead of pretending you didn't exist.

I'll try to write again, but it won't be easy. Mamm sat us all down and said you've done things that we should all be fearful of and that you should be terribly guilty about. And that until you make everything right (marry Graham!) we should do our best to not think of you.

We're not even supposed to speak of you. Ever.

That will be hard, however, because I surely miss you. Lydia has pushed her way into the room and she snores.

Love,
Your sister Ruth

Raising a fist to her mouth, Jenna choked back tears. Never would she have imagined that one bad decision would influence so many others.

Now her sister was suffering, and Graham was . . . embarrassed.

And shamed.

Remembering their last conversation, Jenna bit her lip. When she'd showed up at his house, she had thought he had really liked her. That he would have jumped at the chance to save his reputation and hers, too. Of course, she'd been wrong. Graham wasn't going to reach out to her at all.

Finally, thinking clearly, Jenna knew she didn't blame him. After all, both she and he knew the truth. The baby she carried was certainly not his.

But that knowledge didn't make the whole truth any easier—there was no way she could ever tell who the father was.

Surely no one would ever believe her if she did tell. But even knowing that didn't make what had happened any easier to forget.

"Jenna, are you ready for hot cocoa?"

Jerking to her feet, Jenna pulled open the door. "Yes, Mary. *Danke*. I'll be right there." Closing the door behind her, she left the open suitcase and letter behind her.

At least for the time being.

Chapter Five

Mattie knew she had no choice. From the moment she'd refused Graham's offer to talk with her privately, she'd been besieged by guilt. She might not understand what had happened, she might feel sad about him being with Jenna, but he didn't deserve her cold shoulder. He certainly hadn't deserved to be snubbed in front of just about everyone at the lunch after church.

She'd meant to see him on Monday, but she'd promised her mother that she'd help clean one of the cupboards in their kitchen, sort out old towels, and make fudge. All of that took far longer than she'd anticipated.

But that busy work led to lots of time to let her mind wander. And as she replayed the conversation with Graham in her mind, the awkwardness between them became amplified.

She'd known this morning that the only right thing to do was to visit him and try to smooth things over.

With a determined step, she walked the well-worn path to his house. In the spring and summer, the path was glorious. Vines and other growth decorated the sides, bringing with it the sweet smell of honeysuckle and jasmine.

Now, as winter quickly approached, patches of dirty snow kept company with patches of black dirt and clumps of leftover fallen leaves. The mixture crunched under her boots.

As she passed the snarled vines of the berry patch, she contemplated what to say to Graham. Over and over she practiced various ways to apologize for her rudeness. But even to her mind, all of it seemed far too light and rang of falseness.

They were too good of friends to gloss over past indiscretions.

She was still wondering how to go about saying what was in her heart, all while preparing to hear about his kindled relationship with Jenna when she arrived at his doorstep.

Warily, she knocked on the door and waited.

His little sister Katie opened the door. "Hi, Mattie. Whatcha doing here?"

Obviously, there was going to be no getting away from the truth. "I thought I'd come over and see Graham. Is he here?"

Katie nodded. "Uh-huh. He's over in the barn, looking at the rabbits."

Though she was a bundle of nerves, Mattie smiled.

Everyone knew how much Katie was fascinated by their never-ending rabbit population. It was something of an aggravation for Graham—it always fell to him to explain why they had so many bunnies. And why they couldn't keep them all.

"I'll go out there and see him, then."

"I could go with you—" Katie suggested, just as Lucy stepped forward and held her tiny sister-in-law back.

"No, you could not," she said gently. "You are going to stay here and help me make a potato casserole. Go on, now." When Katie turned and walked back into the kitchen, Lucy lowered her voice. "A word of warning— Graham's not too happy. Not happy with the world . . . or you."

"I expected that. I'll be fine."

"I hope so. I wish—" The scrape of a chair behind her interrupted her thoughts. "I've got to go. But we should talk soon."

"All right." As Lucy closed the door, Mattie made her way toward the barn, picking her steps carefully over the gray gravel and frozen sections of mud.

When she entered the large barn, she spotted Graham immediately. He was kneeling in front of the hutch, an aggravated expression on his face. In the hutch were a black-and-white mother rabbit and three or four bunnies. Normally, she would have knelt down to take a closer look at the baby animals.

But at the moment, she could hardly bring her feet to move. "Hi," she said.

When he looked her way, Mattie noticed his expression

didn't change. If anything, it looked almost blank, like a fresh chalkboard. "Mattie, what brings you here?"

"An apology."

Straightening, he looked at her curiously. "For what?"

"For you know what. I shouldn't have pushed you away at the lunch, and especially not with everyone else looking on. I'm mighty sorry for that."

He stilled, gazed at her for a long moment, then waved his hand in front of him. Just as if he was shooing a fly away. "It was nothing."

Just the fact that he was being so accommodating meant it was definitely something. If he hadn't been upset with her, he would've been teasing her. "I don't know why I didn't want to talk to you," she said, struggling with every word. "I guess I was feeling hurt. It's hard for me to think about you being with Jenna."

Anger flashed in his eyes. "I wasn't with her. At all, Mattie. She's lying. I don't know why, but she is."

A secret part of her felt that he was, indeed, telling the truth. Which, of course, made her feel even worse. She needed to make amends, and quickly. Stepping closer, Mattie lightly touched his arm. "Do you have time to go for a walk now? If so, I'd be happy to walk with you."

His eyebrow rose as she curved her hands around his elbow. "You sure about this?"

"I am. I told you I was sorry, and I came all the way over here to apologize, too. You ought to believe me, Graham."

Almost imperceptibly, his shoulders relaxed, then he glanced at her again. "Now that I'm not so angry, I'm be-

ginning to see why you might not want to be seen with
me. People might talk."

"I wasn't worried about gossip." Struggling with her
roiling emotions, she blurted, "Graham, I was upset about
you and Jenna. I didn't want to think of you two like that."

"And now?"

"And now I realize that I have been terribly foolish.
Come on, Graham. Let's go. If you can leave those bunnies."

Graham chuckled under his breath, an unhappy, deri-
sive sound. "This is a nightmare. I've been found guilty
without ever getting a chance to speak."

"Don't worry. People know you. Things will get better."

"Not without more pain."

"Your faith will help."

By mutual agreement, they kept walking, away from his
house and the barn—back onto the path that their footprints had marked so many times over the years.

Above, dark clouds began to blow in, darkening the November sky. As the silence between them dragged and the
clouds continued to roll in, hanging low, Mattie felt as if
the whole world was closing up on them.

Graham was still terribly angry with her, that much was
evident. As she felt his anger and sadness float over her, his
reaction made her ache. She was so used to his open af-
fection and support; more than anything, she wished she
could take back the past two days and do things differently.

The fanciful thoughts brought a chill to Mattie's spirits,

and to her skin. Glad for her thick cloak, Mattie wrapped her arms around herself. The cancer drugs had left her immune system low, and now she got cold so easily. And sick easily, too.

As a breeze sailed through the valley, she trembled, then glanced at Graham to see if he noticed. Out of habit, she'd become used to Graham always noticing her physical condition.

She'd gotten accustomed to him fussing over her, doing his best to make sure she added layers. She couldn't count the number of times he'd wrapped one of his knit scarves around her neck, or slipped a warm arm around her shoulders.

But today he was oblivious to the drop in temperature and how it affected her. Or perhaps he didn't care.

She supposed she didn't blame him. But it was time to discuss things before they had to turn back. "Graham, what is this about you and Jenna?" she finally asked. "What happened between the two of you?"

His eyes narrowed. "You're asking if Jenna is indeed expecting my baby?"

She was embarrassed to hear the question put so plainly. But she couldn't deny her curiosity, either. *"Jah."*

He stopped. "So you believe what you heard?"

His voice was so harsh and accusing, her feelings were hurt. Getting further chilled, she rubbed her arms again. "I don't know what to believe. I only learned the news from Corrine yesterday at lunch."

Abruptly, he stopped. "Is that what everyone's calling this? The news?"

She didn't appreciate receiving the brunt of his anger. "Well . . . yes." She swallowed. "Graham, why didn't you tell me that Jenna is expecting?"

"Because I didn't know until she showed up at my house the day we got stuck on that elevator."

She blinked. Oh, but that felt like it was months ago instead of just days. "I see."

"Do you? Do you see that her condition has nothing to do with me?" Pain filled his eyes as he stared at her. "Mattie, I don't even know if Jenna is really pregnant or not."

"Why would she lie?"

"I have no idea. I've given up trying to figure out why she would lie about me."

When Mattie couldn't help but gape at him, he charged ahead.

She rushed to catch up. "Graham?" she said hesitantly. "Are you sure she's lying?" Oh, the question hurt, but a lie would be worse . . .

"I'm positive. Mattie, I don't know who the father of her child is, but it certainly isn't me. It's not possible." Finally slowing, he said, "Do you hear what I'm saying? There is no way I could have fathered her child. Ever."

So he hadn't had relations with Jenna. Mattie felt a surge of relief, though she knew she didn't really have any reason to feel so possessive over him. He had every right to have relationships, she supposed with a sinking feeling.

"You aren't saying anything," he murmured.

"There's not much to say."

"You always have something to say." A flicker of amusement filled his gaze before it faded into seriousness again. "So, do you believe me?"

"I'm trying to," she said honestly.

"Mattie, I need you to trust me. I need you to believe in me, no matter what."

They were still walking, mounting a slight hill in their path. The cold breeze whipped around them, flattening their jackets to their bodies. It wrapped the skirts of her dress around her calves, and caused another fierce shiver to reverberate through her.

"I'll try," she murmured, reaching out to him as her breath became labored.

It was the best she could do. Because she knew more than most how hard it was to tell people the truth all the time. With her cancer and her treatments, she'd learned that.

She'd learned that, too, when she'd viewed Lucy's bruises from her first husband. And knew Lucy never told anyone.

Looking disgusted, Graham shook off her hand. "Look. Don't worry about it. You're going to be too busy to worry about me, anyway."

"Why's that?"

"Because a man I know from work wants to pay you a call."

"You did as I asked?"

"I always do as you ask, Mattie," he said, sounding a bit put out that she didn't realize it. "His name is William."

Though she knew it was inappropriate, her ears perked up. "Graham, really? What is he like?"

"He's Amish. I don't know him real well, but the other men seem to think highly of him. He seems nice enough, I suppose."

"When will I see him?"

"I'm supposed to tell him tomorrow if you want to meet him. If you do, he's going to stop over at your house tomorrow after work." He paused. "You don't have to go through with it, you know. I can tell him you changed your mind."

"I haven't."

After studying her face again, he shrugged. "All right, then." Though the wind was still biting into their cheeks, Graham pulled off his hat and tilted his face up to the fresh air. While the breeze ruffled his hair, he murmured, "Mattie, I cannot believe I'm playing matchmaker for you."

"I'm grateful." She couldn't resist smiling. "I promise I am."

Looking back at her, he murmured, "So. You do want to see William? Should I tell him to stop by?"

Slipping two fingers under the brim of her bonnet and *kapp*, Mattie fingered the peach fuzz on her scalp. "Does he know about my hair?"

"*Jah*. And about your cancer and your surgeries, too."

"And he still wants to meet me?"

All at once, the anger fell from his expression and the wonderful, beautiful kindness that had always been there for her appeared. "He does, even though I tried to warn him that you were a bossy, greedy woman."

She felt her cheeks heat. "Oh, Graham! You didn't tell him those things, did you?"

"*Nee*. I told him you were a great lady, one of my best friends." He paused, looking almost uncomfortable with what he told her. "And, um, I told him that he'd be lucky to get to know ya. So you want me to tell him to stop by tomorrow?"

Nervously she nodded.

"All right, then. It's settled." Looking around them, he whistled low. "My word, Mattie. We walked too far! And the wind has picked up something awful. Why, you're going to get chilled if we're not careful." Two steps closer brought his arm around her shoulders.

She shivered, so happy to feel his comfort, his warmth once again.

"Ach, Mattie. You are chilled." Tsking under his breath, he brought her even closer to his side, opening his coat slightly to give her more protection. "We'll go back to your house together, *jah*? I'll take you home and get you some tea. All right?"

Overcome with gratitude, she merely nodded as they slowly walked together, Graham's heat and scent making her feel secure.

Making her feel like she was special to him. No, more than that. Like Mattie Lapp was the most important person in his world.

But that had to be the truth, wasn't it? Their disagreement had proved something to her. Graham Weaver was the most important person in her life.

Chapter Six

"*Onkle* John, how come you don't come over here as much as you used to?" Katie asked.

John looked up from the puzzle they were doing together and scanned his niece's expression, trying to figure out if she was truly sad about his absence of late . . . or if she was wanting something. One could never be sure with Katie.

But when she merely stared at him with her big blue eyes, he kept his voice soft. "Katie, dear. You know I still visit you all the time."

"Not as much. Not like you used to. You used to come almost every evening."

"I'm busy, Katie. I've got the store to run, you know."

"And other things, too?"

Ah. There was the reasoning. Katie was wanting some answers. "Yes. I've been making new friends."

"I heard Lucy tell Calvin that you sometimes see Mrs. Zehr."

John shook his head. "Sounds like your hearing is as good as ever. For your information, I have been seeing Mary and Abel. Just a little bit. When they come into the shop."

"But not Ms. Donovan?"

"No, not Jayne." To his surprise, he still felt a momentary pang of guilt whenever he thought of the pretty librarian with the violet eyes. If he'd been willing to stay English, he thought he might have been able to be happy with her.

Or perhaps not. Though she appealed to him, he'd never felt like she'd needed him. Not really. And after living thirty-some-odd years for the most part by himself, he was eager to be needed.

"I see Ms. Donovan when I go to the library."

"I know you do. You see Ella there, too."

Katie nodded importantly as she picked up a red puzzle piece and put it in the red pile. "You know, one day you could bring Mary and Abel over here."

John privately thought that might be a little awkward. So far, he hadn't even gone to her house for dinner. Besides that, he had a feeling that Mary was more than hesitant about the community commenting on their relationship. "One day I will bring Mary here. But for right now, I just want to spend time with you."

"That's why I like you coming over, Uncle John."

"Why is that?"

"You always have time for me. And you bring us potato chips."

Looking at the bag of Lays, he had to smile. His niece was a junk-food junkie. "Katie, I don't think you've met a bag of chips you didn't like."

She smiled his way, then scooted closer. "You won't ever leave Jacob's Crossing again, will ya?"

"I hope not." Of course, he already had a trip planned to go back to Indianapolis. He wanted to make sure everything was going well on the sale of his place. And he wanted to take one last look at the city he'd come to love before turning his back on that life for good.

"I hope not, too." Nibbling her bottom lip, she rearranged two pieces together until they snapped into place. "I got a match."

"You did indeed, Katie. Those fit together perfectly. Just like you and me. We're a good match, child."

Oh, but their conversation was as wobbly as a loose wheel on a buggy! For the last fifteen minutes, Mattie and William had skittered from one topic to the next. Trying—without success—to find a common thread to grab ahold of.

Mattie was sure this was going to be the longest buggy ride in the history of Jacob's Crossing. Why, her time with William was starting to feel as long as a chemotherapy treatment, and she'd thought nothing could ever be longer than that.

"The snow sure makes everything pretty," she said, feeling slightly bored and more than a little frustrated. "I like winter."

"I enjoy snow, too," William said from her left side. "It's so fresh and cold."

Mentally, Mattie rolled her eyes. Snow was *pretty and fresh? . . . and* cold? *This* would be the extent of their conversation, stilted as it was?

Almost against her will, she compared William's words to what Graham would have said. Graham would have laughed off her inane comment, then would have volunteered to toss her out in the snow.

As the minutes dragged by like hours, she looked longingly at the fluffy layers that blanketed most everything around them. Only tiny bird tracks disturbed the pristine surroundings.

Yes, Graham, indeed, would have joked around with her comment. Or he would have suggested they make a snowman. But of course, William wasn't like that. During their brief time together, he had seemed buttoned up and stiff. Almost wary. Mattie was starting to wonder if he would ever unbend enough to joke around with her—or even with anyone, for that matter.

As she noticed him shift uncomfortably, Mattie realized that he most likely was feeling the strained tension between them as well. She needed to give him a chance. After all, it wasn't his fault they were strangers.

What she needed to do was try harder.

"Perhaps one day we can go out walking in it," she ventured. Unable to stop thinking of Graham and his carefree attitude, she added, "Maybe even make a snowman?"

He blinked. "You can go out in the weather? It won't make you sick?"

"The cancer didn't give me colds," she blurted before she thought to temper her words. "It only attacked my body."

A red stain colored his cheeks. "Sorry. I just thought that maybe you weren't strong enough yet. I mean, that you could catch cold . . ." He slumped. "I promise, I didn't mean any disrespect."

His honest apology made her blush, too. She truly needed to become less prickly.

What a joke it was, to think that she was treating her disease without hardly a spare thought. *Nee*, it was becoming brutally obvious that the cancer was always with her. "No, William, it is I who am sorry. I know you are trying to make sure I stay healthy." His quiet, undivided attention made her bare her soul even more. "See, I've been living with my condition so long that I forget everyone else is still wary about it."

"I can see how one might do that."

She smiled at him, grateful that he was trying so hard to listen and be supportive. "You were right. It used to be that anything could make me sick. But I'm getting healthier and more fit every day. Even strong enough for a little walk in the snow." She held up a foot. "I even have my boots on."

He looked at her black, thick-soled foot, then glanced upward. As he did, William's deep brown eyes softened enough to make her think that maybe she'd judged him too hastily.

She looked down and smiled.

"If you have your boots on, then I suppose we'd best make use of them, *jah*?" William asked as he carefully reined in his horse.

Now she just felt silly. Had she always been so childish? Had she always pushed others in order to get her way?

When he glanced at her again, she smiled weakly. Nothing needed to be said.

After pulling the buggy to the side of the road, William easily hopped out and tied his horse to a nearby fence post. Then, with the same economy of motion, he walked to her side.

"Are you ready to walk now, Mattie?"

"Of course." Slipping her hand in his, she clambered down. When her boots landed on the ground, fresh snow crunched underneath them. A few bits splattered around her skirts.

"Hmm. I have to say that I've never been much for wandering around in the snow and ice, but if it's what you want . . ."

"I think it will be fun."

"Then let's walk for a bit, shall we?"

When they stepped forward, her right boot slipped a bit, nearly bringing her backside to the ground.

With little fanfare, William reached out and gripped her elbow, then slowly slipped his hand down her forearm until their fingers linked together like two well-hewn boards.

His touch, though chaste, felt impossibly familiar. Too familiar. His palm tightened around hers as they walked over a slippery section, then started toward a thicket of pine trees. Mattie couldn't help but notice that his hand felt different than Graham's. A little wider. A little softer, too.

When his fingers folded around hers for a brief second and when his thumb rubbed her knuckle, she grew embarrassed and pulled away. For the briefest of moments, his grip tightened—refusing to let her hand drop. Then, as if he had just realized what he was doing, he let her hand go.

Feeling embarrassed and slightly wary, Mattie clasped her hands in front of her. What had just happened between them?

Her mouth went dry as she dared to wonder about her reactions to him.

As the tension grew between them, she cleared her throat. Then spied the perfect distraction. "Look, William, rabbit tracks."

"Ah." He pointed to another set of tracks. "These look like deer tracks." After a second, he grinned at their own tracks, now looking so big and clumsy next to the animal's perfect prints. "I fear our tracks don't look near as neat."

Mattie smiled at him, pleased he was trying.

Around them, the sun was peeking through the branches of the trees, casting faint shadows on the snow. A few cardinals and blue jays were fluttering, their bright colors looking strikingly beautiful against the pristine snow.

It was a beautiful day. A happy day.

At least, it should have been.

She glanced William's way. For a brief moment, he looked bored. But then when he noticed her looking, he lifted his head and smiled. "Happy?"

She wasn't. It was now obvious that no matter how beautiful the surroundings—or how hard they tried to converse—they were not a good match. "Oh, yes."

"Then I'm happy, too," he said. Obviously lying. "Though this wind is cold."

At least he had hair on the top of his head! Graham would've had his arm around her shoulders, just to warm her up. Or would have pulled her over to inspect a squirrel's nest or an interesting-looking juniper bush. Or he would have told her the names of all the birds.

Or he would have been just content to walk with her, saying nothing.

But William did none of those things.

Once more, she was beginning to get the feeling that he never would.

Chapter Seven

John felt as clumsy as a teenager as he clasped the dish of green beans that Mary had just handed him. *"Danke,"* he murmured, spooning up a few and tossing them on his plate.

But of course, three of the beans wobbled off the spoon before they reached their destination and flew onto the white tablecloth. Immediately, an angry blotch stained the cloth.

Right after, he felt his cheeks heat. Across from him, Abel snickered.

Now what to do—pick them up with his fingers? Pretend they weren't decorating the space to his right?

"Just pick them up with your fingers," Jenna whispered from his left. "Mary didn't see. Besides, your spill doesn't mean anything. Spills happen to everyone."

He needed no more reassurance than that. Still reluctant to look at Mary, he set the bowl down, tossed the run-away beans onto his plate, then wiped his now oiled fingers on his napkin.

Making his cloth napkin stained well and good, too.

Inwardly, he sighed. His clumsiness with the beans was only the latest in a string of misfortunes that had happened since he'd arrived.

He'd tracked mud onto her floor, knocked over a glass of water, shattering the glass on the countertop, and had inadvertently told Mary that he wasn't all that fond of peanuts. Just before he'd discovered she'd made a peanut butter pie for dessert.

Right away, she'd started looking for something else to serve for dessert—and he had begun to wish that he'd learned to keep his mouth shut.

As everyone around him ate silently, John's nerves began to get the best of him. Perhaps this dinner was a worse than bad idea. Maybe they were rushing things a bit . . . eating all together like they were. At his sister-in-law's house, he often stayed in the background, not wanting to make any waves.

Here, Mary was treating him like her honored guest . . . and Abel was treating him as an unwanted one. Obviously he had a lot to learn about family-style dining.

He glanced Mary's way.

However, Mary didn't do anything but smile sweetly.

After a moment, she cleared her throat. "Abel and I started something the other day that was mighty fun. We shared one good thing and one not-so-*gut* thing about our day. Shall we do that now?"

With a sideways glance in Jenna's direction, Abel groaned. "Mamm, let's not."

"Oh, come now, Abel. When it was just the two of us, I thought it was great fun."

Ignoring her son's put-upon expression, she clasped her hands in front of her. "All right, then, I'll go first. My good thing is this, dinner together. Jenna, I'm so glad you've come to live with us, and John, it's a pleasure to share something besides donuts and *kaffi* with you!"

John couldn't resist smiling right back. He was eager to do anything that brought the attention away from his string of mistakes. "And the not-so-good thing?" Oh, he hoped she wouldn't say him staining her good tablecloth!

"That's easy." She lifted her hand, to reveal a row of three neatly applied bandages to the side of her palm. Right below her pinky finger. "I cut myself on the buggy wheel this morning."

John leaned forward. "Mary, I didn't even notice your hand. What happened?"

"Oh, nothing too earth-shattering. Something must have ripped at one of the wheels. When I rested my hand on one, hitching up Daisy, I scraped myself."

"So that's why I saw those cloths soaking in the stationary tub!" Jenna exclaimed. "I wondered what had happened. Mary, you must have bled something awful."

"It was nothing. Truly."

John grew concerned. "Mary, perhaps you should go to

the doctor or urgent care? You might need stitches or a shot."

Her cheeks pinkened, just as if she wasn't used to anyone fussing over her at all. "Oh, goodness. I'm fine, John. It was nothing more than a minor inconvenience."

"Will you at least let me look at it later?"

"Of course. I mean, if you want to . . ."

Feeling that connection between them, he nodded, though he sensed Abel glaring at him. Well, that was fine. He didn't care. Someone needed to look after Mary, and it might as well be him. She needed someone to fuss over her!

After a brief pause, Mary looked at Jenna and Abel. "Now, who would like to go next?"

"I will," Jenna said. "My good thing is that I think I got a job today. Ms. Donovan at the library offered me a part-time job. She said she's been shorthanded."

A brief moment of silence met Jenna's pronouncement. John knew they were all thinking that the reason the library was shorthanded was because of Dorothy Zook's passing. She used to work at the library, but then was recently killed in a buggy accident. As the uncomfortable moment lengthened, all of Jenna's confidence dissipated in front of them. Paling, she sputtered, "I didn't mean that how it sounded." Biting her lip, she continued. "I mean, of course I'm sorry that Dorothy died. Even though she, ah, put Ella in danger . . ." Her voice drifted off.

For a whole other reason, John felt himself growing uncomfortable. Until he'd made his choice, he'd also been seeing Jayne. While he wasn't sure just how much Mary knew about that, he would have rather not talked about Jayne at all.

John cleared his throat.

Again, Abel snickered, but it sounded forced, like he was struggling to stay aloof and snarky.

Tears pricked Jenna's eyes. "John, I didn't mean to offend. I know Ella is your sister-in-law . . ."

"You didn't offend me at all. It's all right, Jenna," John said. Hoping that God would give him the words to help her and to make the tense subject lighter. "I know what you meant. I'm glad you got a job offer. I'm sure you'll be good at it."

After sending a pointed look Abel's way, Mary folded her hands on the table. "Do you have a not-so-good thing, Jenna?"

A faint blush appeared on her cheeks. "My dresses are starting to get snug. I'm going to have to see if I can let some of them out."

"I can help you with that," Mary offered kindly.

John's heart expanded as he yet again thought about what a wonderfully kind and generous woman Mary was. Here she not only had taken in Jenna, but now she was offering to help her with her alterations.

Looking briefly at Abel, who was using his fork to spin a lone green bean in circles on his plate, John cleared his throat. "I'll go next. My not-so-good part was spilling food on your tablecloth, Mary. I hate having to cause you more work."

"Cleaning a tablecloth is no trouble."

He thought it probably was, but instead of stewing on

it, he tried to think of something good to share. Finally, he brought up the little girl who'd stolen his heart. "My good thing is that Katie has agreed to let me take her ice skating next weekend."

Abel turned his way. "Do you think it really will be cold enough for them to open the pond?"

"I think so. We've had twelve days below freezing now. That pond isn't too deep. At least that's what the rumor mill announced this morning at the Kaffi House."

Jenna whistled low. "You're a brave man, Mr. Weaver, to take that little Katie anywhere. She's quick to run off."

"She is, but I love her," John said. "That little girl has enough spunk for several people."

Mary's eyes warmed as she looked toward Abel. "Your turn."

After darting another glance at Jenna, Abel sat up. "All right. My *gut* news is hearing about the skating pond. And my not-so-good news is that I failed today's spelling test."

Mary gazed at her son with sadness. "That's okay, Abel. I know you studied."

"Not that it did any good."

Jenna leaned forward. "I could help you, if you want."

"I don't see how. No matter how many times I write the words down, I still forget their spelling." Pure pain entered his features. "I don't know why I'm so bad at school. I just am."

"Now, Abel—"

"I used to not be a good speller, too," Jenna said quickly. "I learned tricks to help. It's worth a try, right? I mean, if you want some help."

John noticed that Abel's shoulders straightened again and silently blessed Jenna. Only a teenage girl would remember how sensitive a teenage boy could be.

"Sure," Abel said after a pause. *"Danke."*

"You're welcome."

Mary looked as pleased as John had ever seen her when she stood up. "This was such a nice conversation, Jenna and Abel, that I'm giving you both the night off from the dishes."

Abel's eyes widened. "Truly?"

"Truly." Her gaze softened on John. Feeling just like a caress. "I mean, you were going to look at my finger, right?"

"I haven't forgotten."

"And then you could help me for a bit?"

"I don't mind at all," he murmured.

Jenna met John's gaze; then, with a small smile, he walked to Abel's side. "Why don't you go show me your words?"

"Now?"

"Oh, yes. Now," she said with a wink John's way as she ushered Abel out of the room.

John picked up two plates and followed Mary to the kitchen. "I think that Jenna might end up being a blessing to you," he said. "She's sure helping tonight."

Mary tilted her head up to look at him. "I think she's going to be a blessing for me in many ways. I'm sorry that she's disappointed her family so much, but I can't help but be grateful for her help and company here."

"I'm grateful she's letting us have some time alone." He looked at Mary's hand. "Now, come over here by the overhead light," he said, motioning to a gas-powered light in the center of the table. "Let's see just how bad that cut is."

"It's not all that bad . . ."

He walked over, got a couple of paper towels, and picked up the Band-Aid box she'd left on the counter, too. "If it's not that bad, this will be quick, then."

Looking put upon, she held out her hand to his.

He stepped closer and carefully peeled the bandage from her finger. As he did so, John was amazed at how soft and creamy-looking her skin was. How did Mary keep her hands so smooth? Most other women he knew had far rougher skin, or at least a few calluses.

But then he saw the cut, and whistled low. "Mary. This is pretty deep. You should have gone to the hospital."

Her eyes widened. "Truly? I didn't think it was that bad . . ."

Though it wasn't swollen, it did look red and angry. When he tilted her hand, she winced. Mindful of her pain, he said, "How about I take you to the hospital now?"

"Certainly not."

She attempted to pull her hand from his, but he held it firm in between his own. "I bet it needs at least three or four stitches," he protested. "If you don't get those, it will leave a scar."

"I don't mind a scar."

"Mary, I think you're being silly." Wondering if she was avoiding the English doctors, he said, "I promise that I'll stay with you the whole time."

"That wouldn't be necessary. Besides, it's just a cut."

"It's more than that."

"If it gets worse, I'll go to the doctor. But it's fine. Now let's do the dishes."

After bandaging back up her finger, he let go of her hand with some reluctance. "All right. But I'm going to wash. You can dry."

"Of course I can't let you do that."

Looking over her lovely brown hair, neatly twisted and pinned under her *kapp*, and the way her dark red dress illuminated the creaminess of her skin, John was sure he'd never seen a prettier woman. Or a woman more stubborn. "Of course you can. Mary, I think you really hurt your hand. As soon as these dishes are done, you're going to take a break and sit down for a bit."

To his amusement, she hid her hand in her skirts. Just as if he couldn't see it, he wouldn't remember the cut. "That's not necessary . . ."

"But it would be yet another 'good' part of my day. Don't deny me, Mary. I know you fussed all day to prepare this delicious dinner. And it was delicious, in spite of my clumsiness with the beans."

"I hardly noticed."

He knew she was lying. But he didn't care. "I'm glad," he said. "Now, let's get these dishes done so I can have a few minutes to just sit with you." Lowering his voice, he said, "That's why I came over here, you know. I've been wanting to spend time with you and catch up. Just the two of us."

Her mouth popped into a little *Oh*, just as if his words shocked her. Then she swallowed. "John, the things you say."

Secretly, he thought she hadn't heard anything yet.

More and more, he found himself biding his time with her. Trying to be patient. To not scare her or spook her with too many touches or long looks.

But he was a grown man, and all this waiting was getting old. There were lots of things to tell her. Things about how pretty he thought her skin was, and how he hated the idea of it getting scarred or damaged. And how he was entranced by her personality. By her sweet manner with Abel.

And by the sadness that seemed to constantly shroud her. The veil was thin and he could tell that she ached to put her grief behind her.

All he wanted to do was make her happy.

Since they were alone, and he was tired of hiding, he reached out and ran his hand down her arm. He felt a tremor from his touch.

One glance told him that she wasn't afraid. On the contrary, she was feeling a lot of the same things he did. Encouraged, he linked his fingers through hers and rubbed her knuckle with his thumb.

With a smile full of whimsy, she turned and faced him. "John, what are you up to?"

"Nothing. Just trying to get a little closer."

An eyebrow arched. "Because?"

"Because I want to kiss you. Just once."

Instead of looking shocked, he was pleased to see true amusement enter her gaze. "Only once?"

Now it was his turn to feel flustered. Of course he wanted to kiss her more than once. But he would make do with what he said. "Just once right now," he amended, then leaned close and brushed his lips against her slightly parted ones. Unable to stop himself, he wrapped his arms loosely around her and kissed her again, pleased when she kissed him back.

Perhaps the whole thing lasted one second.

Maybe one minute.

Whatever it was, it was over far too quickly. But it had been nice.

Being with Mary was nice. Peaceful. Perfect.

With reluctance, he stepped away and rolled up his sleeves. He squirted some dish soap into the sink and started the faucet. "Mary, please go fetch me some dishes, if you would."

After a pause, she answered. "I'll be right back," she promised, scurrying from the room, making John think that this was just about the sweetest moment he'd had in a terribly long time.

Chapter Eight

Just yesterday, they'd been treated to a newly fallen snow.
Now a good foot of fresh white powder covered the whole
area, making the path that Mattie often walked between
her farm and the Weavers' look like a secret passageway.

The ground crunched under her feet as she forged a
path, and she enjoyed seeing how her footprints were the
only ones mixing in with the deer and raccoon tracks.
Every once in a while, she saw a sleepy squirrel scamper
among the pines, the only bright green dotting the land-
scape. All the rest of the elms, maples, and oaks were bare.
Their dark silhouettes surrounded the path like protective
arms shielding her from outside elements.

At least, that was always how she'd come to think of
them. The trees had been figures she could count on.

Things she could see. For a time, they'd been far easier to depend on than the mythical being of their Lord.

A deep sadness and a sense of loss filled her as she recalled how empty she'd felt when she'd been in the middle of her chemotherapy treatments. For a time, she'd felt completely alone in her pain. Not even Lucy's careful considerations had alleviated Mattie's feeling of dark isolation.

Yes, for a few terrible months, she'd thought she was not only going to lose her life to cancer, but her faith, too.

And then something changed. Maybe it was finally coming to realize just how difficult Lucy's life had been before her husband's death. The reality of her friend's pain and layers of protectiveness that she wore like a suit of armor to protect herself from further pain had been eye opening, for sure. Little by little, Lucy's complete faith had inspired Mattie.

After all, Lucy firmly believed that the Lord had held her hand during all her trials. That though she'd lived through two years of abuse and pain, she would have suffered through so much more if she'd had to survive alone.

So Mattie had opened her heart. The experience Loyal had with Ella in the fall had only cemented Mattie's faith. Surely God had been present when Ella had been in the buggy accident, held hostage by her former "best" friend. Perhaps He was always with them . . . even when things weren't wonderful.

"Mattie, how long are you going to be staring at those bare trees?"

Startled, she turned from her contemplation of the trees to the one man who she knew she could always depend on. "Not much longer," she replied with a smile. "They were keeping me company until you got here."

The wide brim of his felt hat shielded his eyes as he approached, making it difficult to see his expression. But though she couldn't quite make out his smile, she listened for the usual teasing lilt in his tone.

When he paused, she was afraid it would be absent as well. "How goes it with you today?"

"About the same," Graham replied.

She hurried to his side. "What is wrong?"

"You know. I'm practically suffocating under the community's scorn about Jenna."

"Perhaps you should speak to Jenna again," she said gently. "Perhaps she'll be able to explain things?"

"If I thought it would make me feel better, I would. But I'm still so mad at her, I don't think I'd listen to anything she had to say." Reaching out, he picked up a dead branch and snapped it in two. "Do you think she'd even *have* anything to say?"

"I don't know." Clearing her throat, she said, "Graham, don't be so down. The gossips will move on soon. They always do."

"Not this time, I fear." After staring out at the snow for another moment, Graham rubbed his chin. "Let's talk about something else. Anything else."

"What do you want to talk about?"

"Well, um . . . you saw William the other night, didn't you?"

"I did."

A muscle in his jaw tightened. "Did you enjoy your time with him?"

Remembering their awkward conversation, followed by the awkward way in which they left things, she shrugged. "It's hard to say."

"Why?"

"It was different, walking with him," she tried to explain but knew she wasn't being completely truthful. It had been different because William wasn't Graham. "But perhaps just because it was new."

"You don't have to rush into anything with him, you know."

"I'm not rushing." Heaven knew she'd been alone for a long time.

Graham's sour mood and snippy behavior was turning her mood, too. Plus she was getting cold, simply standing next to the trees with him. "Where should we go? Do you want to go to your house? Or would you rather go to my home?"

He hesitated. "I'd rather not go to either, if you don't mind." Looking at her mittens, he said, "If we continue to walk, will you be warm enough?"

Now the cold permeated her heart instead of only her bones and muscles. "I will be fine."

"Let's go this way, then, toward Ella's property."

He pointed to a small, thin trail that snaked in between the two oldest oaks. Obediently, Mattie started following him. Because his posture was so stiff, she let him take the lead, choosing to stay a good two paces behind him for a bit. As she watched his forceful steps, not even trying to place her own black boots in his footprints, she began to worry. "Graham, things will get better."

"They'd have to, because they're pretty bad right now."

Trying to imagine what would have brought Jenna to tell such lies, Mattie frowned. "Poor Jenna."

He turned back his head to glare at her. "Poor Jenna? What about me?"

"You, Graham, are the innocent here. You have nothing to prove. And besides, even if you did, uh, have sex with her, people would shake their heads at you, call you too impatient . . . but your reputation wouldn't be ruined."

"But hers is."

"We both know it is. And we both know you're not surprised to hear that. I always thought it was something terrible, that the woman carries the baby and all the shame, whereas the strong man can escape that burden."

"She's tried her best to saddle me with it, Mattie."

She caught the first glimpse of doubt in his voice. "But?"

"But now I hear what you are saying." After a beat, he said, "It would be a difficult thing, to be thrown out of a home."

"Her parents never were ones to see anything in shades of gray."

"For this, they probably shouldn't. After all, she's pregnant out of wedlock and a liar. The babe isn't mine."

"I know. Of course it isn't."

Reaching out, he squeezed her hand. "*Danke*, Mattie."

"For what? For believing in you?"

"Of course. I've been needing your belief. I've needed someone to believe in me."

"Well, you definitely have that."

Ahead of them, the outline of Ella's farmhouse and barn loomed bright. Surrounding the buildings were neatly pruned holly bushes and trees. "What do you want to do, Graham? Visit Ella and Loyal or turn back around?"

"Perhaps we should go see them?"

She was glad he said that. She loved Ella and Loyal and knew Graham felt the same way. Plus, though they'd been walking at a fairly quick pace, her nose was freezing. "I hope Ella has a kettle on. Some hot tea would taste *gut* now."

"Let's go then. We'll see what they're up to this afternoon."

Mattie smiled at him, glad he looked more relaxed. Glad some of the awful tension had eased from his body.

And because she was glad of that, she kept her last question to herself.

If Graham was not the father of Jenna's baby . . . *who* was?

And why was Jenna so afraid to tell that man's name?

The dirt path widened a bit, making it easier for the two of them to walk side by side. Little by little, he eased her fingers down his arm, finally curving them securely around his palm. Though both their hands were covered in wool, Mattie slowly felt their body heat combine. Warming each other.

Chapter Nine

"So I heard you've got a heap of trouble on your shoulders," Uncle John said when Graham entered the Kaffi Haus early on Tuesday morning.

Inwardly, Graham slumped. Though he'd figured it wasn't likely, he'd hoped there was still a chance that word of his problems hadn't reached his uncle's ears. Though he was very different from his father, Graham respected John's opinion and didn't want to do anything to damage it.

And he'd hoped to push his problems away and pretend they didn't exist for a while, but he steeled his shoulders and prepared himself for the worst. "Uncle John, what have you heard?"

For once looking sober, his uncle walked around the counter and pressed his arm on Graham's shoulders. "Only that a certain girl named Jenna tried unsuccessfully to get you to accept responsibility for her baby."

Hearing that, he felt worse than ever, and more angry, too. "It wasn't like that. John, no one will believe me, but I promise you—"

"Settle, I'm just teasing you."

"There's not much to tease about." Didn't his uncle realize that Jenna was ruining his life? "I promise, all that's happening is that my life is getting ruined. In fact, things just seem to be going from bad to worse."

"Ruined, hmm? What is happening?"

Graham narrowed his eyes at his uncle. For a moment there, he could have sworn he'd heard amusement in his uncle's tone.

But surely his uncle wouldn't be making light of the situation?

"Everyone believes her and doesn't understand why I'm not offering Jenna marriage. But how can I? Her babe isn't mine." Once again, his anger rushed forward, stifling all the rest of his emotions. Pushing all his other emotions away until there was nothing left inside of him but anger, confusion, and resentment.

But to his surprise, instead of quickly turning serious, his uncle merely winked. "Don't take this the wrong way, but sometimes when you are facing a crisis, there are only two choices to make. To laugh or cry. I've found that laughing is easier on your eyes."

"I hear what you're saying, but I can't laugh about this. Everyone is whispering about me, and there's nothing I can say to defend myself."

After guiding Graham to a chair, John went to the coffee bar, poured Graham a generous amount, then opened up the bakery door and carefully set a flaky golden cherry turnover on a plate.

Graham watched his uncle with a bit of bemusement. When he'd first gotten reacquainted with his uncle, the initial impression had been that Uncle John was an impatient man, and one used to being in control. Now it was becoming obvious that John was far different than that. Instead of an impatient *Englischer*, he was a patient, reflective man, uneager to jump to conclusions or incite conflict.

In short, he was a Christian man, a good man. Graham knew for certain that his father would have leaned on him had he still been alive.

"Here you go," John said. "This should help. I think you need some sustenance."

Though he wasn't hungry, Graham took a bite. At once, the pastry gave way to a burst of bittersweet cherry juiciness, the flavor exploding in his mouth. "This is *gut*. Did Amos make the filling?"

"No. The filling is, um, Mary's."

Graham felt a reluctant smile light his face. "Mary, hmm?"

"Yes, well, when I had supper at her house, I noticed that she had almost a dozen jars of cherry filling. I offered to buy a few jars from her for the turnovers. Kind of a test run, you know."

"It's a good test."

"I'll let her know."

"I've noticed that the two of you have gotten close."

"Some. Maybe even a little closer in recent weeks." After pouring himself a cup of coffee, he added, "I had dinner at her house the other night."

"How did Abel take that?"

A faraway look entered his eyes before he blinked. "Grudgingly, to be sure."

"He'll come around. It's hard for a boy to think of his *mamm* as anything other than a mother."

"I have a feeling it's going to take a very long time, Graham. But, that's okay. I've got time. I just want everything to be good, even if I have to wait longer than I intended."

"I've got a lot to learn from you." Looking away, he said, "I don't know what to do about Jenna. I feel like I need to go talk to her and tell her to clear my name."

"She's staying with Mary, you know."

"Yes, but you didn't see her, did you?" Surely Mary wasn't letting her Christian charity overrule her better judgment?

"Of course I saw her. She shared a meal with us."

"And Abel, too."

"The girl is having a difficult time of it, Graham," John said sharply. "Sometimes it's *gut* to remember that your problems are not the only ones."

Graham pursed his lips. Privately, he thought that though his uncle might be right, in this situation, things were different.

Luckily, the door opened, accompanied by a cheerful chime at the front of the glass door. And in came a trio of people, his little sister, Katie, leading the way.

Uncle John jumped to his feet, his face a wreath of smiles—as it always was when he spied her. "Who could this small person be?" he asked, approaching the little girl well covered in a black cloak, a thick red scarf, bright green mittens, and boots.

"It's me, *Oncle*!"

A line formed between John's brows as he obviously pretended to be confused.

"Who?"

"Katie! Katie Weaver!" With a whoosh, she unwrapped her scarf from her face. "Do you see me now?"

After staring at her for a full second, he widened his blue eyes. "Now I see you!" With a laugh, he scooped her in his arms and gave her a twirl. Katie squealed with delight as she clasped her mittened hands on his arms and held on tight.

After twirling in a circle one more time, John set her on the ground. "I like your scarf, Katie Weaver. Is it a new one?"

"For sure." She looked over her shoulder. "Miss Ella made it for me."

John stepped back and smiled at Loyal's wife, who was smiling at John's antics like the rest of them. "It's a pretty one," he said.

"*Danke*. I thought Katie might be needing a red scarf for the holidays. And, someone here wanted to come over and say hello before we went to the library today."

"I did," Katie exclaimed.

"I'm glad you did. What is going on over at the library this fine morning?"

"We're going to be making Thanksgiving crafts."

"What kind of crafts are those?"

Ella grinned. "We'll be making turkeys out of egg boxes."

"I'm going to make a special one, *Onkle* John."

"I can't wait to see it."

Graham stood up. "*Gut* morning, Ella. Hiya, Katie. Ella, did I miss you when you stopped by at my house?" He'd been trying to make a point to make sure Ella felt as welcome as possible around their family.

"*Nee.* Loyal picked up Katie at your house and brought her over. But you didn't miss him, either. Your *mamm* said you'd already left."

He had. He'd worked early in the barn, then had left, anxious to spend some time away from his worries. But here he was surrounded by family again.

The door chimed, and this time brought in a crowd of *Englischers.* John became all business, deliberately walking around the counter and smiling pleasantly at the tourists. Katie—being Katie—followed him around the counter, turned on the faucet, and started washing her hands.

Obviously, she was eager to be her devoted Uncle John's assistant.

"Katie—" Graham called out sharply. "Don't be a pest."

"She could never be that," John interjected. "Let her be."

Ella scooted her chair closer. "Your uncle spoils her," she said with a smile.

"He does. I need to talk to him. Let him know he doesn't always have to let her have her way."

"Oh, I don't think he does. I think he's just enjoying her

company. I happen to think they need each other sometimes."

"Really?"

"John is the closest thing she has to a *daed*. You and your
brothers are very good men, but you're not father figures."

"I never thought about that."

"Like I said, it's just an idea." Biting her lip, she looked
him over. "How are you doing, really?"

He shrugged. "I've been better."

"Your brother is worried about ya."

"I know. But I'll be fine."

"That's all I needed to know, then."

"And you, Ella? How is the *haus*?"

"As messy as ever. I don't know if Loyal and I will ever
have things organized and in proper places. Right now,
we're remodeling the bathroom."

"I didn't think Loyal knew how to do plumbing."

"He doesn't. He's decided there's nothing like on-the-
job learning." She laughed merrily, her merriment ringing
out loud through the bustling room. One by one, several
of the *Englischers* looked at her, smiles brightening their
faces. Graham didn't blame their appreciation. To an out-
sider, Ella was somewhat of a plain woman. But whenever
anyone heard her in person, all of her flaws faded; and
before a person knew it, he was sure he was staring at the
prettiest woman in the room.

She had a zest for life that was infectious. Now everyone
in the family realized that their handsome, very outgoing
brother had chosen well with his bride. By his side, Ella

bloomed. And by her side, Loyal was more approachable. Easier to get along with.

"We will continue to pray for you, Graham," she said.

"*Danke*, but what, exactly, will you pray for?"

"That you will soon know our Lord God's will, of course. That's all you can do, *jah*? One by one, we are all at his mercy."

"Ella!" Katie called out, darting away from the counter with a very important expression. "We must go to the library now or we'll be late."

"You're right. Let's get you bundled up again, child."

With one last reassuring smile, Ella turned to Graham. "I'll see you at dinner on Monday night."

As still more customers came in, Graham poured himself more coffee, then settled to watch his uncle. By his side, Ella bundled up his sister, said goodbye to John, then shuttled Katie out the door.

After a time, the crowd in the restaurant slowed.

And then it was time for Graham to leave, too. But for the first time in his life, he didn't know where to go.

Chapter Ten

"These are movies that have been turned in," Jayne Donovan told Jenna. "All you have to do is check to make sure the movie is in the case, put them back in the plastic security holders, and then put them on the cart alphabetically." She paused. "Am I going too quickly for you?"

"I understood," Jenna said. She'd graduated at the top of her class from the Amish school. She'd learned how to study hard and how to learn things that gave her trouble. And though it was prideful, she'd been very pleased to make straight A's year after year.

Used to be, most everyone had looked at her with respect. And though it had been prideful, Jenna had accepted their admiration. She'd worked hard and had wanted to be someone the others looked upon with at least a little bit of envy.

And in return, she'd done her best to include others and help them, too. For most of her life it had been like that, anyway. Being the oldest girl in the family meant she'd needed to not only watch over her siblings but to also be a role model. In school, she'd merely accepted that role. Later, she'd even come to take it for granted. Years living like that made one accept things, for better or worse.

Now she saw it for what it had been—vanity and pride. And, she was realizing with some dismay, vanity and pride didn't help a person so much when she was all alone.

Or when she was starting over with her life.

As her boss left the back room, Jenna reflected again on how different things were now. Whereas her sisters used to look to her for guidance, now they were forbidden to speak with her.

And where once everyone used to want to be her, now no one in her community did. Taking a seat, she pulled out the stack of DVDs and began sorting them as she had been directed to.

First were several Disney movies. *101 Dalmations*, and *Aristocats*. Others were shows she'd never heard of, some series from the TV.

One by one, she checked to make sure the movie matched the case.

On the other side of the wall, she heard Ella Weaver's kind, bright voice, as well as lots of children's cheery laughter. Usually she would have wanted to help the children make crafts, but today she was glad to be designated to the back room.

There was plenty to do. She wasn't ready to see anyone.

And most of all, she didn't want to see him. *Him*.

The man who'd first turned her head with a kind smile, the one who'd insisted she spend more time with him than was wise. The man who'd offered her promises she was now certain he'd never intended to keep.

The man who still lived in Jacob's Crossing. Still worked at the market. She, on the other hand, had been forced to live a new life almost entirely alone. She was working for an *Englischer*, being pushed into doing something she never would have dared. In a few months, she'd be looking after a babe, too.

Indeed, that man had ruined her life.

So why were the sweet memories of her time with him so hard to push away? Closing her eyes, she tried to concentrate on bitterness and anger, not on how good it had felt to be held in his arms. She'd focus on how they would never suit, not on how good it had felt to simply be Jenna with him. Not the oldest. Not the example. Not anything but herself.

But her mind flickered with images of him smiling at her, listening to her . . . looking so happy and content with her—

She opened her eyes, and forced herself not to dwell on him.

No matter what, she couldn't see him again, because one thing was very certain, at least to her. Though everyone thought she was a terrible person, lying about her relationship with Graham, becoming pregnant out of wedlock . . .

Now living with a widow and working in a library . . .

The truth, she knew, would have been even harder for everyone to know.

The truth would not set her free; it would only make things worse. And if things could be worse than this, she didn't want any part of that at all.

"Jenna? Can you come out here, please?"

"Of course." When she walked out into the main area, she was startled to see Ms. Donovan standing with two little girls.

"These girls need help finding information about airplanes, Jenna. Would you mind helping them look in the children's section for books about airplanes?"

"Not at all." She smiled at the girls, then felt her heart sink when she realized she knew one of them.

"You're Jenna!" Elizabeth Henderson said.

"I am." Trying to smile, Jenna played the game. "And you are Elizabeth, Chris's sister."

"Jenna and Chris were boyfriend and girlfriend," Elizabeth said to her friend. "But they're not anymore."

Jenna was shocked. She hadn't known that anyone knew how close they'd been. Before she could stop herself, she asked, "How did you know about Chris and me? Did you see us together?"

"No. He told us all about you." With a mischievous grin, Elizabeth explained, "He said you were Amish."

"I am."

"He said your family is real strict."

Well, there was another truth she couldn't dispute. "That is true as well." To her surprise, talking about Chris made her sad, and for once it had nothing to do with her pregnancy. Instead, she realized she simply missed him. She missed his company and the easy way about him. "Well, let me take you two over to the reference section and I'll see if I can help you find lots of books on planes."

The little girls followed her and took the books she offered. But just as Jenna was about to leave them at a small circular table, Elizabeth said, "Chris is going to be so happy I saw you here."

Pure panic overwhelmed her. Leaning closer, Jenna said, "You don't have to tell him, do you? I mean he probably won't care too much."

"He'll care," Elizabeth said with confidence. "I bet he'll come visit you once he knows I saw you here."

And that, Jenna realized, was what she was afraid of. "Elizabeth, let's keep our meeting a secret, okay?"

"Why?"

"So I can surprise your brother." She attempted to smile. "Wouldn't that be something?" she asked, her voice all conspiratorial. "Wouldn't it be something if Chris found out that you knew something he didn't?"

Even as she asked, Jenna felt her stomach knot. Here she was, lying again.

Elizabeth's eyes widened. "He would be very surprised about that."

"And you'd be so happy you kept a secret, right?"

Reluctantly, Elizabeth nodded.

With a sigh, Jenna relaxed. "Let's keep our meeting a secret for just a little bit longer. Will you try?"

Eyes wide, Elizabeth finally nodded. "I'll try," she blurted before she turned and ran out the door.

As Jenna watched the little girl leave, she remembered a past conversation with Chris. He'd taken her to a park, a children's playground. No *kinner* had been around, just the two of them. He'd taken her hand and had linked his fingers through hers as they'd sat side by side on a pair of swings. His hand had been warm, but his gaze had been warmer when he'd looked her way.

"Jenna, take me to your house. Introduce me to your family."

She'd been shocked. "*Nee.* I mean, no."

"Why?"

"It wouldn't work out."

A line had formed between his brows then. Obviously, his feelings had been hurt, thinking that she didn't think he was good enough for her family.

Of course, the opposite had been true. She'd known if he'd seen her parents and witnessed their disapproving expressions, he would never come around her again.

And she hadn't been ready to give their relationship up.

"Why wouldn't it work out?" he had finally asked. "What could go wrong?"

"Everything," she said, speaking the truth for once. If she brought him to her house, one thing was terribly certain. No matter how kind he was, or how hopeful she would have been for a future with Chris, everything would go wrong.

As Jenna watched the little girls fade from view, she realized that at least this once . . . she'd been exactly right.

* * *

Downtown Indianapolis looked exactly the same, John realized with a burst of amusement as he drove through the crowded one-way streets in his truck.

He'd been back only twenty-four hours. First, he went to his old condo and talked with the property manager. After being assured that everything with the sale was going smoothly, he spent a good three hours at his storage unit, packing up the rest of his belongings.

After he packed, he visited his old place of employment and shared a burger with a couple of the guys. But beyond hearing about their families and meeting a few of the new guys, there wasn't much to say.

He left the building feeling curiously empty.

Now he was going to have lunch at Rocco's, the Italian restaurant where he'd found employment when he'd first come to the city. Giorgio and Maria Rocco still owned the place, and they still served plenty of food, too.

"John!" Giorgio said, ignoring his outstretched hand and engulfing him in a warm hug. "I was wondering if you were ever going to come our way again." He patted him with as much force as ever. "It's been too long since I've seen you."

The reminder shamed John. "I'm sorry, Mr. Rocco. I should've kept in better touch."

"No way am I 'Mr. Rocco' now." The big man peeked up at him over his half-moon glasses. "No matter how many years go by, I'm still Giorgio to you, yes?"

"Yes," John found himself answering automatically. Looking at the man's stretched-too-tight white button-down and his black apron and slacks, he found himself smiling. Giorgio Rocco was all Italian, and his grandiose bearing and easy smile was as great to see as ever.

Giorgio beamed. "I'm so glad to see you. We'll have to make plans for the holidays."

Growing more uncomfortable, John said, "Actually, I only stopped by to tell you and Mrs. Rocco that I'm leaving Indy for good." He took a deep breath. "I decided to go back home."

"Ah. So you finally decided to be with your family." The restaurant owner smiled. "I wondered when you were going to do that."

The comment took him by surprise. "You really thought I'd return one day?"

"Of course. You love your family too much to leave them forever." He tapped a table. "Sit down and let me bring you some baked ziti. Or, are you too busy to eat?"

His mouth watered. "I'm never that busy."

Giorgio laughed. "Oh, John. You never could pass up a good meal."

John chuckled to himself as he soaked in the familiar sights and smells of the restaurant. As he looked around, he noticed the same wallpaper, now patched in places. And the same clock over the doorway. And the same mouth-watering aroma that wafted through the kitchen doors.

Twenty years ago, when he'd first come in looking for a job, he'd been so hungry it had taken all he'd had not to eat everything in sight. But Mr. Rocco had read his mind—or had just known what boys his age were like. For his first break, he'd sat John down at the butcher block table in the corner of the enormous kitchen and had placed an overflowing plate of baked ziti and garlic bread in front of him. "Eat," he'd said simply, then left before John could even think about asking a question or refusing the free meal.

"Here you go, son," Giorgio said as he now placed another heaping plate of pasta in front of him. "Eat."

John's fork was in his hand before he thought to wait to see if Giorgio was going to join him.

"I'm not eating just yet," the elderly man said. "I prefer to sit here and watch you for a bit."

The first bite was delicious, filled with the fresh flavors of stewed tomatoes, liberal amounts of garlic, and lots of mozzarella. "I don't know how you do it," he said when his plate was half empty. "I've watched you make this dish a hundred times, but I've never been able to duplicate it."

"Of course you can't. You're not Italian. It needs to be in your blood. You're Amish."

"No, I *grew up* Amish."

"Your past is still there." He tapped his heart. "Inside you. Yes?"

Giorgio was right. It was becoming apparent that his religion and his roots were as much a part of him as those same things were to the man in front of him. "Yes."

Shaking his head sadly, Mr. Rocco said, "That Angela never understood that. She always hoped to make you different."

"I tried to change. And I did change. Some," John said, remembering their first few months of married life. He'd been so enthralled by her, he had attempted to change himself completely, just to keep her happy.

Of course, he'd learned soon enough that he was never going to change enough for her.

And then, when he found her with another man he realized the simple truth. Angela had wanted a different man, not a different John.

"How is she?" he asked.

"She is good. From what she tells me. She lives in Chicago now, you know."

"I heard she married." John wasn't ready to admit he'd come across Angela's picture on Facebook a few months before.

"She did. She married a man with two children. They're good. They're a good family. What about you, John? Are you now ready to move on?"

Was that what he'd been doing? "I think so." He said the words quickly, hoping his blunt answer would be all Giorgio needed to hear.

But of course it wasn't. Like the ziti, things here didn't seem to change much over the years. "So, have you found someone?"

For a moment, he considered shaking his head. It wasn't that he wanted to keep his personal life close to his chest, but he just wasn't sure how to reply.

Or how he was destined to fit in with Mary Zehr. But just like the old man's forthrightness and the Italian cooking, much of his honesty had remained intact. "I think so. Her name's Mary. She has a twelve-year-old boy."

"Is she Amish?"

"She is."

"What does that mean for you?"

"It means that I'm going to have to join the church and change again."

A self-satisfied look entered Giorgio's dark eyes. "I was just telling Maria that I thought you might go back one day. When is this event happening?"

"I don't have a date yet." John was too flustered to hedge. "I came here to tell you that I probably wouldn't be back any time soon." Maybe never.

He couldn't actually say that he'd come to say goodbye.

"I'm glad you did," Giorgio said simply. "And I'm glad you came to eat."

John glanced at the dish in surprise. Somehow over the last few minutes, he'd eaten the entire helping. "It was good."

"I'm glad you enjoyed it. Now, don't go anywhere. I'm bringing you out some spumoni."

"I couldn't possibly—"

"Refuse? I know you won't refuse, John," he said with a wink. "Now, you stay here. I'm going to have Maria bring out the spumoni." He paused. "Yes?"

"Yes. I'll stay here. I wouldn't think of leaving yet."

Giorgio nodded. "Good."

As John watched him leave, he contemplated their conversation. And thought again about what they'd discussed. That for better or worse, most things still stayed the same.

Chapter Eleven

Two months before, the city council members of Jacob's Crossing implemented a new program, asking for volunteers to help with a new community project. There was a need in their town for some helping hands, as more and more people were visiting the food banks.

Churches and other community groups were getting involved, but the city leaders suspected even more people would help with food drives if it was made as easy as possible for them. As the weather got colder, everyone knew it would be a tragedy to send even one person home with less than a full bag of food. With this in mind, and in order to make sure they had something to send home with the needy, volunteers had been asked to go door to door once a month to collect canned goods.

Since John vividly remembered just how hungry he'd

been the first few weeks when he'd been living in Indianapolis and subsisting on his one free lunch a day, he'd eagerly jumped on board. The first outing had gone so well, he'd brought in over a hundred cans and boxes to the pantry.

So much so that his back had ached that evening.

So this time, he brought a helper. Abel wasn't all that thrilled to be giving up his Friday afternoon to walk the streets of Jacob's Crossing and collect cans, but so far, for the last hour, he'd done a good job with it. In no time at all, they'd implemented a perfect system for collecting. John and Abel took turns pulling the red wagon down the sidewalk; they'd approach the houses together, then would take turns carrying the food from doorsteps.

After five or six houses, they'd empty the wagon into one of the boxes in the back of John's truck.

With the two of them, they were making good time, going up and down the streets. John's back was thrilled that the boy was carrying half the load, too.

And his mind, well, his mind was getting a pretty good workout along the way. It turned out Abel had a lot to say.

"So how did you know?" Abel asked again as they walked up yet another path to a front door, the cement sticking out like a trail leading them to the goods that the person had left out on the front stoop.

Neatly, John picked up two boxes of cereal and one can of soup, and led the way back to the sidewalk . . . as Abel asked the same question he'd asked at least four times that day.

"How did you know you were ready to leave Jacob's Crossing?"

And yet again, John tried to deflect it. "I don't know," he said flippantly. "I just did."

A flash of pain seared through Abel's eyes before he turned away, leaving John to feel guilt ridden. How could he have forgotten how fragile a young boy's ego was? "I'm sorry," he said quickly. "You asked a serious question, and you deserve a serious answer."

"Do you have one?"

Well, he probably deserved that. "I think so," John said as he briefly glanced in Abel's direction before leading the way to yet another front door.

"There's nothing here."

"I'll knock." Two minutes later, John explained what they were doing, then was handed four boxes of tuna casserole mix.

Abel read the directions carefully as they headed back to their wagon. "Do you think this is any good?"

"I've had it. It's tasty."

"I'm going to tell my *mamm* about it."

"You think she's going to make it for you?"

"Maybe."

When they started toward the next house, John pulling the increasingly heavy red wagon behind him, Abel spoke up again. "So, do you really have an answer for me?"

"The problem with you, Abel, is that you want easy answers for hard questions. I can't give you those."

"Do you think they're hard?"

"Of course. I left my parents and my brother and my community. That wasn't easy. I loved them."

"What did you find in Indianapolis?"

"I found differences," he blurted, then realized how much of that answer was the truth. Hmm. Maybe answering quickly was the way to go. "Here, as you know, everything is the same. At least it's that way on the surface. Our clothes lend us conformity. Our habits and our faith lead us to community. For me, it was exciting to think about being a part of a group of people who weren't like me."

Abel's eyes widened. "Did you like them better?"

"Not all of them. Some I liked fine. Others I liked more than just a little bit." On the tip of his tongue, he was tempted to tell Abel about his failed marriage and the subsequent divorce, but he knew that was a bad idea. He had a feeling Mary wouldn't appreciate him sharing such stories about his past.

And divorce wasn't something their community ever considered. Abel would most likely be shocked.

"So why all the questions? Are you thinking of leaving one day?"

"Would you tell my *mamm* if I wanted to?"

"Not right away."

"That's not much of an answer."

"I bet you're discovering that I don't have as many good answers as you were hoping for." By now, the wagon was near to overfilling.

By mutual agreement, they rolled it to John's truck and started piling the boxes in the back.

Boy was he going to miss that truck.

"Come now, why all the questions? Are you unhappy here? In Jacob's Crossing?"

"*Nee*. I like it here. It's home."

"Then . . ."

"I just want to know more about you. Because you're so interested in my mother."

Abel's comment hit John like a sledgehammer. He stilled. "Does that bother you?"

"Maybe."

Feeling as if they'd just neatly switched places, John spoke. "I like your mother, but I don't want to hurt her. And I don't want to hurt you, either."

His chin lifted. "You can't hurt me."

It took everything John had not to betray his amusement at the boy's bluster. "Sure I can—if I hurt your mother. And I don't intend to do that."

"So . . ."

"So I want to court your mother. But I want her to take her time. I know she loved your father a lot."

"*Mein daed* was the best."

John swallowed a lump in his throat. He heard the wistful tone in the boy's voice. And felt for his loss. "I know your *daed* was a good man. You should be proud to be called his son. More than one person has spoken of him well."

"Really? People talk to you about my dad?"

"Of course. And I want to hear about him, too. Your mother loved him. Plus, no one can replace him. I don't even want to try."

Abel looked at the ground as he visibly weighed his next words. "I didn't expect you to say something like that."

"Maybe today's a day for surprises, then? You can carry far more than I thought . . ."

"And today hasn't been near as bad as I thought it would be," Abel finished. "But I still don't want to like you courtin' my *mamm*."

Lightly, John squeezed his shoulder. "That's fair. Let's go finish this street and turn all this food in."

Mattie had locked her door. She wanted to see herself without worrying about her mother bursting into the room.

Pulling out the mirror the nurse at the hospital had given her, Mattie stared at her face and head. Little by little, her hair was growing back. Luckily, it was coming up the same shade as before, a deep brown. Some of her eyebrows had grown back, too.

When she remembered how hard it had been to deal with her hair loss, Mattie shook her head. Oh, she'd been so vain!

Or perhaps, she'd simply had enough. She'd lost so much during that time—her independence, her health, her appetite. Losing her hair had seemed terribly cruel.

Satisfied that her one-inch hair growth would soon be two, she carefully replaced her *kapp*.

And then she unpinned her dress and looked at herself.

Her mother had warned her against looking at her chest, saying concentrating on her scars would be wrong. But privately, Mattie figured their Lord God had created both men and women the best way He knew how. Surely she was allowed to sometimes be sad that she was now very far from His creation?

Angling the mirror, she winced at the dark red angry scars. The doctors and surgeons had said the lines would fade in time, though Mattie didn't know if that mattered all that much. No matter what, she wouldn't be the same. She'd be forever marked. And forever reminded that the future was never certain.

"Mattie?" her mother called out. "You've got company."

"I'll be right there," she said from her side of the door, then hastily slipped the mirror in between her mattress and bedsprings and took care to pin her dress up again.

Just so.

When she walked down the hall, her pace slowed. "Lucy? What are you doing here?"

"Trying to keep you company, you goose," she teased.

"I thought you were going to stay home and clean out the linen closet with your mother-in-law."

"I was going to. But then Mary left with Katie and I was all alone. And then, well, I had to stop."

"Why? Did you start to feel bad?"

"Not at all. I started to think there was nothing worse than sitting in an empty room and sorting out old sheets! But look what I did."

Mattie grinned as Lucy displayed at least forty neat squares of fabric. "And what are these for?"

"I thought we could make some circle quilts. What do you say?"

"I say that it's been at least four years since I've made

one." Mattie bit her lip. "I'm not even sure I remember how to make them," she added. Actually, the last thing in the world she wanted to do was quilt. But how could she tell Lucy that?

"Really? We used to love to make circle quilts. And they're so easy, too." Her voice turned anxious. "Remember how easy it is to gather the circles and then piece them together?"

For a moment, Mattie was tempted to continue the charade for just a little longer, then she noticed that the skin around Lucy's lips was a bit strained. Crossing the room, she took a seat on the sofa cushion next to Lucy then held out her hands. "What's wrong?"

"Nothing."

"Lucy?"

She looked away. "Oh, it's nothing." But unbidden, her lip started to tremble.

"Luce? Are you hurt? Is something wrong with Calvin?"

After a brief pause, Lucy nodded, then two twin tears rolled down her face, followed by a loud sob. With a gasp, she pushed a fist to her mouth. "I'm sorry."

Mattie hugged her close. "Is Calvin sick?"

"*Nee*. We g-got in a f-fight!"

Startled by the admission, Mattie pulled away. "Truly? What happened?"

"He got upset with me."

"Over what?"

The tears started coming again. Just as another knock was heard at the door.

After one quick glance their way, Mattie's mom opened the door. "Calvin! Hello."

"Mrs. Lapp. Good afternoon."

"And the same to you."

He nodded, looking uncomfortable.

With a curious look Mattie's way, her mom said, "Did you need something?"

He pulled off his hat and looked across the room toward Lucy. In response, Lucy covered her face with her hands.

Alarmed, Mattie stood up to shield her cousin. "Calvin, perhaps you could come back in a bit?"

"*Nee.* I need to see my *frau.*" He stepped inside without another word, his face stormy. He approached the couch.

Lucy was still crying, and looked to be doing her best to burrow into the cushions. Mattie stepped forward and held up a hand. "I'm sorry, but I don't think you should see her right now."

Just a few feet from Lucy, he stopped. "Why on earth not?"

"Because I don't want you to hurt her," she blurted, old feelings surfacing. Remembering how helpless she'd felt during Lucy's first marriage.

At that moment, Lucy's head popped up and Calvin's expression became one of complete amazement. "What are you talking about?" he asked.

"You know," Mattie said weakly. "Lucy's been through so much. She doesn't need your temper."

He stepped to his right, obviously trying to catch Lucy's

eye. "Lucy?" he whispered. "Lucy, is that what's wrong? Are you afraid of me?"

After the slightest of hesitations, she shook her head.

But Mattie saw that Calvin had seen the hurt on her face.

Eyes dark, he scowled at Mattie. "I don't think you understand. I would never hurt Lucy. Never."

Still determined to shield Lucy no matter what, Mattie lifted her chin. "I know you wouldn't mean to, but . . ."

With an irritated look, he stepped toward Lucy and knelt at her feet.

Mattie was so dumbstruck by the action, she moved to the side, then looked toward her mom, who also wasn't even trying to be inconspicuous. Mattie stepped closer to her mother and grasped her hand.

"Lucy, *mein lieb*," he whispered, grasping her hand. "I thought you knew my words stemmed from worry."

"Y-you were so mad."

"Lucy, you were holding that bag of flour."

"I know."

"Did you know it was mighty heavy? Perhaps too heavy for you?"

Mattie looked to her mother in confusion. Little by little the worry left her mother's features and a sweet smile appeared.

Just as Calvin spoke again. "You know I'd be so upset if anything happened to you, or the baby."

Baby? Shock coursed through Mattie as she gaped at her mom.

Her mom pressed a finger to her lips, signaling for her to stay quiet.

"But I told you I wasna helpless," Lucy said.

"I know that. But you are special to me. You are everything, *jah*? You and the *boppli*." Right then and there, he leaned forward, held Lucy's jaw between his two hands, and kissed her.

As she watched the happy couple, Mattie smiled. Then started to laugh. Oh, it was so good to not be thinking about her problems.

It was so good to think about blessings! "Lucy, you've got something to tell us, *jah*?" she said with a giggle.

Her mother squeezed her shoulder. "I don't think she heard you, dear."

When Mattie glanced at Lucy and Calvin again, they were still kissing, Calvin at Lucy's feet. Just like there was no one else in the world but them.

A lump formed in Mattie's throat. That was what she wanted. Love. Love like that. A love so consuming that no one else existed.

She wasn't sure if she'd ever find it, but Mattie knew she was willing to try.

Even if she wasn't perfect. Even if she was scarred.

No matter what, a love like that was surely worth everything indeed.

Chapter Twelve

"Graham, the day's over, man," Scott, Graham's shift manager, called out with more than a touch of exasperation in his voice. "It's time to call it a day and go home."

Still trying to get a hinge in place, Graham mumbled, "I will. As soon as I finish this project."

"Leave it, why don't you? It will still be there tomorrow. Honestly, you work harder than any man I know."

Finally giving him his full attention, Graham glanced at his boss with amusement. "That's supposed to be a good thing."

"It is, except when you're making the rest of us look bad," Scott teased right back. "Now, go put up your tools and join us if you want. My wife made peanut butter bars this morning and dropped them by for everyone."

A glance to the large, white-faced clock above him on

the wall told the rest of the story. It was ten after five, and time to go. The owners of Crossing Construction and Doors didn't pay often for overtime. They valued family and church, and didn't see any need to impose on other areas of their workers' lives.

"I'll be right there." Peanut butter bars sounded good. And, now that he thought about it, stopping for the day sounded good, too. Though it was as cold as could be in the large, cavernous space, he felt sweat trickle down his back. For the last three hours, he'd been intent on putting brackets on some decorative pieces. The job had been as frustrating as it had been difficult, manipulating the big pieces of wood around like he had. After wiping off his worktable, he headed to the washroom to clean up.

Minutes later, he was sipping a glass of icy cider and biting into his first bite of the peanut bar. Both were very welcome. "Thanks for pouring me a glass, Scott."

"It's a fair trade. You brought me those two loaves of bread the other day. My wife is still talking about how good they were."

Graham drained his glass. "I'll let my *mamm* know," he said. It had been no trouble to ask his mother to make an extra loaf of bread or two. He'd also learned that Scott and the other managers treated the employees more like friends than hourly workers. With that in mind, men were often bringing in drinks or treats to share.

"Don't know what we used to do without you, Graham," Scott said. "I'm always eager to see what you've got in your lunch pail. It's truly amazing, the amount of food you can put away."

He'd always been on the skinny side. Because of that, he'd never been shy about eating his share, and anyone else's too. "Hard work makes me hungry," he said with a laugh.

Scott grinned. "Plus, we're getting mighty used to your jokes. No one makes as awful ones as you."

"It's a gift from God, I'm sure."

"You're a *gut* fit here, Graham," Scott finally said. "I'm glad you're here."

"Danke." Ever since he'd started, Graham had been happy that he'd made the choice to work in the factory thirty hours a week instead of only helping Calvin farm their land.

He'd needed his own identity, and he'd needed time to himself, in the company of other men. Unlike Calvin, who could talk to his horse all day long, and Loyal, who was content to only farm and flirt with Ella, Graham had a need to be around other people with different interests.

So far, the men at the factory fit the bill. Well, all except for William.

Though he'd first thought he was nice enough, further conversations with him led Graham to believe that they had little in common.

Beside him, Scott's easy grin tightened.

Graham stiffened as well. While William seemed to get along with everyone else, no matter how hard he tried, Graham couldn't seem to warm up to him.

At first, he thought it was because he'd made the mistake of introducing him to Mattie and was feeling jealous. But now Graham was slowly realizing that there were other things about William that he wasn't completely fond of.

He had a way about him that seemed to announce that he thought his way was the best, and that the Amish way was the only way.

After exchanging greetings with everyone, William stopped next to Graham. "I would have thought you would be the first one to leave today."

"And why is that?"

"You've got celebrating to do, of course."

Both William's tone and the self-satisfied way he was talking grated on Graham's nerves. "What in the world are you talking about?"

"The party your family is hosting tonight, of course. To celebrate your sister-in-law's pregnancy."

Beside him, the other men shifted uncomfortably. Graham felt just as awkward. William was speaking of women's issues, and private, personal ones, too. Once more, it was obviously not his place to be sharing such news.

But Graham was caught. He couldn't very well ignore William, but if he encouraged the conversation, he felt he'd almost be violating Lucy and Calvin's privacy. "Are you speaking of my sister-in-law Lucy?"

"Of course. Unless Ella is expecting, too?"

Graham shook his head, at least not that he knew of.

William took a seat, joining the other men—and then proceeded to ignore them all as he peppered Graham with more questions. "So, I guess Calvin is pretty excited and proud."

"I wouldn't know. It's private, *jah?*"

"Oh. Sure. I guess I only brought it up because when I saw Mattie yesterday, she was so happy about her friend's news. And you know, they are especially good friends."

He knew that. Of course he knew that. He nodded again and moved to stand up. Usually he looked forward to visiting with Frank, Scott, and many of the other men, but William's arrival had cast a shadow on Graham's mood. "Well, next time I see Mattie, I'll tell her you were thinking of her."

"There's no need for you to do that. I'm going to be seeing Mattie tonight. Again."

Even thinking about William being alone with Mattie made his heart beat a little faster. Though at first he thought they might be a good match, Graham now was certain that Mattie deserved someone so much better than William. He was a foolish man, prone to gossip and half-truths.

Though if he was being completely truthful with himself, Graham knew he'd have to remember that he'd half-hoped Mattie wouldn't care for William at all.

Actually, he'd secretly hoped that Mattie would realize that no one was as perfect for her as he was.

But of course he could never admit that out loud.

"I hope you will have an enjoyable time."

"Oh, we should. I told her we could go for a walk."

Scott spoke up. "In the dark? In the cold?" He curved his hands more thoroughly around his cider cup. "You're braver than I am. The last thing I'd want to do is go out in this if I didn't have to."

"It's not that cold."

"It's near freezing," another man in their group added.

"She must be some girl if she likes walking in temperatures this low!"

"She is." William smiled broadly. "Of course, she doesn't get too chilled walking next to me. I keep her warm."

Graham stilled. Pushing aside his decision to not talk about Mattie here, he asked, "What do you mean by that? What are you doing with her?"

William countered his question with a cool look. "What do you imagine we are doing?"

Graham could imagine too much. His temper was flaring, and his fists were clenched in spite of his best intentions. Desperately striving for control, he said, "Mattie is a vulnerable woman . . . she shouldn't be out in the cold . . ."

"I'm taking care of her." William grinned again.

"You shouldn't be saying such things."

Scott glanced Graham's way, coughed, and then stood up. With a staying hand on William's shoulder, he said, "If I were you, I'd leave right now."

But, fool that he was, William kept talking. "She's not helpless, Graham. And though she hardly has any hair, she's still plenty pretty."

"She had cancer."

"That's what I mean. She's pretty if you don't dwell on her faults." Getting to his feet, William smiled again.

Though the other man probably hadn't meant to be offensive, Graham only saw red. Before he could think the better of it, he jumped to his feet and stood right up to William.

Though his pride was showing, Graham was pleased to see that he stood at least four inches taller. In addition, though he was wiry, he was solid. In contrast, William looked smaller and far more slight.

Graham used this strength and size to his advantage.

"Listen, I want you to leave her alone. Don't see her anymore."

"It's too late. I'm courting her."

"But—"

"It's not your place to say anything to me, Graham. We both know that. And listen . . . before you know it, Mattie and I will be making plans." He turned away then, leaving Graham fuming as he and the crowd of men around him watched William's cocky form fade into the shadows of the hallway.

After a brief moment of silence, Frank crossed his arms over his chest. "This isn't Christian, but a part of me really hopes that man starts messing up. He's not a person I'm anxious to work beside anytime soon. Are you all right, Graham?"

"*Jah*. I mean, yes."

"Is Mattie a special friend of yours?"

She was everything to him. "Yes. She's been my neighbor forever."

"She's who you left work for the other day, right? Didn't you take her to a doctor's appointment or something?"

Graham nodded. "Because of her illness, she still needs a lot of checkups. I don't like her to go alone."

Scott rolled his shoulders into his thick wool coat, buttoned it, then grabbed his lunch pail. "It's no business of mine, but if you like that woman, I'd do something."

"I like her . . ." But how did he describe their relationship? Were they just friends? Were they much more than that?

"You sound pretty close."

"We are. But what can I do? Mattie seems to only want to be my friend."

"You better try harder. Graham, you don't want her getting attached to that guy. If she does, things might go badly for her. What you have to do is start making her want to be more than just a friend."

"It's not that easy."

Scott laughed. "You're a handsome guy. It can't be that hard. Make your move, or you're going to lose her." With a grimace, he added, "And personally, I can't think of anything worse than having to listen to William talk about the girl you like every day."

That would be more than difficult. "I think you have a point."

"I'm glad you think so," Scott replied. "Frankly, I'm almost tempted to tell William that he needs to watch himself. I like this workplace to feel comfortable, and want my men to feel relaxed enough to talk about their families and such. But he is almost crossing the line."

Graham nodded and said he'd think about what the man said, but as he drove his buggy home, he took his friend's words to heart. Yes, something had to be done. He was going to have to make his move . . . or he was going to lose Mattie.

And worse, she was going to end up with a man like William.

And that wouldn't do. Not at all.

Chapter Thirteen

Jenna was running late. For the last hour, she'd been in Jacob's Crossing finishing up the two errands Mary had asked her to accomplish before she returned home.

The first had been easy enough. Mary had asked her to bring home two cookbooks from the library. Jenna was discovering that Mary loved to cook and try out new recipes, much to Abel's dismay. That morning, Mary had given Jenna a list of four choices of cookbooks. "See if you can get any of them, wouldja?" she'd asked hopefully. "I'm so anxious to try out some new recipes for hamburger casseroles."

Mary had said hamburger like it was something wondrous and special. It had taken all Jenna's restraint to not tease her, but of course she hadn't. Jenna was learning that just about everything was special to Mary. She had a way of looking about her that was full of interest and fresh hope.

After she collected the cookbooks and checked them out, she slipped on her cloak, scarf, and mittens, and headed into the chilly weather.

Her next task should've been easier, but in fact it was far more difficult to complete. She needed to go to the market and pick up a dozen eggs. And there was the problem, really. Because if she had her choice, Jenna was sure she'd never step foot in the grocery again.

All because Chris was there.

Though she usually walked as fast as possible in the cold, she found herself slowing down to look at one family's Thanksgiving decorations on their front porch, then stopped to pet a particularly friendly poodle that two girls were taking for a walk.

As Jenna wasted time, the sun continued to fall. Soon the twilight glow would fade into night, and walking back to Mary's home in the dark wasn't something she wanted to do.

So she steeled her shoulders and pushed open the glass door, then exhaled in relief as she realized the store was fairly busy. This was *wunderbaar*! All she would have to do was scurry to the dairy section, grab the eggs, and walk to the cash register.

If she kept her head down, she wouldn't see him, and maybe he wouldn't see her, either.

After a quick glance at the signs at the beginning of each aisle, she darted down aisle three. At the very end was a refrigerated case holding the eggs. With the end in sight, Jenna quickened her pace, determined to finish her chore and escape. All she had to do was pass the woman in the denim skirt and get to the eggs—

"Jenna? Jenna, it *is* you!"

Startled, Jenna stared at the woman who'd just called out her name. Ah. It was Mrs. Berch. Her neighbor.

Well, her parents' neighbor now.

"Hello, Mrs. Berch," she said politely. "Good evening to you."

"My evening is even better now that we've crossed paths here at the market." The woman examined her over the rim of her reading glasses. "How are you doing, dear? I haven't seen you lately."

"I am fine."

"I asked your mother if you wanted to come over the other day to babysit Jeremy, but she said you weren't available."

She wasn't available because she wasn't around! But her mother's evasive words weren't a surprise. Mrs. Berch was English. Never would her family have told an *Englischer* about their personal troubles. It just wasn't done.

"Actually, I've been living with a friend."

"Really? Why? Is anything the matter?"

Jenna knew the lady well enough to know that the question was asked with the best of intentions. She really was a kind person, and someone with whom Jenna would've confided in, if she had felt comfortable doing that. "Everything is fine. I took a job at the library, and I'm tutoring, too. The woman lives within walking distance, so it's easier."

After looking her over again, Mrs. Berch nodded. "Well, I guess that makes sense. You always have been such a hard worker. You take care, dear. I'll tell your parents not to let you be a stranger."

Jenna flashed a weak smile before moving forward, hastily dipping a hand into the cold section, pulling out a dozen eggs, and then, holding the carton securely in front of her stomach, started walking to the front up the next aisle. She was in no hurry to say anything else to Mrs. Berch!

Aisle four was far more crowded. She kept her head down as she darted in between parked grocery carts, a stroller, and a pair of elderly gentlemen examining two packages of bacon.

But all of that rushing did little good. She had to wait for the six people in front of her to pay for their goods. Time seemed to inch along slowly, suspended, as her heart beat quicker and quicker.

Behind her, chatter and conversations floated forward. Mothers talking about school with their children. An *Englischer* was talking far too loudly on his cell phone.

A pair of Amish teenagers were looking through magazines and chuckling.

And then she heard *his* voice. Laughing and joking with someone.

Just like he didn't have a care in the world.

Anger, strong and sharp, filled her as she thought of how unfair that was. Why was she the one who'd gotten kicked out, and now was reduced to skulking around the market, practically afraid to see her own shadow?

"Two sixty-five," the blond teenage girl said as she stuck the eggs in a plastic bag.

"Pardon?"

"You've got to pay for your eggs." She chomped on her gum, looking bored. "Anytime, now."

Fumbling with her wallet, Jenna pulled out a five. "Oh. Yes. Yes, of course."

With little fanfare, the cashier took the five-dollar bill, opened the cash register drawer, then gave her change. "Here you go."

"Thank you," Jenna said. Quickly, she stuffed the change in her tote then strode to the exit. But yet again, she was forced to stop as a mother got her toddler settled in a grocery cart.

Which delayed her far too long. "Jenna? Hey, Jenna. Hold up."

He'd said almost the same thing the last time they'd been together. She'd been trying to find a way to tell him that she was pregnant. He'd been fiddling with something on his laptop computer.

As she'd sat beside him and waited, her already frayed nerves pulled tighter and tighter until she was sure her temper was going to snap. Well, that, or the tears would start falling and never stop.

In a rush, she'd left his side and ran . . . and he had stood and called after her.

Though it shamed her to be running again, Jenna pushed the glass door open with a fierce shove and practically ran down the sidewalk.

"Watch it!" a man said as she practically knocked him down.

"Sorry!" she called out, cradling the carton of eggs to her chest. Afraid to look back to see if he followed, the tears started to fall.

Making her realize yet again that there was going to be no hiding. No hiding from him.

Or from herself.

Not any longer.

When Mary heard the door open, she turned around to greet Jenna with a smile, but instead saw that the new arrival was Abel. "What are you doing home so early?" she asked. "Did Mr. Carpenter not need you today?"

Abel walked to the sink. *"Nee."*

Mary winced. After two days of being almost happy, Abel was back to his sullen ways. "Well, then? What happened? Usually you don't come home for another three hours."

"I had to stay after school."

Oh, this was like pulling teeth! "Why?"

"I messed up my homework." With a bitter expression, he added, "The teacher said I messed it up good. I had to stay late and redo it all."

Seeing the disappointment in his eyes broke her heart. "I'm sorry, Abel. Do you understand things better now?"

"Nee." He turned off the faucet and started drying his hands. "Mamm, I don't want to go to school no more. Can't I stop now?"

"Oh, no. You've got two more years."

"But I hate it. Everyone makes fun of me because I still can't write good."

He had problems reading, too. "I'll ask Jenna to help you more. You said she helped last time, right?"

"She helped, but I'm still the worst in the class."

"You won't be if you keep studying extra hard. All you need is more time, I bet." Thinking quickly, Mary added, "I'll offer to watch her baby when it's born and she goes back to work. That will be a wonderful-*gut* trade, I expect."

But instead of looking hopeful, Abel just slumped. "Jenna can't help me do things for the next two years, Mamm."

"I'll go talk to your teacher. Maybe she can give you some special help before school, too."

"None of that's going to make a difference."

"It might. You just need to be positive. That helps me."

"Stop talking to me like a child, wouldja?"

"Abel, I'm not—"

"Stop. Just stop."

When he rushed off, anger apparent in every step, Mary was tempted to run after him, but she decided to let him go. This anger inside of him had been brewing for some time. The only way to make things better was to make drastic changes, and frankly, she'd been too unsure of herself to do that.

But now that she had Jenna and John, she felt stronger. Amazing how much easier it was to make decisions when she knew there was a person or two on her side. Available to help her solve problems.

With a new resolve, she pulled out the flour, sugar, and

yeast. When Jenna arrived with the eggs, she would make pretzels. Their warm goodness used to always make Abel feel better. Perhaps it would today, as well, even though Abel was growing up.

She was still stewing on Abel's problems when the door opened again. Seeing it was Jenna, she smiled. "Jenna! Did you remember my eggs?"

"Jah." Moving like a wooden doll, Jenna stepped forward. "Here you are. I'm going to go lie down." As soon as she set them on the counter, she walked down the hall.

Concerned, Mary followed. "Jenna, are you all right? Are you sick?"

Finally, Jenna lifted her chin and met Mary's gaze. "I'm not sick," she said. Right before she burst into tears.

Mary wrapped an arm around Jenna and gathered her into her arms. "Oh, you poor dear. Tough day?"

But to Mary's dismay, Jenna didn't answer. Instead, she only cried harder.

Closing her eyes, Mary held her closer, and gently patted the girl's back. The girl really was distraught. Once again, Mary wished Jenna's parents would bend a little and reach out to their daughter. What Jenna really needed was her family's love and support.

But since that wasn't available, she had to make due with Mary.

Opening her eyes, Mary saw Abel standing at the end of the hall, watching them. By his gaze, she couldn't tell if he was upset by Jenna's tears, or upset that she was getting his mother's attention.

When he turned away and closed his door, for about the

thousandth time, Mary closed her eyes and prayed. "Lord, it's me again. I know I was asking you for companionship, and I'm truly grateful for Jenna's company, but I'm afraid I still need more from you. When you have a moment, could you please send me some guidance? There's too much going on in my life to tackle it alone!"

Chapter Fourteen

Graham heard laughter coming from his mother's kitchen before he actually saw anyone. He was glad of that, because it gave him the time to school his tense features into something far more easy and relaxed.

If he didn't, his mother would catch on and immediately begin asking too many questions. Questions that he was in no mood to answer. No, what he needed to do was push his troubles aside and not bring his black mood into the house. Lucy didn't deserve it, and he wouldn't welcome the attention, either.

But all his stern warnings and intentions didn't seem to make a bit of difference. No matter how hard he tried, he felt desolate and out of sorts. And no amount of warnings enabled him to push everything away easily.

He gripped the doorframe for support.

He was still so terribly angry at William, and—though it made no sense—at Mattie, too. Didn't she understand how careful she needed to be around men? Especially men like William who surely had the wrong things in mind? What had she talked to him about when he visited, anyway?

Guilt and regret slammed into him like an uneasy horse when he thought of how he should have never even talked to William about Mattie. How he should have never promised Mattie he'd help her meet a man. For that matter, he should have been praying while they'd been sitting in that elevator, not thinking about kissing Mattie.

Yes, this whole situation was surely all his fault.

He was still standing at the door, doing his best to push his worries away but somehow still stewing on them, when Loyal exited the kitchen and turned the corner, a box of oranges in his hands.

When he almost ran straight into Graham, he jerked to a stop. "What are you doing, standing here by yourself like a stranger?"

"Nothing. Just getting settled."

"Well, it's taking you awhile," Loyal said with an older brother's disdain. "It's near freezing here, too. If you're going to stand around doing nothing, you should do it somewhere warmer, don't you think?"

"Ha, ha." With a push at the wood behind him, Graham stepped forward and finally slipped off his black wool jacket and blue scarf. Without looking at his brother, he hung both on a peg. "What's going on?"

"About what you'd expect," Loyal said drily. "Everyone's eating and talking. Our Katie most of all."

As if to punctuate Loyal's words, Graham heard a shriek of laughter from his little sister drift down the hall. It was loud and unconstrained and altogether infectious.

It was also far different than anything he, Loyal, or Calvin had ever done. When he had been six, his mother had constantly encouraged him to behave himself. He could only imagine that it had been the same for his two older brothers.

When Katie's laughter and chatter burst down the hall again, Graham shook his head in dismay. "Mamm never let us carry on so."

"She wouldn't have, but of course, I never thought about shrieking like that. Did you?"

"*Nee.*"

As they heard Katie giggle again, Loyal smiled. "Though, I think Daed would've enjoyed Katie's silliness," he added. "As a matter of fact, I think our father would've been carrying on right there with her, cracking jokes and being merry. He always loved having a *gut* time."

"You're right. He surely did." A flash of a long ago memory surfaced. In it, their father was teasing their mother about the wishbone on their Thanksgiving turkey. Their mother had blushed and told him not to be so fanciful, but it had been obvious to the three boys that she was enjoying every single minute of their father's banter.

"Before you go in, hold on a minute, would you?"

Graham waited for Loyal to exit the back door, drop

off the box, and come back in. Just when they were about to start walking down the hall, Loyal looked him over. "You got out late from work today, didn't you? We thought you'd have been here before now."

"I am late. I, uh, lost track of time. I got caught up talking with the other men at the factory."

"Oh." Loyal blinked, then shrugged. "Well, that's *gut*. I hope you don't mind me saying so, but I've been kind of worried about you, starting this new job at the factory and all. Maybe you're pushing yourself too hard."

"I'm not."

"Mamm told Ella she was worried about you working so much."

"She shouldn't worry. I'm fine." Curious, he asked, "Loyal, do you think I should have never taken a job at the factory?"

"Honestly? A little. But not for the same reasons. I knew you were a hard worker. We all are."

"Well, then, what were you worried about?"

He paused. "I wasn't sure how you'd get along with all the men in a factory setting. I'd have worries about myself, too. It's a pretty quiet life we lead, here on the farm."

Hearing his brother's matter-of-fact appraisal made Graham realize he'd practically been holding his breath until he heard the answer. Graham sighed. When in the world had he started worrying about pleasing his older brothers?

And when had he become so sensitive, anyway? "I'll tell Mamm I'm sorry I'm late."

"I don't think she minded. I mean, it's not like this dinner was something special, anyway."

"Oh, it sounded plenty special to me. As a matter of fact, I heard we were having a true celebration. Someone had heard about Lucy's news."

Loyal beamed. "It's wonderful-*gut* news, *jah?* Calvin's about to burst, he's so pleased."

"I can only imagine." As far as Graham could tell, Calvin thought nearly everything Lucy did was special. Remembering Loyal's armful of oranges, he said, "Where did those oranges come from?" They definitely weren't something they usually had on hand.

"Calvin, of course." With a wink, Loyal rocked back on his feet. "He asked Uncle John to take him over to some fancy store in East Cleveland today. It turns out nothing makes Lucy happier right now than cold, sweet clementines."

He laughed. "I'll make sure I don't swipe any, then. At least not when he's looking."

"I wouldn't even swipe *one*," Loyal said with a laugh. "Calvin's right proud of that gift."

"And Lucy? How did she receive them? Was she pleased?"

Loyal's eyes softened. "Oh, *jah*. Very much so. She started crying and carrying on, saying how our brother spoils her."

Knowing her history, Graham nodded. "I'm glad of that."

Finally they started walking down the hall. "So, are you

sure you're okay? You have a strange look about you. Like something big is on your mind."

"I'm fine. Just working through some things."

"Well, we'd best go on in then before all the fine food is gone. Mamm and Ella have been cooking all day."

His brother was right. The closer they got to the kitchen, the more tantalizing the aromas. His mouth watered as he smelled the unmistakable scent of sweet potato casserole, roast chicken, and roasted winter vegetables. But overriding it all was the wonderful scent of homemade yeast rolls.

Graham doubted anyone could make a batch of rolls like his mother.

He pasted a smile on his face, then strode into the kitchen, where everyone was gathered around the large oak table. As he approached, Calvin, Mamm, Katie, Lucy, Ella, and Uncle John each popped their heads up and smiled.

Lucy was the first to speak. "Graham, I'm so glad you made it here in time to join us."

"And just in time for the big celebration, I see," he said softly as he crossed the room to the butcher block table in the middle of the room and gently squeezed her shoulder. "Congratulations, Lucy. I hear you're going to be expanding our family."

She blushed. "That is true."

Calvin walked to her side and took her hand. "She's a miracle, don'tcha think?"

Graham wisely refrained from doing anything but agreeing wholeheartedly. "Absolutely." He slapped Calvin on the shoulder. "When I came in, I ran into Loyal lugging about the biggest box of clementines I've ever seen."

"Lucy loves them, so don't eat any."

Graham lifted a hand. "Believe me, I won't."

"Don't listen to him, Graham," Lucy said with a shy smile. "There is plenty to share."

"You may share the fruit if you want, but just don't forget about yourself," Calvin said. " I want you to have something special."

"He spoils me," Lucy said.

"Nonsense," Ella said, coming forward, her full cheeks bright pink and shining under the usual wire-rimmed glasses. "I don't think any of us can ever spoil Lucy too much."

As if she was made of spun glass, Calvin gently pulled his wife closer to him, then slipped his hand around her waist. "How are you feeling? Lightheaded? Do you need to sit down?"

"Of course not."

"If you do—"

"I'll tell you." Looking back over her shoulder, Lucy threw Graham an exasperated look.

Graham winked at her as he made his way to the sink. While washing his hands, he mused that Calvin's and Lucy's love for each other felt cleansing, too. If they could overcome all their problems, then perhaps there was someone special for each person in the world.

Unable to help himself, he said, "Is, uh, Mattie coming over?"

Lucy shook her head. "I asked her, but she said she had other plans. William is stopping by to see her tonight."

Just as he expected, irritation and anger coursed through him again.

Uncle John stepped to his side. "Why don't you take a seat and I'll serve you some chicken."

"There's no need. I can do it . . ."

"Let yourself be helped, son," John murmured. Lowering his voice, he added, "It's obvious you're troubled. I've already finished my meal. Let me help you."

It was good advice. Graham did his best to push his worries to the side as he ate and caught up on the day's events.

And listened about Lucy's doctor's appointment. And looked at Katie's new picture book.

And heard about the new baby goat at Loyal's and Ella's farm.

He tried really hard to push all his worries about Mattie and William away. To forget about the fact that many in his community still thought he'd ruined Jenna.

Doing his best, he tried to care about little things, and to take the time to listen to Katie tell him about her day, too.

Later, he pulled out a dishcloth and helped the women dry the dishes, then went outside and helped Calvin bring in more firewood and stack it by the fireplace.

Hours later, when Loyal, Ella, and John left, after Calvin and Lucy and his mother went to prepare for bed, Graham knew he couldn't wait a moment longer.

He grabbed his coat and a flashlight. He was going to go see Mattie and talk to her about William.

It didn't matter that it was late. Or that he should probably visit her when his emotions weren't running so high.

All that really mattered was that he wasn't going to be able to rest or sit until he knew things with her were all right.

Only when he was walking in the dark did he dare admit the truth. He wanted to make sure things were all right with himself, too.

Chapter Fifteen

"Graham. Oh, my goodness! What's wrong?" Mattie's voice rose. "What's happened?"

Graham realized that his late, unannounced visit had scared the wits out of Mattie. "Nothing's wrong."

Visibly relaxing, she rested against the door. Then stared hard at him. "So there's nothing the matter? You're here for no reason?"

"No." Then, thinking about how confused he'd been feeling about William—and how he really did need a better excuse for his call—he amended his words. "Well, there might be."

She blinked sleepily. "I still don't understand. Is someone hurt?"

"*Nee*. Nothing like that," he said quickly. "I, uh . . . I just wanted to speak with you about something."

Mattie's eyes narrowed as she closed the door a few inches and hid the majority of her body behind it. "If you're not here for a purpose . . . couldn't you have waited until morning? It's late."

"Not that late. Come on, Mattie. Let me in. It's freezing out here."

"It's also after nine." Pointing to the clock resting on the table behind her, she said, "Actually, it's almost ten."

Graham was on the verge of teasing her about the time—she was acting like it was midnight—when he realized she was right. It was late. Too late for him to show up unannounced. It was inappropriate for him to visit at that hour.

But he felt so twisted and confused, he didn't dare apologize. Instead, he pressed forward. "Obviously, I wouldn't have come over if what I had to say wasn't important. I really need to speak with you. Can I come in?"

To his surprise, she still didn't move to the side. "Of course you may not."

"Why not?" Now he was getting slightly irritated. "Mattie, have you felt the air? My feet are turning numb. Plus, we need to talk. Really."

"If you had wanted to talk to me so badly, you should have come over earlier."

"Come on . . ."

With a scowl, she waved a hand over herself. "Have you even looked at what I'm wearing? Don't you even see that I'm not dressed?"

He blinked, realizing that she was dressed in a white and blue striped nightgown and thick ivory robe, and her feet were bare.

As he looked her over, the first thing that he thought of was that she looked adorable. Then, well, he was more than a little bit embarrassed. Here he'd been so intent on his own agenda that he hadn't even taken the time to really look at her.

And hadn't that often been his problem with Mattie? He took her for granted? He was not about to turn away now.

"You're covered, though you really should've put some slippers on."

"You are actually going to stand there and tell me I should put something on my feet?"

Her voice had risen. Graham knew she was uncomfortable. But the walk had been long and cold and his worry hadn't tempered one bit. Raising his chin, he changed his tone to lofty. "Oh, come on, Matilda. Stop being so silly. Besides, we both know I've seen you in that same outfit when you were sick."

"This isn't the same. And Graham Weaver, don't call me Matilda."

"Then let me in." Giving it one last try, he smiled at her the way he always had when he'd wanted something. "Come on, Mattie," he coaxed, making his voice as wheedling as he could. "Just long enough to let me warm up. My nose is cold, too. And my fingers. Let me come in."

"Graham—"

"Please?"

Finally, he saw wavering.

"Mattie, I was with you when you were practically lying on the bathroom floor. I promise, I've seen you looking worse."

Her eyes narrowed. "Is that right?"

"Sorry, but you forced me to say it."

Without another word, she inched open the door. "Come in, then. But you may not stay long."

"I won't." After he got inside, he pushed the door shut with a satisfied thump, then followed her to the living room.

"Ah, you've got a fire. Perfect!" Within seconds, he had his gloves, scarf, and hat tossed on the floor. "I needed this. Why, my fingers were practically turning blue, they were so cold." He stood for a moment, enjoying the warmth spreading through his hands and face. "I tell you, I think this must be one of the coldest nights of the year."

"Winter has come with a vengeance," Mattie said, almost grudgingly standing next to him and holding her hands out to the flames.

Unable to stop the impulse, he reached for her hand. When he felt how cool her skin was, he covered her hand with his other and gently rubbed them between his. Trying to warm them up.

Looking bemused, she let him rub her hand. When he threaded a set of fingers through hers, she spoke. "What in the world are you doing?"

"Your hand is chilly. I was just trying to warm it up."

Smiling slightly, she shook her head. "I doubt that will help much. I seem to be always cold now."

"Mattie. Are you going to be cold forever, do you think?"

A flash of desire, and of something he couldn't decipher entered her eyes, then with another blink she pushed it away. "I was perfectly warm until I opened the door to you."

He grinned at her sharp tongue. "I can wait here while you go put on slippers."

"If you speak quickly, I won't need to put them on."

Oh, that tone! She was obviously at the end of her patience with him. Pretending to be contrite, he said, "Thank you for letting me in."

Her lips twitched. "You're welcome. Now stop beating around the bush. What in the world is so important?"

"You."

As quick as one of those flames in the fireplace, she yanked her hand away. "What about me?"

Uh-oh. Things weren't going as smoothly as he'd hoped. "How about we sit down?"

Mattie followed him and sat, but he could tell she was becoming impatient with his beating around the bush. He could hardly blame her, it wasn't like him to hedge so much.

"Graham, please talk. *Now*," she commanded, hardly blinking when he turned to face her, close enough that their legs touched. "What about me?"

Having already decided to try not to tell her that they'd been talking about her at work, he approached the topic in a roundabout way. "Well, you see . . . I heard William was coming over to see you this evening."

"He did."

"And I heard that he's come over before. Several times."

"Well, yes. Not several. Twice. But you knew that."

"I knew he'd visited you once," he corrected.

Tilting her head to one side, Mattie looked at him curiously. "Why do you care?"

"I have my reasons."

"Such as?"

He cleared his throat. "Actually, Mattie, I've been think-ing, and I believe it would be best if maybe you didn't see him anymore."

"I don't understand. Why?"

He wasn't ready to tell her all his suspicions. "When you are alone with William . . . how is he?"

"He is fine."

Why was it now that Mattie decided to be so close-mouthed? "Well, what do the two of you do together?"

"We—" As if she had just realized what she was doing—giving him exactly what he asked for—Mattie stopped and glared. "Why do you ask? What has got you so spun up?"

"Nothing. I mean, well . . . he told me he was going to see you . . ." His voice drifted off as he realized he now had no idea how to tell her what he was worried about.

After a long pause, her eyes widened. "Graham, did he say something about me?" Self-consciously, she put one of her hands to her *kapp*. "Did he say he thought I was ugly?"

"Of course not." Not wanting to hurt her, he shook his head. "No. No, nothing like that. It's just . . . it's just, I don't think you should see him anymore. I don't think he's the man for you."

"But he likes me . . ."

"Mattie, you can find a better man. I'm sure of it."

Pure hurt flashed in her eyes. "I doubt that. No one's come around yet."

Why was he only now realizing just how glad he was

that he wasn't one of her relatives? Everything he was feeling for her had little to do with brotherly love.

No, it was more of a possessiveness that was catching him off guard and keeping him awake at night. He didn't want another man to be important to her. He wanted to be the only one she thought of.

He wanted the two of them to be courting.

But of course he couldn't say those things. Why, if he did, Mattie would either kick him out of the house or run away, scared of the things he was spouting. To her, he'd always been her friend. Her pal.

Folding her arms over her chest, she raised one very faint eyebrow. The hair there had only recently started to sprout. It was so baby-fine her brows reminded him of an angel's wings. Delicate and fragile.

"Graham? Are you even going to try to explain yourself?"

Well, all right. He could definitely try. "Mattie, we are good friends. Mighty good friends. That gives me a reason to offer my opinion, don'tcha think?"

"That is true . . ." She paused, then walked toward the doorway. "But that is not a good enough reason to come running here at night, offering your opinions."

"But Mattie—"

"I'm sorry, Graham. But I'm out of patience with you. It's not like you're my brother."

Once again, he thanked the good Lord that Mattie Lapp wasn't his sister. "I know that."

She crossed her arms in front of her and shifted. "Well, then . . . *gut naught*, Graham."

He had to say something quickly. He had to give her a reason or this moment would be gone and he'd be stuck backtracking for days. "I overheard him talking about you," he blurted.

One by one, her arms dropped. "And?"

"And, uh, I don't think he understands just how difficult your cancer was."

A wrinkle formed in the middle of her forehead. "And why should that matter?"

"He needs to treat you gently, that's why."

Mattie had the gall to laugh. "Oh, Graham. Listen to you! I don't want to be treated gently."

Stunned, he stepped back. "But of course you do . . ."

"I'm not made of glass. In fact, the doctors say I'm as good as new." She bit her lip. "Well, almost as good as new."

He knew she was talking about her surgery. "You're perfect now. But you do need special care . . ."

"I don't." To his dismay, her voice rose. "Graham, just so you know, I like seeing someone who doesn't always look at me with pity. William definitely does not."

There was a gleam in her eyes that brought out every bit of jealousy he'd been holding close to his chest. It made him start to wonder just how, exactly, William had looked at her.

Pure irritation coursed through him. Oh, but no one could irritate him like Mattie Lapp.

"Not everyone who is concerned looks at you with pity," he snapped.

"You do."

"I certainly do not."

To his aggravation, she rolled her eyes. "Yes, you do."

He'd seen her white as a ghost in the hospital room. He'd held her on the bathroom floor when she was too nauseous to move. And in a flash, he recalled all the emotions that had run through him while he'd tried to be everything she needed. Pain, helplessness, worry. And yes, even pity.

He'd hated that she'd been so sick. "I do not pity you now."

"*Now*, huh? Well, William doesn't, either." Her chin lifted as pure defiance entered her eyes. "As a matter of fact, he told me tonight that he wants to court me."

"You hardly know each other. He shouldn't be so pushy."

"It's not pushy. It's what I want."

"I doubt that."

"And why?"

"Because you're only now feeling better. You need to wait and let your spirit heal along with your body. Mattie, I promise, you'll have time for courting."

"But don't you see? I don't want to wait any longer. I want it now, Graham."

He stepped forward. "What do you want? Excitement? Attention?"

She didn't flinch when he stopped mere inches from her. Only looked into his eyes. "*Jah*," she said. "I want everything. I want attention. I want excitement. I want a man to put his arms around me and hold me close."

He'd done that. But of course, it had been when she was so ill she could hardly stand up. "Mattie—"

But Mattie continued just like he wasn't there. Just like

she was standing by herself, talking to the Lord. "I want a man to hold me close like he cares for me."

His mouth went dry. He cared for her.

"I want him to kiss me," she said after another beat.

He was shocked. "Mattie!"

Her eyes flashed. "Like William said he wanted to."

Graham was so furious, he could hardly find his voice. "What do you mean? Did he try to kiss you?"

"Oh, stop being so prudish. Men and women kiss sometimes, Graham. Even when they aren't married. Sometimes even when they're not engaged. Sometimes things happen." More softly, she said, "Sometimes emotions take control and push all reasoning aside."

"And I suppose something has happened between the two of you?" Even though he knew his voice sounded harsh, he asked again, "Has he kissed you?"

"It's none of your business."

"Mattie. Just tell me."

"Not yet," she said finally. "But I'm hopeful."

He couldn't help it, he reached for her. Held her shoulder, held her so Mattie couldn't turn away and make some stupid flippant remark. "You had better not let him."

"I haven't yet. Of course I haven't."

"*Gut.* You have to worry about your reputation, you know."

"You're worried about my reputation? I'm not the one who is accused of getting Jenna Yoder pregnant, Graham."

Even the mention of Jenna made his stomach clench—like he was receiving a fist in his gut. "I told you that nothing happened between us."

Oh, but he was so tired of everyone thinking he had done something he hadn't. Of being blamed for something when he'd been trying so hard to be the man his father was. The type of man his brothers were.

"I know you say that, and I want to believe you. I do! But I can't help but wonder what did happen. Now, stop ordering me about—" She stopped, hands on her hips. "And you can drop your hand, too."

Stop ordering her around? Stop touching her?

Instead of dropping his hand, he curved it farther around, cupping the small of her back. His breath caught as he waited for her to push him away.

Instead of pushing, she dropped her arms. Instead of stiffening, Mattie sighed. Relaxed. Her body moved slightly closer. Their eyes met.

And that was all he needed. Before he thought things through, before he pushed himself away, he leaned forward and did what Mattie said she wanted. He let his emotions take charge instead of his brain.

He finally gave into temptation and kissed her. Carefully. Like she was made of spun glass, even though that was exactly what she wasn't.

Oh, her lips were as soft as he'd always imagined. He lifted his lips, half afraid he'd scared her.

But instead of pulling back, Mattie sighed and leaned into the kiss.

Giving him the invitation to kiss her again. He cupped his palms around Mattie's jaw and held her still and pressed his lips to hers. Again. Just to make sure they both knew it hadn't been a mistake. Eyes closed, he breathed in her scent. The faint combination of lemons and spice that was Mattie.

Desire spun forward. Making him imagine things he shouldn't. Shocked, he broke away, breathing hard. Knowing he should apologize.

But he couldn't. She glowed in the dim light of the burning embers of the fireplace. Her beautiful dark eyes were gazing at him with awe, her lips slightly parted in surprise. After a split second, she opened her mouth, then closed it.

Then opened her mouth again. Obviously searching for the right thing to say to him, but coming up at a loss.

If he had been able to, he would have smiled. For once in her life, Mattie Lapp was at a loss for words.

Well, so was he. "I should go," he said. Because he couldn't help himself, he brushed his lips against hers one more time. Then he turned, grabbed his gloves, scarf, and hat.

He opened the front door and stomped down her steps, putting on his hat, wrapping the wool scarf around his neck, and thrusting his fingers into the gloves as he did.

After finding the flashlight he'd left by the oak tree, he turned it on and began his long journey home.

The wind was cold against his skin, and the air was so silent he could hear the ground crunch under his feet.

Nothing was resolved. Everything was even more confused than ever before.

He shouldn't have kissed Mattie.

He certainly shouldn't have kissed her more than once.

But when he recalled how she'd felt in his arms. How

her eyes had shone when he'd lifted his head . . . how perfectly right holding her felt . . . Graham smiled.

His heart was full and his spirits were high. All the worries that had been plaguing him all evening had dissipated.

As he shone the light in front of him, guiding his way, Graham began to whistle.

Chapter Sixteen

The moment Graham left the house, Mattie ran to her room. Closing the door swiftly behind her, she rushed to her bed and crawled inside the thick layers of sheets.

"Mattie?" her father called out. "Is everything all right?"

"It's fine!" she called right back. Then burrowed deeper under her covers. As the darkness of the room eased her mind and the down comforter and quilts soothed and warmed her skin, she sighed deeply.

Graham had kissed her!

She wasn't sure whether she was pleased by it or just plain shocked.

No, that wasn't true, she realized as she felt her cheeks heat. That kiss had been like everything she'd ever imagined it would be, back when she'd been twelve or thirteen and had still thought she and Graham would have a chance together.

Graham's embrace had been tender and sweet . . . but not too sweet. He'd treated her like a girl he liked—not as someone who was just a cancer survivor.

Of course, given the way he ran out of the house, there was no telling what he thought about what had happened.

Maybe he regretted it? Or maybe . . . just maybe . . . he had felt that certain something between them, too?

As her eyelids grew heavy, Mattie sighed and snuggled deeper into her pillow. And, for the first time in a long time, thought about weddings and wedding nights . . . and more kisses from Graham.

"Couldn't stay away, hmm?" John asked.

"I needed coffee," Mary countered as she entered the Kaffi Haus.

"And here I thought you were only coming here for my sparkling personality."

Well, John's eyes were sparkling, that was true. In addition, there was a new playfulness in his expression that made her feel like there were a hundred little special feelings between them that couldn't be denied.

But even taking all of that into account, she surely wasn't going to let him know her thoughts! "That most definitely is not the case. I'm only here because your coffee is almost as good as mine."

He paused. "Almost?"

"Almost," she returned with a smile. "But I have to admit to always appreciating your conversation."

"Well, I'll take that." His voice warmed as he looked at her like he always seemed to—as if he was genuinely glad to see her. "Have a seat and I'll pour you a cup."

As she watched him open up a clear glass-fronted cabinet and pull out a white mug, Mary cautioned herself to keep her expression serene and not too interested in his every move.

That was harder than she imagined, because he made her so happy. In fact, John Weaver made her feel younger than she had felt in a terribly long time. It was a gift she couldn't ignore.

As he handed her the mug, she caught a whiff of his scent. Ah. Fresh soap and leather and coffee and donuts—for her, a terribly appealing combination.

Eager to put even more distance between them, she said, "I'm rather hungry, too. Perhaps you could give me a donut as well?"

"I thought you were giving them up," he teased as he went to the case, pulled out a glazed one and slipped it onto a plate. "Though, if you're hungry, you probably need more than one."

"One is enough. I did say I was cutting back." She would've said something more, something more interesting than her need for food and drink—but the door chimed, signaling more customers.

John winked at her before turning back behind the counter.

Mary glanced at the new arrivals, then felt herself blushing when she saw it was her neighbor, Ruth. Ruth was older by twenty years and had never failed to give her opinion on most anything.

"*Gut matin*, Ruth," Mary said politely. "Lovely day for November, wouldn't you say?"

But instead of coming right over to chat for a spell, Ruth only looked down her nose at her. "Mary. I must say that I'm surprised to see you here."

A feeling of unease rushed through her. "And why is that?"

"I would've thought you would be far too busy with your houseguest to leave, let alone be sitting here like this. Eating pastries and sipping coffee."

Mary didn't like busybodies. Especially not busybodies who seemed to find problems in even the tamest of activities. "How kind of you to be thinking of me," she said, letting a hint of sarcasm tinge her tone.

If Ruth was taken aback or embarrassed, she didn't let on. "Yes, from what we've heard, that girl is keeping you plenty busy."

Mary didn't miss Ruth's use of "we've" to signal that Mary had been a topic of conversation for some. "Jenna is no trouble at all. Actually, she is a wonderful-*gut* houseguest."

Ruth narrowed her eyes over the rims of her glasses. "Even if that is the case, I must say I'm surprised you took her in."

"I don't know why. Jenna is a mighty nice girl."

Ruth pursed her lips. "She was. Now, though, I would worry."

To Mary's relief, John entered the conversation. Pretending to wipe the counter near them, he said, "And why is that?"

"Don't tell me you haven't heard about her and Graham Weaver."

John folded his arms across his chest. "I've heard malicious gossip—but I, for one, know that Graham did nothing untoward with Jenna."

"So he says . . ."

"So I *know*."

John's voice was so hard and unforgiving, even Mary was taken aback.

And, by the look of Ruth's flushed cheeks, the woman finally had decided to back down. "All I meant to tell Mary was that she should be careful, given that Jenna Yoder has quite a reputation now."

"Perhaps," Mary allowed. "But I think we all have a reputation of one sort or another." No longer caring about being rude, Mary glared at Ruth.

Ruth continued to flush, but lifted her chin. "All the same, you might want to watch her around your son."

"Abel?"

"Of course. She could be a Jezebel, don't you know." Her voice rising, she added, "In fact, she could very well threaten every good thing you've done for that boy. If they're ever alone together, he might get in trouble."

Mary stared at Ruth, stunned. They'd known each other for years. Ruth had even organized dinners for Mary and Abel when her husband had passed. Though they'd never been especially close, Mary had never imagined the woman could think such venomous things. "I don't think so."

"Still . . . you never know . . ."

"I would know. Even though Jenna has made some mistakes, she still has a good heart. I think we could all name many instances when Jenna has either helped us cook or quilt, or helped watch our *kinner*." Did the other woman really imagine that a lifetime of good choices could really be unraveled with just one houseguest?

"If you don't wish to heed my warnings, that is your business. I just felt that I would say my piece."

"I'm glad you did," John said. "Now, may I help you with your order?"

"I need a dozen donuts."

Though Ruth had turned her back on Mary and was now looking in the case of donuts, Mary felt like she needed to defend Jenna.

"Ruth, though I respect your opinion, I have to tell you that I think Jenna needs all of our prayers and support. The book of Matthew says that 'God blesses those who are merciful, for they will be shown mercy.' "

Ruth's lips thinned. "Indeed, she does need our prayers. And she needs to repent."

"Her family put her out. She had nowhere to live."

"That is her consequence," Ruth said primly over her shoulder.

Mary's hands shook with anger as she sipped her hot coffee and watched John quietly fill a bakery box with a dozen donuts, then take Ruth's money.

Once Ruth left the shop, John walked to Mary's side.

"Are you okay?" he asked. To her surprise, he put a hand on her shoulder, offering comfort.

It took everything she had not to grip his hand with hers and hold him close. "Of course."

"I'm sorry about the things she said. She was pretty harsh." Sliding onto the stool next to her, he added, "Don't let her get to you. I've never had much patience with narrow-minded people."

As she gazed into his eyes, Mary's stomach did a summersault. Suddenly, the donut looked like the absolutely worst thing she could imagine eating. With two fingers, she pushed it a few more inches away from her.

John noticed. Slowly, he got to his feet and took two steps back. "Not hungry anymore?"

"*Nee.*"

"You're not actually giving her insinuations credence, are you? Abel is a good boy and is on his way to becoming a good man. Even if I worried about Jenna's reputation—which I do not—I wouldn't worry about your son."

His words were so good to hear. "Thank you, John. You're right. Abel is most definitely a good boy." But even Mary heard the strain in her voice.

No, she wasn't worried about Abel, but suddenly, she was worried about herself. Leaning too much on John was dangerous. Though she liked John's conversation, he wasn't Amish. Not yet.

Abruptly, she got to her feet. "I think I'll go now."

"You don't even want to stay for my very good, very fresh coffee?" Lines formed around his eyes, drawing her attention to his handsome face again.

For a moment she yearned to sit back down and not think about the future . . . but she didn't dare. "The day has gotten away from me. I should really get home to do my chores."

"How about I come by tonight?"

"Oh, John . . ."

"Tomorrow night? Thursday?"

"*Nee.* Thursday will be a busy day."

"Mary, I know things are crazy, what with Jenna there . . . but I want to see more of you. I thought you felt the same way."

"I did."

"Then don't shut me out."

With some surprise, she realized John was exactly right. She'd been pushing him away. Pushing all her feelings away, just like she used to do right after her husband had died.

She'd thought she was stronger by now.

"Mary? Please?"

"All right. This weekend."

His gaze softened. "I'll see you this weekend, then. Goodbye, Mary."

She walked away before she spoke. Before she was tempted to say something silly. Before she was tempted to tell John that she'd look forward to seeing him again very much.

Most likely, too much.

Chapter Seventeen

In the days since Graham had come by, Mattie kept herself busy. It wasn't hard to do. After a year spent mostly being sick or bedridden, much of the usual spring and fall cleaning chores had been pushed to the side.

Now there was much to do to help get the house back in order. And because there was so much to do, Mattie was happy to help her mother in any way that she could.

For the last two hours, Mattie had been helping her mother organize and clean her sewing closet—and what a mess it was! Stacks and stacks of fabric, shoe boxes packed with knickknacks, sewing notions, and old mementoes filled every corner. Not even a year's worth of sickness could create this nest of a mess. No, this was only possible after years and years of being a packrat.

As Mattie opened one old shoe box and found six sets of laces and two skeins of yellow yarn, she sighed. Had her mother ever met an item that she couldn't justify keeping and storing away?

"*Muddar,* we need to get rid of some of these things."

Over her shoulder, her mother glanced at the contents of the box. "Those items are perfectly useful."

"Indeed. They are useful for someone who will use these things. You haven't knitted in years."

"But I still remember how."

"And the shoelaces? Mamm, no one has worn the shoes these go with since I was in school."

Her mother wavered. "Perhaps . . ." She reached for one, held it up, and inspected it. "Or, they might be useful for trim? Or cording?"

"Maybe for someone else." Encouraged that her mother was at least thinking about clearing up some of the mess, Mattie held up a large basket filled to the brim with scraps of all different shades and colors. "And look at all this. We could surely get rid of all these scraps."

"Oh, no we could not. These scraps can make a very good crazy quilt."

"Mamm, we're not going to be making crazy quilts anytime soon."

"We might. Daughter, you need to learn to be thrifty. Everything can be used for something."

"That is true. But, Mamm, some of this fabric you've had for years." She pulled out a piece from near the bottom of the stack. "Plus, it's all mighty dirty and dusty!"

"It can be washed . . ."

"Really? You want to spend the afternoon washing old scraps of fabric?"

"*Nee.* But it's still useful."

"Why don't we make a sack of scraps and take it to some of the older ladies in our community. You know how they like to make crazy quilts. They will put it to good use. They are always passing out blankets and quilts to people in need."

Her mother bit her lip, obviously wavering. "But—"

"And then I will have made good on my promise to Daed," Mattie said, talking as quickly as she could. Pressing forward, she added, "You know Daed asked me to help you clean this out. If I don't help you, Daed will wonder what we did today."

"Your father has enough to worry about without concerning himself with storage closets." Her mother seemed disgruntled as she looked up from inspecting a violet-colored floral cloth about the size of a pillowcase. "If we don't tell him, he won't know."

"I will. Come now, Mamm. Let's make a dent in this."

"All right." After treating Mattie to a disappointed expression over her shoulder, she left, then returned with a large paper grocery sack. "We will fill this to the brim, but that is it for today, *jah?*"

"That will be enough," Mattie replied. There were more boxes of half-filled spools of thread, needles, buttons, and thimbles, but Mattie knew better than to push her luck. Getting her mother to give up anything was a true accomplishment.

She settled for pulling the fabric out for her mother,

then folding the discarded pieces and placing them neatly in the sack.

They worked together in unison for a time, hardly speaking. Mattie relaxed, enjoying the easy, mindless task, as well as the sense of accomplishment. In no time, they would have the sack filled, then could dust a bit.

On her knees, her mother competently lifted the fabrics and sorted. Then spoke. "So, dear. What did Graham want when he came over the other night? It seemed terribly late for him to come calling."

Now, where on earth had that come from? Just like that, the tables had turned. And now she was the one who was worried about coming up with the right answers.

Though in this case, she wasn't even sure if she had the right answers to describe what had happened between them.

"Mattie? Did he want something special?"

Right then and there, she thought about his kisses. And the way he'd held her close.

And the way she'd felt in his arms. So right. So complete.

But of course she couldn't tell her mother any of that. Fumbling with her folding, she attempted to school her voice and features. "Oh, it was nothing," she muttered at last. "He only came over to say hello."

"To say hello? So late at night?"

"He had forgotten the time." Oh, the lies were coming quick now!

"If Graham Weaver is forgetting the time, then it surely wasn't nothing. He must have wanted something badly."

Oh, he had.

There it came again. A flash of memory. Recalling the glint of satisfaction that had appeared in his eyes before he left, Mattie felt her neck heat. A hint of wariness coursed through her as she remembered his touch. The way he'd held her in his arms.

Right before he'd kissed her.

Mattie lifted her chin. Deciding that her mother was asking too many pointed questions to be coincidence, she decided to tackle the conversation directly. "Mother, what exactly did you see?"

After picking up a dark navy square her mother eyed it, then set it in her keeper pile. "What did I see? Nothing, of course. Your father and I were half asleep."

Mattie relaxed. For a moment there, she'd thought her mother had spied on her and Graham.

"But I would be lying if I didn't tell you that I heard his tone, Mattie." Shifting until she sat comfortably cross-legged on the floor, she added, "He seemed terribly agitated. What was bothering him?"

Mattie shook her head. She was still surprised by what had been on Graham's mind—that she was seeing William. He'd been jealous. Well, until he'd kissed her and made them both forget everything . . . but how good it felt to be in each other's arms. "Oh, you know Graham," she said lightly. "What isn't bothering him? He's such a worrywart."

Her mother raised a brow. "A *worrywart*? Hmm. You know, I never really thought he was much of a worrier. No, he's always seemed more of an easygoing sort of man to me." After picking up two swatches of purple and pink, her mother wrinkled her nose. "I never did care for these. Here you go," she murmured.

Mattie took the fabric and set it inside the sack. "Well . . . he is. A worrywart, that is."

"Perhaps he can't help it. Some people like to fret."

"I would agree with you, except he lets things bother him that aren't any of his business."

"Such as?"

Why do you always say so much? she chided herself. "Such as his brothers' lives."

One of her mother's eyebrows rose. "Why would he worry about them? I've never seen Loyal or Calvin so happy."

"They *are* happy. Which is why Graham shouldn't be worrying," she said lightly.

Pitifully. Oh, but it was so obvious that she was fibbing!

"Mattie, were you arguing about Jenna?" she said softly.

"No. I know he did not father Jenna's baby."

"I hope not. Her mother is so upset."

"As is Jenna. Mamm, they kicked her out of their house!"

"I'm sure they'd welcome her back with open arms if she'd just tell them who fathered her baby. She's been lying, Mattie. That is serious, don't you think?"

"Well, yes. I suppose."

"You suppose?"

Mattie took the four pieces of black fabric and added them to the sack. Now it was almost full. Thank goodness! "I know her troubles are great, but I'd be the one lying if I acted like the world was ending over her pregnancy.

There are much worse things to fear than gossip, or a loss of reputation."

Her mother stilled. "I suppose you are right. After all, we've been through worse. Much worse."

"Mamm?" she asked hesitantly. "Why do you think Jenna lied?"

"I couldn't guess . . ."

"But if you had to?"

Her *mamm* lifted one shoulder the way she did when she was at a loss for words. "Maybe the truth is too awful to admit. Maybe she thought Graham would be his usual easygoing self and not say a word. Or maybe she thought he liked her enough to offer to marry her, no matter what."

"I'm glad he didn't."

"Mattie, the things you say."

"I can't help it. Graham is one of my best friends. I hate the thought of someone trying to trap him into marriage."

Looking at her speculatively, her mother said, "I can see why you'd think that."

"But that said, I still do feel very sorry for Jenna, being tossed out like she wasn't good enough. It seems terribly harsh to me."

"Mattie," her mother said after a pause, "between you and me, I agree with you."

"You do?"

She reached out and brushed her cheek lightly with two fingers. "Most definitely. Daughters are precious things. I would miss you terribly if you weren't with me."

"I'd miss you too, Mamm," Mattie said softly.

Her mother got to her feet. "So now that we've talked

about Graham . . . what are you going to do about William? Will you see him again?"

"I suppose so. He's planning to come over here tonight."

"What if he is not the man who God has planned for you?"

"If he's not, then I certainly hope He will guide me to the right man sooner than later. I want to begin my life again. I want to fall in love and get married and have a houseful of *bopplis*."

Her mother burst out laughing. "Oh, Mattie, but you do make me happy," she said. "I promise, you will have all those things. As soon as you let our dear Lord have a chance. The way you go on, why, He hardly has time to work miracles." She laughed again as she walked to the door.

"I'm going to make us some lunch."

"I'll be there as soon as I finish cleaning up."

"*Danke*, daughter."

As she watched her mother walk away, Mattie thought about miracles. She held her hands to her scarred chest and wondered if she had the nerve to ask God for more than her fair share of them.

After all, He had already given her one miracle—her health. Suddenly it seemed, after a mighty difficult journey, that she was starting to get everything she'd ever wanted. Her body was healing. Her relationship with her mother was smoother.

And then there was Graham. She'd always known he was important to her. She'd certainly come to depend on his friendship. But maybe it was time to see if there was a whole lot more to their relationship?

As she thought of their kisses, she felt her cheeks heat. Everything with Graham had felt so right. Why, one kiss had turned into two . . . then three.

Now all she had to do was decide if taking a chance on an uncertain relationship with Graham was worth jeopardizing the friendship they had. Had God given her and Graham to each other because He knew their love was meant to be?

Could it really be that easy?

Chapter Eighteen

As Jenna continued to organize packets for the new reading club Ms. Donovan was starting for a group of twenty senior citizens, she let her ear drift to the current reading group in the library. The preschoolers who came twice a week to hear Ella read.

Today, they were reading *If You Gave a Mouse a Cookie*. This one seemed to be as popular as Ella's other choices. At least a dozen children were scooted as close as they could to her; and each time Ella turned a page, they leaned forward.

In other parts of the library, people often stopped what they were doing and observed the children watch Ella with pure joy on their faces. Whenever Ella read, Ms. Donovan said, you could hear a pin drop. Jenna figured that was no exaggeration.

She smiled as Ella read the last line of the book, then set it on her lap. But still the children sat motionless, anxious for another word.

"I'm sorry, but I'm afraid that's all there is, *kinner*," Ella said. "You can only give a mouse so much, you know."

Jenna grinned at the joke as she put another stack of cards together.

On the floor in front of Ella, one of the little girls pulled on her skirt. "Couldn't you read us another story, Miss Ella? Just a short one? Please?"

Jenna bit her lip, wondering what Ella would say. Actually, she was half looking forward to another story.

Ella shook her head. "*Nee.* I'm afraid not," Ella said with a look of disappointment. "I'm sure your parents have places to take you."

More chatter followed as one by one the little patrons got to their feet and approached Ella for hugs.

Then the mothers rushed forward, anxious to check out books and be on their way. Ms. Donovan signaled Jenna to leave the worktable and join her.

One by one, Jenna stamped cards and helped Ms. Donovan scan the books. "*Danke,*" little Emily said.

"You are welcome, Emily," Jenna said with a smile.

When the rush was over, Ella joined them at the circulation desk. "Well, I think I had better read that one again soon. They liked it."

"I think they like all the books you read to them," Jenna said. "You are a wonderful-*gut* librarian."

"Indeed you are, Ella," Ms. Donovan said with a smile.

"The preschoolers and I took a vote and decided you are never allowed to stop working here."

Ella laughed. "Until Loyal says differently, I don't think I'll ever choose to stop. I enjoy it too much."

"It's obvious," Jenna said. "You glow when you're with the *kinner*."

"They make me happy." With a shy smile Ms. Donovan's way, Ella lowered her voice. "To tell you the truth, I like too many things here to give up this job. For once, I feel like I belong."

Jealousy struck Jenna hard. With every day that she spent at Mary's, it was becoming more and more apparent that she didn't belong anywhere. Her parents and family didn't want her, and Graham certainly didn't. And though Mary was a gracious hostess, Jenna knew that she couldn't take advantage of Mary's hospitality forever.

Jenna smiled tightly, then went back to her table and picked up the papers. It had been a silly dream, but for a while, she'd truly thought one day she and Graham would be married, too. And that she and Ella would be sisters. For a while, she'd hoped that was where she belonged. With the Weaver family.

Of course, her lies had made almost any sort of relationship virtually impossible.

To her surprise, Ella joined her, pulling up a chair. "How about you compile the papers and I staple and put them into folders?"

"That's fine." Working in unison, Jenna picked up the stacks, straightened them neatly on the table, then handed them one by one to Ella, who in turn stapled and made a new pile. The work was easy, and in no time a rhythm developed as they worked together.

After a bit, Ella glanced her way. "So, how are you feeling?"

"Me? Fine."

"Truly? You are lucky, then. Poor Lucy is sick all day long." A whimsical smile appeared on her lips. "You should see Calvin fuss over her. I tell ya, you would think no woman had ever been with child before! He constantly watches every move Lucy makes, and even bought her a case of fancy oranges." She shook her head slightly. "Have you ever heard of such a thing?"

Jenna smiled weakly as Ella continued. "We are glad for the both of them, to be sure. But we can't help but smile at Calvin, ya know? My Loyal thinks his brother is mighty amusing."

"Yes. I can just imagine that."

As Ella stopped her stapling to give a preschooler who approached a hug, a fierce longing for some of Lucy's attention burst through Jenna before she could tamp it down.

Though she knew it wasn't fair, Jenna privately thought Lucy's terrible morning sickness most likely stemmed from being allowed to be sick. After all, she had someone who would care for her.

Jenna, on the other hand, wasn't nearly that lucky.

When Ella returned to stapling, Jenna tried to move the conversation along. She shouldn't punish Ella for her own misfortune. At least she had asked how she was feeling. "I was a little queasy at first," she admitted. "But I'm better now."

"I'm glad of that. How far along are you? I mean, do you know?" As the question sat between them like an uninvited guest, Ella's cheeks burned bright. "I mean . . . oh, I don't know what I mean."

Jenna knew Ella didn't have a mean bone in her body—she'd just been trying to make conversation. And the question wasn't a difficult one for her to answer, anyway. After all, she knew to the exact moment when she'd conceived. "About four months."

"Ah." Ella looked at her, then darted her eyes away. "I heard you are living at Mary Zehr's."

"I am."

"I've always thought she was a kind woman."

"She is. She is terribly kind."

"So, have you seen Loyal's uncle John?" Ella asked, her voice low and bright. "Loyal told me John fancies Mary something awful."

In spite of her mixed-up feelings, Jenna felt herself smiling. "I have, indeed."

"What do you think? Do you think Mary will have him? Do they seem like a good match?"

"Perhaps." As she thought about how confused she'd been, thinking about Chris, wondering about Graham, she shrugged. "I think love is out of their hands, if you want to know the truth. Things always seem to happen the way our Lord wants them to."

Ella grinned. "I think you're right about that." After making sure that Ms. Donovan wasn't in hearing distance, she said, "At first, I just wasn't sure what would happen with John; he seemed at loose ends. I'm glad things are better now." After picking up the last two packets Jenna had put together, she stapled them quickly and stood up. "I guess I had better eat my lunch, then get ready to shelve books."

"All right."

"And Jenna?"

She paused. "Yes?"

"I know it's hard, but please try not to worry so much. Everything will work out. It always does."

Jenna wished Ella's words were true, but they certainly didn't feel true. Though Ella had had her share of hardships, now she was married to Loyal Weaver, one of the most eligible and handsome men in their community. She had little to worry about. But as far as Jenna could tell, her own troubles were only beginning.

But that wasn't something she could tell Ella. Instead, she smiled bravely and tried to pretend that there was a light at the end of her tunnel. "*Danke*, Ella."

After another kind look, Ella squeezed her hand, then walked away—leaving Jenna to wonder if things would ever get better. Or if things would continue to only get worse.

"Mattie?" her mother called out. "William is here."

Surprised to see him, she rushed to the entryway. "Hi."

"I happened to be nearby, so I thought perhaps you'd like to go for a walk with me. Want to go grab your coat?"

Mattie paused. Took a closer look at him. William held his felt hat tightly in his hands. He looked happy to see her. And neat. But nothing like Graham.

That's when she knew.

Nothing might ever happen with herself and Graham. Maybe they'd never be more than friends.

But she knew for certain that there was nothing between her and William. "William, I thank you for the invitation, but I don't think that would be a good idea."

His eyes narrowed. "Why not?"

Oh, this was hard! "I don't think we suit."

He looked flabbergasted. "We just haven't spent enough time together. You need to give us a chance . . ."

She walked to the door and turned the handle. "I'm sorry. I can't help how I feel."

"I'm not giving up, Mattie. Don't be surprised if I stop by again."

Now she was feeling a little irritated. "My feelings will stay the same."

"Feelings change. You'll see," he promised as he put his hat back on and left.

Making her feel decidedly chilled.

Chapter Nineteen

"Uncle John, Mamm is terribly excited about you becoming Amish soon," Katie said as she skipped by his side down the sidewalk toward the Dutch Kitchen, a new restaurant that had opened just three blocks from his donut shop. "Everyone is."

When he'd heard his sister-in-law was hoping to get some sewing done, he'd offered to take care of Katie for a few hours. It had been no problem. He really did enjoy the girl's company. Of course, one never knew what she would choose to talk about. Lately, her conversations had been all about her books, Ella, and Lucy's baby.

He was a little caught off guard to realize she'd been thinking about him joining the church, too.

"I'm excited as well," he replied.

"Are you scared?"

Stopping, he looked at her curiously. "Katie, now why would I be scared about reaffirming my faith?"

"'Cause it's something you never did before."

"Ah, do you get scared of new things?"

After a pause, she nodded.

He really did treasure this little girl. Knowing she didn't bring up anything without an ulterior motive, he asked lightly, "And what new things are you worried about?"

"My new teacher."

"What happened to your old one?"

"She had a baby." Katie wrinkled her nose for good measure, making him laugh.

"So who's your new teacher?"

"Miss Yoder."

There were at least three Yoder families in Jacob's Crossing. "Do you know her first name?"

"*Nee.*" She paused. "Mamm said I mustn't ever call my teacher by her first name, anyway. So it don't matter what it is."

"Perhaps you have a point there. Well, maybe she'll be at church on Sunday and we can meet her then."

"Maybe. Do you think she'll like me?"

"Yes. If you're a good girl."

"I'm always a good girl."

"Katie, I love you dearly, but even I know that is not the full truth."

Biting her lip, she nodded. "All right. I'm *almost* always a good girl." Looking at him hopefully, she raised a brow. "Right?"

"Very much so." He laughed. "So when does your Miss Yoder start?"

"On Monday."

"Your mother asked me over for supper on Tuesday. You may tell me all about Miss Yoder then."

"Okay."

Thinking about school made him think of Abel, who was about as far from being an eager student as a child could get. "Katie, do you happen to ever see Abel Zehr at school?"

"Yes, but he don't talk to me. He's big."

"I guess he is. Is he a good boy?"

"Not always."

"What does that mean?"

"Oh, I don't know."

Now he was curious. Rarely did Katie hesitate to offer an opinion. "What does he do at school?"

She shrugged. "He doesn't say much. And he ignores me." She paused. "After you get baptized, what are you gonna do?"

"I'm going to eat lunch with everyone, of course," he said with a smile. Actually, he wasn't ready to tell her more about his plans.

"Are you going to stop driving your truck?"

"I am."

"Are you going to move out by us?"

"I am not."

"Are you going to turn off your lights in your apartment?"

"I am."

"Are you—"

"Katie, enough," he said, exasperated. "You are enough to drive a man to drink."

Her eyes widened. "Uncle John!"

"Perhaps not drink. Maybe just to getting a headache?" he asked as they entered the homey-looking restaurant. Immediately, warmth infused his body. "Ah, this is much better."

"My ears were getting cold."

He laughed. "Two please," he told the hostess, then stilled when he saw Mary and Abel sitting together. Though they'd planned to see each other for dinner on the weekend, he couldn't pass up this opportunity to see them. "Actually, perhaps we could join these two here?"

Mary looked up. "John!"

"Hi. I was just taking Katie here out for soup. Can we join you?"

"Certainly." All smiles, she scooted to the side, and gave Abel a look. "Isn't it nice to have John and Katie join us?"

"Sure," Abel said.

By his side, John noticed Katie shrinking a bit against him. "Katie, are you okay?"

She nodded, but only looked at the table.

Curious as to her reaction, he glanced at Abel again. His expression looked like ice, and he was glaring at her. "Is something wrong between the two of you?"

After a moment, Abel shook his head. "*Nee*. I was just preparing myself to be tattled on."

"I wasna gonna say a thing," Katie blurted.

Mary leaned forward. "Say a thing about what?"

"About how Abel gets into trouble all the time."

"What?" John bit back his words after seeing Mary's shocked reaction.

Abel's eyebrows snapped together. "It's just because I'm stupid, right?"

Mary crossed her arms in front of her chest. "Abel Zehr, you will explain yourself."

"I have a hard time in school," he muttered, a mutinous expression burning in his eyes. "You know that."

She faltered. "Your grades have not been that bad."

"They've never been good, either, Mamm." Brushing the hair from his forehead, he shook his head. "Why, I bet even Katie here can read better than I can."

John looked at Katie, ready to shush her if she started bragging about how she was, indeed, a very good reader.

But instead of looking proud, she looked unsure and doubtful.

Abel continued. "It's not like I haven't been trying. But even when I do, our teacher always gets mad at me."

"You never told me any of this."

"What could you have done?"

"Something, surely."

John's heart went out to her. Though he had no children, he was learning quickly from his dealings with Katie that their problems and needs quickly turned into his own. Right now, he was able to make Katie happy by giving her attention, donuts, and hugs. But it was very hard indeed to realize that one day she would need things he could never give her.

Just as he was contemplating any number of platitudes to tell Mary, Katie interrupted. "We're getting a new teacher," she said.

For a moment, hope entered Abel's eyes, then dimmed again. "Like that's going to make anything better."

"It might," Katie said, sounding older than her six years. "The other kids said Miss Yoder is nice."

"Like that would matter."

Though of course all of this was news to John, he was somewhat surprised to see that it was news to Mary, too.

"Why have you not told me any of this before now?" she asked.

"You've seen my grades."

"I thought you were just behind because you needed to try harder."

"Mamm, I have tried hard. Really hard. The truth is . . . well . . . I have a hard time reading. The letters move all around and get switched up."

"Maybe he should get tested," John said. He remembered reading in the paper about all kinds of learning disabilities a child could have. Needs that only special teachers could help.

"Tested?" Mary lifted a brow.

"You know, like from an *Englischer.*" John racked his brain. "Maybe he has a learning problem." Recalling one of the men he'd worked with at the tire distributor, he said, "Maybe he has dyslexia."

"A disease?" Mary looked like she was on the verge of tears.

"No, no." Seeing that he had Abel's attention, too, John explained. "That's when someone sees numbers and letters all mixed up and backwards."

A flash of recognition entered Abel's eyes before he turned away. "I'm twelve. There's no need to do anything. I'll only be in school another two years."

Mary nodded, but still didn't look relieved.

John was glad of that, because he wasn't relieved, either. "Abel, you might be only going to the Amish school for two more years, but you'll want to be able to read for the rest of your life. You'll need to do figures and such, too."

"Not if I just farm."

"I don't understand why your teacher never told me," Mary said, fussing with the laminated menu. "I wish I had known."

"She never told you because she thought I was lazy," Abel said sharply. "And sometimes you say I'm that way, too. But I'm not."

Tears sprang to her eyes. "*Nee*, child. You are not."

The server came forward. "What will you like?"

John hadn't even looked at the menu, but he knew Katie wanted soup. "Two bowls of soup?"

"Vegetable?"

"Perfect."

Abel scooted his chair out. "Can I go sit on the porch, Mamm? I'm not hungry."

After a pause, Mary nodded. Her brow furrowed as he left. When they saw his shadow on one of the swings, Katie pulled on John's sleeve. "Can I go sit with him?"

"Do you promise not to ask him a dozen questions?"

For once completely earnest, Katie nodded. "I won't even ask him one. I'll be good. I mean, as good as I can be."

"All right," he said, because he was eager to speak with Mary alone. When Katie darted through the doors, and they saw her sitting next to Abel, John exhaled. "How are you?" he asked softly.

Tears were falling now. "About like you'd imagine. Not too well."

"What can I do?"

"You've already done more than I have, John. If it weren't for you and Katie, I wouldn't even know as much as I do now." She bit her lip. "I just don't understand myself sometimes. I thought I knew a lot more about my son than I do."

"I promise you, you didn't know because he didn't want you to know. Boys are good at keeping secrets."

Something new flickered in her eyes. Awareness? "Even you?"

"Especially me," he said, aching to hold her hand. "Back when I was Abel's age, I wanted to leave more than anything. But, I promise, I never told a soul."

"What do you think we should do?"

He loved how she was including him in her worries. "How about I call the English school and ask about testing? I think you can get Abel tested to see if he has any learning problems."

"And if he won't go?"

John thought about that one as he watched the server

approach with two piping hot bowls in hand. "I have an idea, but you may not like it."

"What? I'm open to anything. He needs to be able to read and write, John."

"What do you think about getting Jenna involved?"

"Jenna?"

"He seems to be able to take advice and help from her more easily. And why not? She's a pretty girl."

"And?" She still looked confused.

"And if we can get her to volunteer to go with him, to help him, it might help them both."

Understanding filled her gaze. "Jenna will have something constructive to do, and Abel with get help."

"Exactly. If that sounds like something you want to do, of course."

"But what about me? Shouldn't I be doing more?"

"It seems to me, you've already been doing a lot. God asked your heart to take in Jenna and you did. He also asked you to give me a chance, and you are . . ."

A rosy pink hue filled her cheeks. "I . . . I'll go get Katie and tell her to come in."

"Thank you."

"And then I'm going to take Abel on home."

"All right."

She touched his shoulder. "And John?"

"Yes?"

"God might have brought us together by chance, but I don't think I'm going to let you out of my life easily."

Happiness floated through him, though he pushed

down that giddiness. "I don't intend to leave, either," he said. "You are stuck with me."

She blinked, and a warm, cozy light flared in her eyes, promising all kinds of dreams for him.

He clung to that hope like a lifeline. And held it close to himself until Katie came in, skipping and full of talk about a cat she saw on the porch.

With a hand up, he reminded her to silently give thanks for their food, then dipped his spoon in his bowl. "Now you can tell me all about the cat, Katie."

"You still want to hear?"

"Every word, child," he said with a smile. After all, that was why he had taken her out. Every word she said was precious to him. Every single word.

Chapter Twenty

Mattie had come to hate her monthly checkups at the medical center. Not only did the travel mean that the majority of the day would be used up, but always in the back of her mind lurked the idea that the doctors or nurses would one day discover a problem and need to bring her in for more tests.

No matter how many times the doctors declared she was "cancer-free," she couldn't shake the feeling that this freedom was a temporary thing. She'd heard of too many women who'd been "cancer-free" for years, only to discover another lump or to receive another worrisome test result.

But even tougher to take than the worry about the future were the reminders of the past. Whenever she stepped foot in her doctor's waiting room and smelled the same clingy scent of antiseptic, old buried feelings rose. And with them came all the pain and anxiety she'd lived with for a year. Like a flash, she'd feel clammy and ill again. It was as though even the waiting room's carpet held hints of her past.

Though Mattie tried hard not to make too much of a fuss about her feelings when she had appointments, they seemed to be universally known. Her mother always made sure Mattie had company, whether it was she or Lucy or Corrine or Ella who joined her.

And, then, sometimes, poor Graham had the dubious honor of accompanying her. Like today.

Now he was sitting next to her in the waiting room of the lab, flipping through old magazines while she waited to be called back to get blood drawn.

He looked completely calm and unflappable—far different than the way he'd been when he'd visited her the other night. Actually, from the way he was acting, one would think they'd never argued at all.

Or kissed.

In fact, all their heated words about William and the suitability of him in her life seemed to have been forgotten. At least for the moment. From the time she and Charlie had picked Graham up, he'd been polite and cordial. Friendly.

And that behavior never ceased to amaze her. Yet again, Graham was putting her needs before his.

Graham didn't like to be thanked for coming with her. He'd told her time and again that he liked to come with her, that he would worry about her if he didn't. But still, she couldn't help but thank him. "I really am grateful to you for taking time off work, Graham."

He looked up from the *Sports Illustrated* he was reading. "I told you it was no trouble. I don't work full-time at the factory—only thirty hours. Arranging my day around this appointment was easy."

She had a feeling it hadn't been that easy. "Still, I do appreciate it. I don't know what I would've done if you couldn't have come . . ."

"But I could," he said abruptly, cutting off the rest of her gratitude. "Besides, Mattie, you know I only come with you to the hospital so I can tease you."

He was good at teasing. But he was also good at making her feel at ease, too. Playing along, she said, "And what are you going to tease me about today?"

He set the magazine down and grinned. "I haven't decided yet. The possibilities are endless."

Though his words were full of fun, there was a new light in his eyes. It made her warm and not a little bit flustered. "Not so."

"Quite so."

Self-conscious, she raised a hand to her head. "Are you going to comment on my lack of hair?"

"Not today, Mattie."

The slow, soft tone in his voice was new, as was that warm gaze. Actually, both felt disconcerting, especially since she couldn't help but remember how much she'd enjoyed being in his arms. "My *mamm* asked about your visit the other night," she blurted.

In a blink, his gaze turned intent. "And what did she say?"

"She thought it was interesting that you came so late and stayed so long."

He winced. "I shouldn't have come at all. What did you tell her?" he asked again.

"Nothing."

"Nothing?"

"Not a word." Doing her best to keep her tone light, she fussed with the fabric at the end of her sleeve as she continued. "Actually, she wasn't very happy that I had no news to tell her."

Relief flew into his expression. Just like that, she knew he was thinking about their kiss.

"Mattie, are you sorry I stopped by?"

"Do you mean right now?"

"I mean then."

Of course he meant then! That was what they both had been talking in circles about!

But, what was he really asking? Was he really talking about showing up after nine at night? Or was he asking if she regretted their kiss?

"Mattie, surely you have an opinion."

"I don't know what my opinion is. I can't decide," she finished in a rush.

"That's convenient."

"I can't help it. If you ask me questions, you must sometimes be prepared to hear some answers you don't like." Actually, that was the truth. She didn't know if she regretted their kisses or not.

Though . . . perhaps she would regret them if Graham did. She bit her lip as she studied him. *Did he?*

"Mattie—"

Two women across from them popped their heads up. And though she ached to settle things between them, ached to tell him that she told William that she wasn't interested in him, she certainly wasn't eager to have witnesses. "We can't discuss it here, Graham."

"If not now, when?"

"I—" The office door opened. "Mattie?" the nurse called out. "You ready?"

Mattie practically hopped to her feet. "I am. I'll be back soon, Graham."

"I'm not going anywhere. I'll be here when you come back. And then later on, we'll talk. Okay?"

When she nodded, he picked up the magazine again. Just like he wasn't worried about a thing.

She really needed to be more like him, she decided. She should learn to take every day as the gift it was and stop worrying about romance and consequences. Yes, that was it. She should stop worrying about it all and remember the promise she'd made to herself when Ella had gotten in the buggy accident: she would start trusting the Lord more.

Yes, most certainly. That was what she needed to do. Soon.

As soon as Mattie disappeared through the door and it closed behind her, Graham put the magazine down and sighed in relief. Every day, it was getting harder and harder to pretend that they were just buddies. That night when he'd visited, he hadn't even tried. His emotions had been running so high, no voice of reason was going to get through. He'd had to rely on his willpower alone.

Of course, it hadn't been enough.

For a few minutes there, he'd slipped. He hadn't been able to hide the tenderness he felt toward her. Hadn't been able to hide the feeling of how right it had felt when he'd held her in his arms.

And then there were the kisses.

Even going over to Mattie's house had been a giant mistake. He'd been too emotional.

Okay. He'd been too jealous of William. And because of that, he'd acted too impulsively. His brain knew that. Unfortunately, other parts of his mind couldn't stop repeating what had happened between them. Over and over again.

It didn't help to know that even the slightest hint of encouragement would lead him into her arms again.

Just as the nurse called out a name, and then another woman followed her, Graham picked up his magazine again—and flipped the glossy pages with a new resolution. What he needed was a plan. What he needed to do was tell Mattie how he felt. Then they could face the consequences together.

For a moment, he imagined a future with Mattie by his side. Happy. Enjoying a true partnership.

But what if his imaginings were destined to be nothing more than just a dream? He imagined telling Mattie his true feelings—and he imagined her shock. Heaven knew, she'd told him many times how grateful she was for their *friendship*.

And he imagined her fear, too—what if she got scared and ran into the arms of another man? Like William.

Unfortunately, he didn't know if he could risk doing that anytime soon. He was discovering he'd rather have things rocky between him and Mattie instead of being without her at all.

But maybe it was time to speak his mind to William? Even though he'd set them up, Graham realized they wouldn't be good together at all. And though William would probably get irritated, if he told William how he and Mattie were starting to have more of a relationship . . . surely William would back off.

Most men would. Right? That's what he would do, Graham decided. He would talk to William the next time they worked together and put the record straight. Tell him that Mattie actually had a sweetheart. And it was Graham.

And though things might be a little rocky between him and William, things would settle down. After all, that's what happened. Men and women fell in love all the time— sometimes even stepping on a few toes while they did so.

Love. Graham gulped. Well, he finally admitted it. Now all he had to do was figure out a way to tell Mattie that he had fallen in love with her before she saw William again.

Chapter Twenty-One

All too soon, Jenna saw him again. Ducking her head, she exited the market as quickly as she was able and walked down the sidewalk. It was bitterly cold and the morning's first scattered flakes had transformed into a full-fledged snowfall. Small, delicate flakes were now falling slowly, so slowly that each looked to be suspended in the air for a brief moment in time before giving way to gravity and landing on a surface.

Several had landed on the black leather of her shoes, glistening on the tops like decorations before quickly melting into nothing.

She increased her pace, desperate to put even more distance between herself and the market. And the man inside. As she imagined what a meeting between them would be like, anxiety sank into her bones. Until she got off the sidewalk and into the protection of Mary's home, she wasn't safe.

Then she heard footsteps behind her.

The smart thing to do would be to turn around and see who it was. Jenna didn't.

Tucking her chin closer to her chest, she quickened her steps. The snow didn't abate, falling now on her eyelids. Stinging them.

The person came closer. Footsteps pounded the side-walk behind her, becoming louder with each step. Gripping her cloak, she pulled it tighter around her body. Hoping it would warm her. Hoping it would shield her from the worst.

"Jenna?"

It was him.

Almost running, she increased her pace, weaving past an English couple walking their cocker spaniel. "Watch out!" the man said.

"Sorry!" she blurted, not even sure if she'd spoken in English or Dutch. All she cared about was getting to the next block. Getting away from him. Her breath grew ragged. She crossed the street, hardly looking on either side.

Soon he would have to give up, right?

"Jenna? Jenna, wait!" he called out. With a gasp, he added, "Please?"

Though the temptation was great to ignore him, she slowed.

He was just loud enough to capture the attention of two elderly ladies on the other side of the street. Just loud enough to create more of a disturbance if she didn't do as he bid.

She had no other choice.

With a sense of inevitability, she finally stopped.

"Thank you," he said, his voice breathless and more than a little husky, though whether it was from his run or their meeting, she didn't know. "For a moment, I didn't think you were going to stop."

She definitely hadn't wanted to. Too afraid of her emotions to say much of anything, she stood and stared at him in silence. Watched him approach as the snow continued to fall, decorating her cape and his thick brown jacket.

"I was starting to wonder if I was going to have to chase after you through the whole town."

Her mouth went dry as she noticed the look of intent in his eyes. As he came closer, his footsteps slowed. At the same time, the look of purpose was replaced by wariness. "Hi," he finally said.

"Hi," she answered—almost automatically—as she looked into the eyes of Chris Henderson, the son of the pastor of the local Christian church. "Hello, Chris."

Concern etched his features as he looked her over. "Where have you been? I've been looking for you for weeks." He paused. "I was about to come to your house and ask if I could see you."

Even thinking about that visit made her stomach turn. Her parents had no idea she even knew Chris. If he had mentioned that they'd been dating, it would have made things even worse than they were. "I'm so glad you didn't do that. My parents would've been so mad. And they wouldn't have told you anything anyway."

He shrugged. "I don't think I would've cared what they thought. And I would have stayed there until they let me see you."

"It wouldn't have done any good. I'm not living there."

"What? Where are you living?" Before she could think of a reply, he said, "Where have you been? It's like you suddenly disappeared. I used to see you every other day at the market."

That was because she'd go there just to see him, Jenna realized with regret. Did he really not realize that? For a time, going to see him had been the highlight of her days.

Now, though, her goals were the complete opposite. No matter what, she wanted to avoid him. Wanted to avoid anything that had to do with him.

As a mother pushing a stroller approached, Chris put his hand on her shoulder and guided her to the side. "Watch out," he murmured as they neared a dense thicket of prickly pines that offered them a little bit of privacy, and a little bit of a respite from the snowflakes that were falling.

When they were standing alone, he brushed two fingers down her cheek. Wiping away the snowflakes that had settled there.

Or perhaps it was a tear?

"Talk to me, Jenna," he said, his voice deeper. "Don't block me out."

"I haven't been blocking you out. Just avoiding you."

His expression eased. "I've missed you. I've missed your humor. And I really do want to know what happened."

At one time, his words would have caused a rush of pleasure. Now she just worried that everyone would see the two of them together and ask questions. "I've been busy," she said.

"Really busy, huh?" His tone was flat, revealing his skepticism. He sighed, his eyes scanning her face.

Jenna stood still, aware that she had no real reply to give him. Everything was such a mess. Plus, she had so much to tell him, she hardly knew where to begin.

"Listen, want to come over tonight? My parents have been dying to meet you. We could have pizza . . ."

She knew what he was suggesting, and it had nothing to do with food. One thing would lead to another. Where Chris was concerned, she seemed to have little to no control. "I don't think so."

"We need to talk."

"Chris, we can't see each other anymore."

"Why not?"

"Because of everything . . ."

"You mean because we slept together?"

Her cheeks burned at his boldness. "Chris, you know what we did wasn't right. We shouldn't have done anything in the first place." Actually, she shouldn't have ever even spoken to him.

"Hey." He reached out and touched her shoulder. "Why do you say that? It's not like we aren't of age. I'm twenty-two, you're twenty-one."

"I know . . ."

"I told you that I loved you. I wouldn't have told you that if I didn't mean it."

He had, but did that even matter? Jenna was coming to learn that those words didn't really mean that much. Her parents used to tell her that they loved her all the time. Then they kicked her out as soon as she disappointed them.

And Chris's words of love had been sweet, but they'd obviously only been a way to push her into sleeping with him.

Jenna pulled away from his hand. "Nothing is that easy," she said at last. "Especially not love."

Something new flashed in his hazel eyes. "Why are you making everything so hard? You said there wasn't anyone else. I told you there wasn't anyone else but you. For me, there still isn't." He paused. "I still can't believe that you've been avoiding me ever since."

And for a moment, she wanted to believe him. To think that his earnestness was genuine. Wanted to believe that things were that simple. That professions of love could take the place of consequences. But they couldn't. *Of course* they couldn't. Especially now that there was something else to deal with.

"Chris, there's more going on than just regrets."

"Then tell me, Jenna. What is so wrong? Why did you move out? Why are your parents so upset? Why won't you come over?" His voice became harder, more intense. "Why don't you want to see me anymore? Is it because I'm not Amish?"

"It's not because of that." From the first time they'd met,

she'd never cared about their backgrounds. Not really. He was just Chris; and she, simply Jenna.

"Then what is it?"

She bit her lip, debating whether to tell him the truth. But perhaps that had been her problem all this time. She worried too much about lies instead of trying to do the right thing.

Looking left, then right, she gave into temptation. "Chris, I'm pregnant."

If things weren't so bad, his expression would have been comical. His eyes were wide and his usual half-smile went slack. "From me?"

"Of course." When he still looked stunned, she glared at him. "Chris, you know you were my first. You were also the only."

"But . . . it was just that one time . . . then I never saw you again."

"Once was enough." When he stared at her in confusion, she added, "Look, I'm not blaming you. I'm blaming myself. I should have never let my guard down. I shouldn't have done a lot of things . . ."

Which was part of the problem, Jenna knew. She and Chris had had a flirtation between them that should have never been there in the first place.

But she'd been frustrated with Graham's on-again off-again attentions and couldn't help be infatuated with Chris's flirting ways. She'd grown tired of being perfect Jenna Yoder, the role model for her siblings.

She'd liked how Chris had liked her.

Over the span of a few weeks, they'd talked more and

more, then had kissed one evening behind the market. And then, well, one thing had led to another.

And now she was dealing with the consequences.

"What are you going to do?"

"What do you think I'm going to do? I'm going to have a baby."

"But then what?"

"Get a job. Maybe give it up for adoption," she said, though she doubted she'd be able to give up the baby. "I haven't decided yet."

"*You* haven't decided yet? Didn't you think you should have told me earlier? We have to think about the consequences."

Feeling at her wits' end, she replied with a forced patience. "That's all I've been doing. Chris, I know you just found out, but I've been dealing with this for a while."

"How have you been dealing with it?"

"I told my parents."

He looked crushed. "And?"

"And, what do you think? They told me to move out."

Pure pain flickered in his eyes. "Truly? Jenna, you should never have kept this from me." He swallowed. "Do they want to meet me?"

"They don't even know about you, Chris. They would be even more upset to know that I've been with an *Englischer.*"

"So I'm your secret?" His voice was so hoarse, and Jenna could tell what he was thinking. Was he relieved? Or just shocked?

His confusion made her want to lash out. "Why do you

care, Chris? What are you going to do? Marry me?" she blurted sarcastically.

His cheeks flushed. "I don't know," he said after a pause. "Maybe."

"Come on. I know you don't mean it." Unbidden, she recalled yet another memory . . .

She'd run into the market, her emotions high and her face flushed. So eager to see him. Though they hadn't had plans to see each other, she'd wanted to surprise him. And maybe get a hug and a kiss. After all, he'd said such sweet things the night before.

She'd found him stocking loaves of bread.

And smiling at two English girls.

At first, she'd lurked at the end of the aisle, waiting to approach him until he finished his conversation . . . but then it became all too obvious that the girls weren't going to leave anytime soon.

And that he was perfectly fine with that. Feeling embarrassed, she'd turned and left.

And had never mentioned it to him.

"Don't tell me what I mean and don't mean. And for that matter, stop telling me that I don't know what feelings are, or that I don't know what I want. You don't know everything about me, Jenna." He paused. "Maybe not anything."

For the first time in four months, she looked at him hard and realized that maybe he was right. Maybe she didn't really know him at all. "But it's too late, don't you think?"

"No. If anything, it's probably the best time. The perfect time."

She stared at him in wonder. "What?"

"You heard me." His eyes narrowed. "Look, it's cold. You shouldn't be out here. Where are you living? And don't play games with me, Jenna. I want to know, and I deserve to know."

"With an Amish lady. Mary Zehr."

"Where does she live?"

"Why?"

"Because I'm going to come see you this week and we're going to talk, that's why. Where does she live, Jenna?"

Too stunned to evade again, she mumbled, "Off of Broadway." Before she could chicken out, she told him Mary's address.

"If I call on you there, will you talk to me?"

He deserved that at the very least. "Yes."

"Okay. I have to go back to work, but I'll stop by to see you this week. All right?"

"Yes. Are you going to tell your parents? Aren't you worried about what they might to say?"

"Not so much."

She was stunned. "Why not?"

"Jenna, I promise, I wasn't thinking about them when this happened. I stopped living my life for their approval years ago." While she processed that, he murmured, "So, you promise that you'll open the door for me?"

His lack of belief in her made Jenna feel even lower. "I promise."

"Good."

Before she knew it, she found herself smiling at him. Just like she used to when he'd rush around the counter to see her.

"Good." Surprising her, he put his arm around her shoulders and guided her back to the sidewalk. "Are you walking the rest of the way?"

"Of course."

Reaching out, he flicked a snowflake from the brim of her bonnet. "It's snowing pretty good right now," he stated, his voice all warm and cozy. "Will you be all right?"

Her mouth went dry. "Yes. I'll be fine, Chris."

"Sure? Because I don't want you to get sick."

"I'm not a child, Chris. I am fine."

Looking less confident, he nodded. "Okay."

Surprising her again, he reached out and brushed a finger against her cheek. His lips curved. "Jenna, you should have never avoided me. I promise you, I'm the last person in your life who you need to steer clear of. " Then, before she could respond, Chris turned and walked away.

Now that the snow was beginning to fall in earnest, Jenna picked up her pace and walked faster. Funny how her quick pace seemed to be in time with her rapidly beating heart.

Chapter Twenty-Two

It turned out that Graham didn't have to wait all that long to see William after all. On Tuesday morning, Scott had asked Graham, William, and Frank to accompany him on an installation. When the two other men had to make an emergency run to the hardware store, Graham knew the time was right to bring up Mattie.

Truth be told, he felt mighty uncomfortable about it. After all, he'd been the one to talk to William about Mattie. Furthermore, he'd kept his mouth shut when he'd discovered William had called on her.

But after a moment's pause, Graham shrugged off his misgivings. He'd made his decision and he needed to stick to it.

Steeling his resolve, he joined William at the back of the truck. Picking up a pair of two-by-fours, he plunged in. "Listen, after you told me about you visiting Mattie so much, I've been thinking about it a lot."

William looked at him from the corner of his eye as he scooted a gas-powered generator forward. "Why?"

Why? "I've been thinking about the two of you, and I wanted to talk to you about her."

"Because?"

"Because she and I are friends," Graham said as he made another trip from the truck to their workspace.

William raised his brows. "I know that."

Graham's mild irritation with William's manner churned into a simmering anger. "So, I just want to tell you that lately things have changed between us. Between Mattie and me, I mean."

William set an armful of wood down on the tailgate. "Changed . . . how?"

"We've become closer." Thinking of their kiss, Graham felt himself blush. That embarrassed him. "So close, that, uh, I'd rather you not see·her anymore."

"That's not your choice, Graham."

"Listen, what Mattie and I have is special. It would be best for all involved if you just, you know, moved on."

William shook his head. "I don't think so. I'm planning to see her tonight, and that's what I'm going to do."

Everything inside of him protested. "Look, I'm trying to be reasonable about this. But you have to see—"

William cut him off. "What's wrong, Graham? Having Jenna Yoder wasn't enough?"

"Jenna has nothing to do with this."

"I disagree." His voice hardened. "You can't have all the

women, Graham. You need to get over that, *jah*? Now, are you going to help me unload, or just pry into my business some more?"

In answer, Graham grabbed the toolbox and carried it to the house. Though he did his best to keep his expression calm, inside, he knew he'd never been angrier. He was mad at William for being such a jerk, at Mattie for ever giving William the time of day, at Jenna for ruining his reputation, and at himself most of all.

None of this would have ever happened if he'd been brave enough to admit his attraction and love for Mattie years ago.

Truly, he only had himself to blame.

"There was no need for you to come over on your day off to work like this," Loyal said from the other end of the measuring tape in his back bedroom. "I feel badly, taking up your extra time."

Graham shook his head at his brother. "You know I don't work full-time so I can still help around the farm."

"But this isn't our farm . . ."

"It's yours, you're my brother, so it's mine, too. Right?"

After a pause, Loyal smiled. "*Jah*. I suppose you have a point there. Well, help me line this tape up carefully. The last thing Ella is going to want is crooked bookshelves in here."

Dutifully, Graham held firm to the tape and double-checked the measurements. "Seventy-two inches?"

Loyal nodded. "That's what I have as well. All right, then," he said as he walked over to his makeshift workbench, marked the piece of oak, and then began to saw. "No going back now, eh?"

"I guess not." After Loyal cut that piece of wood, he grabbed another. "I'm still surprised you're making Ella a library of her own here. You'd think since she now works in a library, she wouldn't need another one at home."

Loyal smiled smugly. "That's why she's my *frau* and not yours. She loves books. I'm going to make her a little reading area in here. A place where she can have her books and sit in a rocking chair and relax."

With so much to do around the house and barn, Graham still was having a difficult time understanding why Loyal was making a special room for Ella. It seemed like a waste of time. "What did she do when you told her you were doing this?"

"She cried." Loyal grinned. "It was a mighty happy moment."

Graham paused. It was comments like those that made him wish for something more. "You don't have any doubts or regrets about your marriage, do you?"

Loyal paused in his cutting and looked at Graham curiously. "Not at all. Did you really think I would?"

"No." Realizing how clumsy he sounded, Graham added, "What I meant to say was that I know you've known Ella a long time. I guess I'm just surprised that you fell in love with her so quickly."

"You're forgetting that we hadn't been close. For most of our lives, we merely just nodded to each other in passing." He paused. "We were never like you and Mattie, for example. You two are like two peas in a pod. A matched set."

Graham frowned. "I don't know what Mattie and I are now."

"Really?"

"Things between us are pretty confusing, if you want to know the truth."

"My advice is to talk to her. That's what helped with me and Ella."

"We keep meaning to talk . . . but for some reason we never get to the important stuff." With a sigh, he added, "The truth is, I think I really messed things up between us."

"How did you do that?"

"Things between us changed." For a moment, Graham weighed the pros and cons of telling his brother more, then ultimately decided to tell him everything. He needed help.

After all, that's why he came over, wasn't it?

"She's been kind of courting William from my work. Actually, I set them up."

Loyal shook his head. "Oh, Graham. Then what happened?"

"Well, William turned out to be the wrong person for Mattie. Actually, he's an irritating man."

"So you should tell Mattie that—"

"I did. But when I talked to her about him, she told me that her outings with him were none of my business."

With a wince, Loyal took off his hat and ran a hand through his hair. "And then what happened?"

"I kissed her," he blurted.

Loyal smiled as he left the piece of wood and approached. "It's about time."

"What is that supposed to mean?" Really, did everyone around him have to have so many personal opinions about his love life?

"For years, we've all been waiting for the two of you to come to your senses."

Graham crossed his arms over his chest. "We?"

"Me, Calvin, Mamm, John. Even Katie." With a grin, he added, "I say it hasn't come a moment too soon."

"We've just been friends."

"You've been more than friends. She's depended on you something fierce during all of her treatments."

Remembering how she'd even sent for him sometimes, Graham knew it to be true. "But still . . ."

"She's special to you. So, uh, is everything better with Jenna?"

"I suppose. I've been trying to avoid her," Graham said, feeling the veins in his neck tightening even as he thought of the trouble she'd caused him. Still, there were lots of people who practically refused to acknowledge him. The last thing he ever wanted to do was be in the same room with Jenna Yoder.

But instead of looking sympathetic, his brother frowned. "I don't think anything is over with. At least, it's not for everyone."

"Everyone else doesn't matter." If this experience had taught him anything, it was that it was wrong to depend on other people's perception of him. He could only depend on himself and his relationship with God.

Loyal sighed. "I don't think you'll ever be able to move on if you don't get things settled with Jenna. Find out why she's been lying." With a waving motion of his hands, he added, "Graham, you should go talk to her."

And say what? Graham thought bitterly. It wasn't like he owed her an apology. "There's nothing for me to say."

"Then maybe instead of going to talk, you should go to Jenna's and listen to what she has to say." Sounding almost like their father used to, Loyal added, "There's got to be a reason she named you as the baby's father. Go see what it is."

Though he never would have admitted it, Graham was afraid. He'd never intended to lead her on, had he? Inadvertently? Had she named him the father as some kind of revenge? Out of a twisted spite?

Or was there something else that Jenna was battling? If so, he didn't want to think about it.

"I just want to forget about her."

"You know you can't do that."

"I can try."

"That's impossible, unless you want to do what Uncle John did and move away. But, then, he pretty much proved to us that it was hard to move away, too. Because you always want to come back."

"Sooner or later," Graham finished. Couldn't he postpone things until later?

"Go see her tonight," Loyal prodded. "Even if she doesn't tell you what you want to hear, at least she'll tell you something."

"And what if nothing she tells me makes any sense? What if it's nothing I want to hear?"

"The Lord never promises the right path is the easiest.

But at least you'll have some answers. And those answers would be more than you have right now."

With reluctance, Graham got to his feet. This was going to be difficult, but he had a feeling that it would also unburden his heart and help things between him and Jenna heal. "I hate it when you're right, brother."

As expected, Loyal grinned over his shoulder. "I know. Of course, I kind of fancy the feeling myself."

The doorbell rang. Mattie rushed to answer it, then found herself sputtering. "William?"

"Hi there, Mattie. I happened to be driving by." His gaze skimmed over her slowly. "May I visit with you for a bit?"

"Well . . . I don't know if that's a good idea." Looking at him, she wondered again about Graham's mistrust of the man. Was he justified? Or had he simply been jealous?

"Mattie?" her mother called out from the kitchen. "Who is here?"

"William," she said reluctantly.

Her mother popped out of the kitchen doorway, all smiles. "*Wilkum!* Would you like to come in for a spell and have some banana bread?"

"*Danke*, but . . ." William cast another meaningful look her way. "Perhaps in a little while?"

"Oh. Sure." Her mother looked at them both, obviously curious as to why William had stopped over.

Mattie was curious, too. Especially since she thought she'd been pretty clear about her feelings that last time he'd stopped by.

But when William didn't say anything, just looked at

her in a heated way, Mattie knew they needed some time alone. Some things couldn't be said with her mother's sensitive ears listening for every snippet of conversation.

"I think we're going to go to the barn," she said, suddenly making a decision.

"Barn?"

"Yes. Um, William was interested in our new rabbits." Glancing at him quickly, she added, "Weren't you, William?"

"Very much so."

Grabbing her cloak and black bonnet, Mattie tossed them both on and led the way outside. "I'm sorry to drag you out to the barn," she said to him as they stepped down her front steps. "It's so snowy and cold out. Too snowy to be tromping around. But I thought you might appreciate a bit of privacy."

William smiled. "The barn is fine. I'm glad you thought of it."

When they got inside, the building felt especially drafty and cold. So cold that she felt as if the wind was flowing right through her clothes. The cloak didn't seem to offer any protection from the wind.

She shivered. "Here are the rabbits," she said, showing him a stall lined well with shredded paper and straw. In the middle of it, six Dutch rabbits were snuggled together, looking like angels. "They're sweet, don'tcha think?"

Dutifully, he leaned over the rail and looked at the bunnies. But he didn't seem particularly interested in them. "Mattie, we both know I didn't come to see the rabbits."

She turned to him. "I know that." Because he looked

so ill at ease, she prodded a bit. "But what I don't know is your real reason. Why did you really come over, William?"

"Because I wanted to see you again."

"But I told you I didn't think we'd suit."

He stepped closer. "And I told you that I thought you hadn't given us enough of a chance."

"What are you talking about?" she asked, trying not to let his nearness disconcert her. But when he stepped even closer, effectively trapping her in his embrace, her mouth went dry. Licking her lips, she blurted, "We've tried and tried to talk to each other. You had to have realized that things between us were strained—"

"I didn't come here to talk, neither," he said, then pressed his lips to hers.

Immediately, she lifted her hands to his chest and pushed. But her hands might have been butterflies, they were so useless.

The kiss continued. Hard and nearly violent. She felt his hard teeth against her lips. Little by little, she was finding it difficult to breathe.

Tension rose in her, intertwining with panic. With all her might, she pushed at him and averted her face. *"William!"* she gasped. *"William, stop!"*

But instead of backing away, he grasped her arm. "Mattie, you know you want this."

She most definitely did not. Just as he leaned closer again, obviously determined to trap her in another kiss, she raised her knee into his groin. Just as Graham had taught her years ago.

And, just as Graham had—William grunted, then crumbled in pain.

Mattie used the opportunity to run.

Out of breath and shaking, she raced outside, then ran to the kitchen door in record time. Only when she was safely on the other side of the closed door did she feel the slightest hint of relief.

"Mattie? I heard the door slam," her mother said, walking into the kitchen with a towel in her hand. "Whatever is—"

"Oh, Mamm. I'm so glad to see you."

Tossing the towel on the counter, her mother approached. "What's wrong? Mattie, are you sick?"

"*Nee.* It was William. Mamm, he gr-grabbed me and k-ki-kissed me." Still struggling to catch her breath, Mattie added, "I think he would've done more if I hadn't run away." As she said the words, everything felt more real than ever. Tears started to fall. "I was scared."

Her mother tensed. "Oh, why did your father have to be out of town right now?" Looking at the closed door, she said, "Where is he?"

"In the barn. I left him kneeling on the floor. But I imagine he'll get up again soon." As she thought about how angry he must be, she whispered, "Mamm, what are we going to do?"

"*We* are not going to do anything. I, however, will go talk to him. You need to go lie down."

"Mamm, that could be dangerous."

"After everything you've been through? *Nee.* The last

thing I would ever do is let me leave here without talking to William. But you don't worry, child." With a tender hand, she softly brushed two fingers along Mattie's cheek. "Oh, my daughter. I am so very glad you are all right." And with that, she turned and practically marched out the door.

Mattie knew the right thing to do would be to follow her *mamm*, to lend her support. But she was shaking so badly, she didn't know how she could lend any help at all.

In a daze, she wandered to her room, sat on her bed, then hugged her favorite down pillow tightly.

And tried not to imagine what would have happened if she hadn't fought William.

As she started shaking, she wished she could call for Graham, but it felt too strange.

It was time to stop depending on him and start making do on her own. But, of course, that made her feel even worse than usual.

For a moment, panic set in. A bare, desolate feeling settled in, making her feel completely alone.

Then, she remembered a long-ago conversation with Lucy, back when Lucy's life had been far different. She'd been struggling with Paul's death, and her feelings of guilt surrounding it.

"The Lord is always with you," Lucy had said. "No matter what, you are never alone. During my darkest days with Paul, I held tight to that belief."

Hold tight.

Liking the imagery of those words, Mattie closed her eyes and desperately held tight to that hope. "Please,

Lord," she said to the empty room. "Please hold me in your arms and guide me. I still need you."

She paused, feeling a bit selfish. She'd already gotten her health. Maybe now she was asking for too much.

With that in mind, she spoke again, squeezing her eyelids tightly shut and lifting her whole heart into the silence of the room and the spirit of the Lord who she felt was always with her. "God, I know I've asked a lot from you lately. I asked for your healing touch with my body. I asked you to be with Lucy, to help her find happiness and love. I prayed over Ella and Loyal, asked for your help and prayers for their safety and happiness."

She swallowed. "And most of all, I asked for your trust. For you to believe in me even when I didn't believe in you . . ."

As Mattie heard her words reverberate in the room, she remembered the scripture verse from Isaiah about prayers. *When you call, the Lord will answer. "Yes I am here," he will quickly reply.*

Nowhere in that verse were conditions about when to pray, or that a person could pray or ask for too much . . .

Gathering her courage, she tried again. "Lord, if it's not too much to ask . . . could you help me now? Again? I really need you." Sheepishly, she added—most likely to herself as much as to Him—"I guess I always have and always will."

Little by little, a sense of calm floated over her. Little by little, her muscles relaxed.

After a time, her door opened and her mother poked her head in. "He's gone, Mattie."

Mattie scrambled to sit up. "Oh, Mamm. Mamm, are you okay? He didn't hurt you, did he?"

"*Nee*, Mattie." To Mattie's surprise, her mother smiled. "I'm perfectly fine."

"What did he do?"

"After I yelled at him and told him I'd make sure everyone knew he attacked you, he promised he'd never come near you again." Tilting her chin up, her mother's grin turned mischievous. "Don't tell anyone, but I have to say I quite enjoyed watching him look at me in fear."

Mattie couldn't help it, she started giggling. And when her mother crossed the room, giggling, too, Mattie laughed until she cried.

Chapter Twenty-Three

When the doorbell rang, Jenna's pulse raced. Chris had left a message at the library that he was going to stop by.

"That must be Chris," she told Mary. "What should I do?"

Jenna took one last look at Mary. "What should *I* do?"

Mary motioned her forward with her hand. "Go answer. Chris and you need to talk. Plus, you've sought shelter here, not a hiding place."

Mary's words were true. She was coming to learn that evading didn't solve problems. Things just got more complicated. With that in mind, she opened the front door. But the person on the other side of the threshold was not who she expected. "Graham?" she sputtered. "What are you doing here?"

"We need to talk," he said, stepping right inside, hardly even waiting for her to get out of the way.

Though she moved, Jenna wasn't inclined to follow his directions. "Could we maybe talk tomorrow? Now's not a good time." Before he closed the door, she skimmed the yard behind him. If Chris kept his word, he was going to show up any minute, and if he saw Graham here, it was going to be one of the most uncomfortable moments in her life, ever.

Graham scowled. "It doesn't matter if you think it's a good time or not. We need to talk things through. I can't wait another day."

Graham's six-foot stature loomed over her, as did his discomfort. It emanated off him in waves.

She knew she deserved his anger.

"I'm expecting someone, Graham. Are you sure we can't talk tomorrow? Or maybe even in a few hours?"

For a moment, he looked like he was going to let her have her way, but then a muscle in his cheek tensed and he crossed his arms over his chest. "I don't think so. This won't take long."

Feeling comforted by Mary's presence in the next room, she nodded. "All right. What do you want to say?"

"I want answers to questions, Jenna."

"Does that mean you intend to listen?"

He jerked a nod. "Why did you tell that story? Why did you lie?"

It was almost a relief to tell him. "Because I was desperate."

His eyes flashed. "Desperate? But why would you think I would accept your lie?"

"From something you told me months ago," she said. "When we went to that art show and walked around, you said good friends were willing to put up with things out of their control. You said good friends tried to be there for each other. No matter what."

"I was talking about Mattie. I was talking about caring for her while she was so sick."

"Well, I took it to mean that it also included helping me." Before he could reply to that, she raised a hand. "Listen, before you say anything else, I want you to know that I realize I was wrong. I'm sorry, too. And I fully intend to tell everyone that you are not the father of my baby."

"So who is?"

"That I can't tell you," she said, even as she heard the gravel spit out under Chris's truck tires. "And believe me, you don't want to know."

He froze. "Jenna . . . did someone force you?"

"No." Jenna held his gaze for a moment before tucking her chin again. The look she'd seen there was disconcerting. It reminded her of how she'd hoped he'd look at her when they were at the art show.

Full of concern and care.

Boy, had she messed things up between them. Now that time had passed, she knew she'd been half hoping to see a spark between them. Instead, she now knew the difference. Graham hadn't looked at her with love because he hadn't loved her.

She'd been hoping to force things instead of waiting for the right time, which obviously hadn't come yet.

She cleared her throat. "I wasn't forced," she said, thinking about so much more than just what Graham was asking. "Everything that happened, I did out of my own free will. And the consequences, well, they're mine to bear, too." Glancing toward Mary, Jenna silently begged for help.

Luckily, Mary understood and immediately walked toward them. Just as the front door chimed. "Oh! We have more company!" she said cheerily as she opened the front door.

And then there stood Chris, looking tall and handsome and terribly sweet.

Jenna swallowed hard.

As Graham looked at the newcomer with solemn eyes, she wished she could disappear into the floor. This was really too much.

"Chris, won't you please join me in the kitchen?" Mary asked, taking his arm and practically dragging him to the back of the house.

"Jenna, are you all right?" Chris called out, looking at her over his shoulder.

Graham stared at Mary and Chris's backs as they disappeared into the kitchen. "Jenna, why is he here?"

"To visit, of course," she said. Feeling at odds and ends, she wiped her sweaty palms on her apron, then opened the door to let him leave. "Now, if you will excuse me, I should probably go speak with him."

"Who is he? Is he—" Graham looked toward the kitchen again.

Jenna heard Chris's voice float down the hall as he accepted a cup of coffee from Mary. Her uneasiness about the whole situation forced her to finally say what needed to be said.

"Graham, I'm sorry. I was wrong, I promise I realize that now. I'm sorry. I'm sorry for lying about you. For lying to you. Though my apology will probably never be enough, I don't know what else to say."

He shuffled to the doorway. Grasping the door handle, he paused again, looking toward the kitchen. Jenna felt her cheeks heat as Chris's voice flew their way again.

"I, uh, hope you will have a good evening," she said. "That is, unless you have any more questions?"

"*Nee*. I got the answers I came for," he said cryptically.

Jenna watched him turn and walk away, and with a sigh, she closed the door. As she heard Chris's easy laughter float down the hall, she steeled herself to get ready for the second confrontation of the day.

Graham's mind was racing double time. Far quicker than Beauty's hooves as she clip-clopped along the road.

Though he usually took time to admire the snow-covered landmarks in Jacob's Crossing, all he could think about was his visit with Jenna.

Why had that *Englischer* shown up? And what did he want with Jenna? Or, perhaps he had come to see Mary? Mentally, he tried to recall how old that man was. Younger than himself by at least two years, placing him around twenty-two.

That seemed too young for Mary Zehr. She had to be at least ten years older than him.

No, he'd definitely come to see Jenna.

As he drove through town, he passed John's donut shop. The store was closed, but there was a light shining in John's window. Making a decision, he stopped the buggy.

With heavy feet, Graham climbed the stairs and knocked.

Inside, he discovered that the light hadn't come from the electric lights, but instead from a Coleman lantern.

Then he noticed that John's shirt had no buttons. In fact, John looked Amish.

"Uncle John, what's going on?"

"I decided it's time to make the change." Patting his shirt, he shook his head with a slight grimace. "I have to say I'd forgotten how to pin my shirt easily. Pricked my finger two times."

Spying an open cardboard box on his otherwise bare kitchen table, Graham walked over and inspected it. "Whose clothes are these?"

"Jacob's. I mean, they are your father's."

Graham lifted up one of the shirts. Though he figured it was silly, he pressed his nose to the cotton, on the off chance it would smell like his father.

But of course, it only smelled like the laundry soap his mother favored. "Did Mamm give you these shirts?"

"She did. She gave them to me a few weeks ago, I just hadn't been ready to put them on."

"What's different about today?"

"Mary. I want her to be able to trust me . . ." His voice drifted off. "Graham, does my wearing your father's old shirt distress you?"

He wanted to say no. He really did. He wanted to be more accepting of John, and not feel out of sorts that his uncle—who they'd never seen or heard from much at all until recently—now owned more of his *daed*'s old things than Graham did. "A little bit," he finally said. "I never thought my *daed*'s things would go to someone besides Calvin, Loyal, or me."

"If you had wanted them, why didn't you take them before?"

"Mamm had them in her room. I thought she wanted the clothes near."

"She had the box in your attic. It was obvious no one had looked at the clothes in years. She washed everything again before passing them on to me."

Well, that was convenient. Caught off guard by his sudden anger, Graham put the shirt back in the box and picked up his hat. "I think I'll be going now."

"Wait. Why did you stop by?"

Graham couldn't believe it—he'd almost forgotten. "Oh, no reason in particular."

John's brows snapped together. "Are you sure? You seem pretty upset. Is there anything new with work? Or Mattie . . ." He paused. "Or Jenna?"

Graham was almost tempted to smile. There was quite a lot new: He'd realized he was in love with Mattie, but Mattie was still seeing William, who he worked with.

And Jenna—well, he didn't even know how he felt about Jenna anymore. For some reason, he didn't hate her so much. Instead, he simply felt sorry for her, which caught him by surprise. He'd thought for sure that he'd never feel anything but anger toward the girl.

It was all terribly peculiar. "Everything's mixed up," he said.

"Do you want to talk about it? I've felt that way before."

"No. Actually, I think I had better go see Mattie."

"Are you upset with me? Do you want your father's clothes back?"

Having his father's clothes wouldn't make the man return. Slowly, he shook his head. "No. Keep them, *Onkle.* They suit you."

John's eyes widened as he ran a hand down one of his sleeves. "You really think so?"

"I do," he replied, surprising himself. "I think they suit you just fine." Backing up, he grabbed the door handle. "*Gut naught*, Uncle John."

"*Gut naught,*" he replied. But didn't move when Graham opened the door and left.

Chapter Twenty-Four

"Mattie, Graham has come calling," her mother called up to her room. "Would you rather not see him? I could tell him to leave."

"*Nee*, don't do that. I'll be right there."

She scampered down the stairs, then, unable to stop herself, practically leapt into his arms the moment she saw him. "Graham, it's so good to see you."

To her relief, his arms curved immediately around her as she clung. "Mattie? Mattie, good heavens! What's going on?"

Oh, but no one else on earth felt like Graham. The taut muscles of his chest and shoulders felt just right to lean into. His height was the perfect size for her to tuck her face into his neck. And his embrace felt the way it had always been. Warm and solid, comforting but not too firm.

"Mattie?" Graham was soothing her, rubbing between her shoulder blades—right in the area that had been so sore after her surgery. "Mattie, what is wrong?"

After taking comfort in his arms another minute, she stepped away.

Blue eyes met hers as a lump formed in the back of her throat. Should she tell him the truth? Or not?

If she told Graham the truth, it might change the way he thought of her. After all, he had warned her to stay away from William.

But if she didn't tell him the truth, the lie would always be between them. Even if Graham never guessed the truth, it would be like a cut between them, festering, infecting everything . . .

"Mattie, you can tell me anything, right?" Reaching out, he clasped her hands so they were swinging slightly between them. His grip was easy and sweet.

Slowly, she met his gaze again. When the corners of his eyes crinkled, she saw the unabashed truth there. And that's when she knew there was only one thing to do.

Mattie gathered her courage and spoke. "William came here."

Holding her at arm's length, he gazed at her in confusion. "And?"

"And he kissed me, Graham."

In a flash, cold hurt filled his gaze. "I see."

Stepping close to him, she shook her head. "*Nee!* You don't see. Graham, he kissed me without my wanting. And then . . . he upset me," she added in a rush. "So I hurt him like you showed me."

He blinked. "You did what?"

Pulling him into the living room, she stopped in front of the fireplace. "I jabbed him with my knee, Graham," she said, barely blushing at all. "Your trick worked well."

It was obvious he was fighting a smile as he sat. "He went down on the floor, hmm?"

She nodded. "He was terribly hurt."

"*Gut.*" Taking her hands, he rubbed his thumbs along her knuckles again. "Did he hurt you?"

She shook her head. "No. He scared me, though."

"I'll talk to him, you can be sure of that. Believe me, he'll be sorry for coming over here."

"It may not be necessary. My *mamm* talked to him, already."

"No. He needs to hear from me." His voice was hard as stone. "What he did wasn't right. Besides, I told him to leave you alone."

That caught her off guard. "Why?"

"Because—" His cheeks turning red, he stopped. "Never mind. Now isn't the time to continue our talk. Now, are you sure you're okay?"

"I'm fine. Well, I mean, I will be soon." It was then that she noticed he seemed off—a tension emanated from him, making him seem almost like a stranger. Actually, Graham looked as down and out of sorts as she'd ever seen him.

Slowly, she realized that he must have been upset about something when he arrived. "Are you all right?"

"Truly? *Nee.*"

"I see." Mattie noticed his lips were pursed so tight that a faint sheen of white surrounded them. His body was stiff, too. All he did was stare at the fireplace.

As the flames crackled and her hands and face warmed, Mattie wondered how to help him. Was he waiting for her to say something—just the right thing?

She didn't know what that was.

Perhaps she should offer him comfort? Maybe she could remind him about that Bible verse from Isaiah? As far as she knew, Graham's faith had never wavered. Perhaps that would comfort him more than anything she could think to say.

But just as she was about to speak, Graham stretched out his legs and finally looked at her. "I've just come from seeing Jenna."

Unable to stop herself, she winced. And though it made no sense, being her old, familiar friend, jealousy settled inside of her. "Oh?" she asked in what she hoped was a terribly offhand way. And how did you find Jenna?"

"Full of news." Graham was looking at the flames again, but a bit of humor, dark and ironic, tinged his voice. "I went to her house, full of anger and self-righteousness . . . but when I left, I felt humbled."

Humbled? "Graham, what happened? What did she say?"

He turned to her, his beautiful blue eyes full of questions. Making Mattie realize he was only half with her. Part of his mind was back at Jenna's house, back with their conversation.

Feeling completely confused, Mattie wrapped her arms around herself and waited. Too much had happened today to understand.

Finally Graham spoke again. "Mattie, I have a lot to tell you about our conversation. But suddenly, it doesn't matter so much anymore. And I'm realizing, too, that I don't want to think. I'm exhausted. Would you mind if we just sat together for a bit? If we sat together and I held your hand, and we just watched the fire?"

There was only one response she could make. "Of course, Graham. We can sit here as long as you want." Without another word, she held out her hand.

Chapter Twenty-Five

Three days had passed since Graham had come over and she'd told him about William's kiss. Three days since he had told her he'd talked to Jenna and felt humbled.

Three days since they'd put off yet another important conversation.

And though they hadn't seen each other—Graham had work and Mattie had been busy with chores around the house—he was never far from her mind.

When he came over today, he'd been full of smiles, much like the Graham she'd known all her life. Easygoing, happy. Relaxed even though the weather outside seemed to get darker and the rain didn't let up.

But as the minutes passed, Mattie began to realize Graham was still as troubled as he'd been Wednesday night. And still reluctant to share his burdens.

Though the stormy weather outside had her on edge, she doubted the storm warnings were the source of his edginess. They'd never worried him before.

"Graham, don't you think it's finally time we talked? Really talked?"

Instead of answering her right away, he clenched his hands.

Fear flew into her chest. Was he still thinking about everything she'd told him? Did he now think badly of her because of what had happened between her and William?

He opened his mouth, looking to be on the verge of speaking, but then closed his mouth again and shook his head. "I'm fine, Mattie. Please don't worry. I've only had a long day."

But his expression told a different story. His face looked so set in stone, it seemed as if a hard knock would crack his skin. With another person, she might have ignored her concerns. Tried not to be intrusive. But this was Graham. And he deserved her pushing—even if it might prove to be uncomfortable for them both. "I've had a long day, too. I spent a good three hours washing walls in our guest bedroom and helping wash comforters and quilts." She shook her arms out. "My arms feel like they're about to fall off. Time and again, things happen to remind me that my body still has a mighty long way to go to get back to normal."

"You shouldn't try to do so much."

"I'm not complaining. Just trying to talk to you." She gave him an encouraging smile. "So . . . what have you been doing? What caused your day to be so long?"

For a moment, she didn't think he was going to answer.

Then, leaning back, he crossed one foot over another knee and swallowed. "I went back to speak with Jenna today."

Now it was her turn to feel like she was made of stone. Mattie quickly tried to steel herself for his news.

"You said when you talked to her last time you felt humbled. Are things better now?" Really, she was proud of herself for acting so nonchalant.

"Good enough," he said with a sigh. "Well, I think so." He shifted again, moving his leg off his other knee, bracing his elbows now on his knees. "I think we got some things ironed out."

"Such as?"

"Well, I told her she's going to have to tell everyone who the father is. Or at least, that it's not me."

That sounded like the very least Jenna could do! "Do you think she'll do that?"

He shrugged. "I hope so. She said she would. I guess the man who she, uh, was with . . . is back in her life."

"This is *wunderbaar!* If she tells everyone the truth, she'll clear your name and we can go back to how things were."

"I doubt they ever will be the same. I tell you what. I think some people are going to think the worst of me no matter what I say." His eyes darkened. "Or what Jenna says now."

Mattie noticed that the lines of tension around his mouth hadn't eased a bit. Actually, he looked even more perturbed. "Graham, you're going to have to learn to get control of your anger."

"I don't know how I'm going to be able to do that."

"Then I guess you'll just have to try harder."

"It's not that easy, Mattie."

"Believe me, I know that. For months after my cancer diagnosis, I wanted to be mad at everyone, but it wasn't the right thing to do. I had to learn to ease my anger. Most of all, I had to learn to give my hurts and worries over to the Lord."

"I'd gladly give this burden to the Lord, but it isn't even my problem. Jenna's baby isn't mine."

"I know that. But don't you see, Graham? The baby was never the Lord's trial for you. The gossip and losing your control over your reputation was."

"Why would God give me something like this? It makes no sense."

"You're right. It doesn't. But you don't need to analyze it, Graham. I promise, I've learned the hard way that we all have burdens to shoulder. Some are more evident than others. If I've learned anything over the last year, it's that it would be foolish to imagine that one person's problems are more important than another's. I've also learned that when times are tough, it's best to depend on the only thing that is our constant: Faith."

Hesitantly, she gazed at him. *Please let me in*, she silently pleaded. *Please don't push me away. Don't put up more guards.*

"Well, this is sure new for you," he said sarcastically. "I didn't know you'd made such a pact with the Lord."

Well, he'd obviously made his choice. A deep sadness flowed through her as she realized that he was far from moving on. Instead, he was mired in his grief and anger.

Choosing her next words carefully, she said, "Graham, I haven't made a pact with Him. I merely chose to listen." *Finally*, she added silently.

"I'm not ready to do that. It might surprise you, but the other night I actually did pray and I asked Him for help. But He didn't answer."

"Maybe He did."

He waved a hand. "Things aren't better, Mattie. I don't think He was of the mind to listen. Or at least not of the mind to do a thing about it."

Mattie knew it would do no good to press him any longer. Graham had made up his mind, and was sticking to his decision, no matter what. "Where does this leave us?"

He blinked. "I'm not sure what you're talking about."

"I think you know." Bracing herself, she dived in. "Graham, you told me that you cared for me. We kissed. I thought we would start courting . . ."

Her cheeks burned as he looked at her like he'd never seen her before. As if such a thing had never even occurred to him.

Just when she thought she couldn't be more embarrassed, she felt the heat flow from her cheeks, down her neck, and across her chest.

"We can't, Mattie," he said finally.

"Because of the rumors?"

"Because of that. And because of where I am right now. Mattie, I'm so angry and confused right now, I don't think I can be everything you need me to be."

"Graham, all I want is for you to be yourself . . ."

"That wouldn't be enough."

As she thought back to all the times they had together . . . both the good and the bad, she shook her head. He'd been there for her when she could hardly get out of bed . . . and hardly get off the bathroom floor, she was so nauseous.

He'd teased her when she came home bald, and had given her hope when she thought she would never feel hopeful again. "I promise, Graham. Just for you to be you is always enough."

A fierce, sweet yearning flashed in his gaze, giving Mattie hope . . . then, just as quickly, anger and desolation flew back.

"Not yet, Mattie. I can't start pretending nothing in my life is wrong. Not when everything is." And with that, Graham stood up. "I'm going to leave now. I think it would be best."

"Yes. Probably so."

"I hope you're not too mad . . ."

"I'm fine." Well, she would be. One day. "Don't worry about me."

He paused. For a brief moment, a flicker of something so familiar and sweet entered his gaze, bringing with it a thousand memories of easier times.

"I am sorry, Mattie. I'm sorry if you expected more."

"I'm sorry, too," she said simply, and looked at her folded hands on her lap when he paused, obviously looking for something to say. Giving up, he turned and walked away.

When her front door closed, she leaned her head against the back of the couch and breathed deep. Had she expected more?

Oh, yes.

Was she disappointed?

Definitely.

Was there anything she could do about it?

Of course.

Closing her eyes, she opened her heart. "Lord, I know you hear everything. I know You already know what is deep in my heart, and what is deep in Graham's, too. If it's your will, I could sure use some help. And, if you don't mind, the sooner the better would be best. Amen."

Half imagining God grumbling about her impatience, Mattie kept her eyes closed and breathed deep and smiled.

Oh, it felt so good to give up her burdens to the Lord!

Chapter Twenty-Six

"Thanks for letting me come over again," Chris said the moment he entered Mary's front room. Wearing jeans, brown suede hiking boots, and a gray wool sweater with a bulky navy coat over it all, he looked big and out of place among Mary's sparsely decorated room.

He was also soaked. "It's really pouring out there. Crazy weather, huh? First snow, now rain and storm warnings." Holding out a sleeve, he shook his head. "Sorry. I should've put on a slicker or something."

"Don't worry. You look fine. Wet, but fine," Jenna said with a half-smile.

Actually, Jenna thought their differences had never been more obvious. Here she was in her purple dress, black apron, *kapp* and black tennis shoes. In contrast, his

English clothes stood out like a sore thumb against the plain-looking living room.

Or maybe he looked especially perfect, Jenna decided as she watched him sit down on the oak Shaker-style chair next to the matching coach she was perched on the edge of. He was so very handsome. And when he looked at her, his hazel eyes warming her skin, she still felt the faint awareness of his regard.

When he leaned back, he said, "Actually, I was half afraid you wouldn't even let me in here."

"I told you we could talk more . . ."

"I figured you were going to change your mind."

"Really?"

"Really. After all, you've been avoiding me for weeks."

He did have a point. "You're right. I was avoiding you, but it wasn't because I didn't think we had anything to say to each other." It had been about so much more than that. She'd been confused about her feelings. And she'd been ashamed that she'd let one night's passion undo a lifetime of trying to be perfect.

Of course, she'd been scared, too. Her parents weren't the type of people who smiled and hugged when they were disappointed. No. They punished.

And she'd felt so completely alone.

"I was upset," she finally said. Though, of course, "upset" didn't really cover all she'd been feeling.

"I deserved to know about the baby, and about how you were feeling," Chris countered, his voice flat. "No matter what you thought about me, it was my right. It should have been your first priority, Jenna. Even if you were mad at me—or mad at yourself."

"I know." Glancing his way, she saw the surprise in his eyes at her ready acceptance.

But she couldn't deny that he had a point. Now that everything was out in the open, all the pros and cons she'd been weighing didn't seem so insurmountable. Now that everything was out in the open, Jenna felt almost free. Well, at least less angry and confused. "I should have told you about the pregnancy," she stated again. "It would have been easier for both of us if I had."

"You shouldn't have been afraid of my reaction, Jenna."

"How could I not be? My family was very upset."

"I'm not your mother or your father. Besides, I knew better, too, Jenna. We weren't ready. I should've waited. Being caught up in the moment is no excuse."

"I never expected you to say that."

"Why? Because I'm a guy?" Chris shook his head. "I'm also a pastor's son, Jenna," he said softly. "Like you, I knew better. I'd been taught to respect myself better."

Goodness! Though they'd spent hours in each other's company, she'd fooled herself into thinking that he was selfish and immature. But now maybe it was she who had some of those qualities? "You can't take all the blame. What happened isn't only your fault. It's mine, too."

"Jenna, how about we move on?"

"What do you mean?"

To her surprise, he leaned forward and his voice softened. "Jenna, I'm tired of describing what's happened between us as a mistake. We can't go back in time and change our actions. Obviously God doesn't want us to do that either. It's time for us to move forward."

"You really think God even cares?"

"Of course," he said softly. "God always cares about us. And maybe most especially now. After all, hasn't He been by your side when no one else was?"

Jenna nodded. Funny, how talking things out was changing her original opinions. When she was alone, she'd turned bitter. Sure that no one else could ever understand her. But she should have recalled that no one is ever truly alone. Not if they embraced the Lord's companionship.

Holding out his hand, he said, "Jenna, since we can't change the past, we might as well concentrate on the future. We might as well start thinking about this baby as a blessing."

His words made so much sense. But the last thing in the world she wanted to do was trap him into some kind of responsibility he'd never asked for and wasn't ready to take on. Ignoring his hand, she murmured, "Chris, that's not necessary."

"Sure it is." He looked at her for a moment, then, as if he had finally made a difficult decision, he stood up and moved to the cushion beside her.

"What are you doing?"

"Getting closer. Coming to sit right next to you." A faint sheen of amusement entered his expression as she stared at him. "See, this is the deal. I'm not going to walk away. Fact is, I'm not going anywhere."

But if he wasn't going to walk away, where did that leave her? "I'm afraid I don't understand."

"You're going to have to start seeing me more often. At least every day. Now tell me about how you came to be here."

"There isn't much to tell. Like I said, my parents were mighty upset about the news."

"I understand that. But why—"

"Chris, they asked me to leave."

His hazel eyes, the color of the grass at twilight, flickered. It was obvious that her parents' actions were unfathomable to him. "They didn't even want to talk to me?"

"I lied about who the father was," she sputtered, feeling so terribly ashamed. "I lied and told them it was an Amish friend of mine."

"How could you do that?"

"I was scared. I didn't think we'd have a future. Of course, the boy denied it. Then I got kicked out."

Chris seemed to take a moment to process everything she'd told him. "Do you still think we have no future?"

"No. I mean, I hope we do."

"Jenna, I really liked you. I still do. You are special to me. Did you think that wasn't the case?"

"I'm afraid I started listening to stories and gossip about *Englischer* boys. About how they use girls." Now that she heard her words out loud, she began to get even more embarrassed. She'd taken so much for granted, and based it all on hearsay and rumors. "I should have talked to you, I suppose."

"I wish you would have." Looking troubled, he said, "Jenna, did you really think I was such a loser?"

"Loser?" She didn't know what that meant.

"A loser is a guy who would tell you things but not mean them. A guy who would sleep with his girlfriend and not care about her."

Shocked, Jenna realized that she had thought the worst of him.

But maybe that was because she'd been feeling so bad about herself?

Not waiting for an answer, he reached for her hand and rubbed his thumb across her knuckles. "Never mind. Everything that happened before is all in the past now."

"It can't be that easy."

"It is, if we're together. Okay? I mean, if you want to be together."

Did she? Scanning his face, Jenna realized that she had missed him terribly. She'd missed him but had been too afraid to hope for a future with him, so she'd pushed everything off to the side, her feelings, too.

"I do."

"Good. Now, how are you feeling?"

Looking at her stomach, how it was now protruding, she winced. "Big."

He laughed. "You don't look big. If you hadn't told me you were pregnant, I would have never guessed." Brushing his fingers along her cheek, he added, "As a matter of fact, you look as pretty as ever."

"Yeah, right."

"I mean it, Jen. I think you look beautiful."

His words sounded heartfelt; his gaze felt like a caress, coaxing her with warmth. Making her feel valued and special.

That was why she'd missed him, Jenna realized. Chris said what was on his mind, regardless if it was too personal or maybe even too forward. So different than the Amish way.

"Have you gone to the doctor?"

She nodded. "Once. Mary took me."

"And what did the doctor say?"

"That everything is fine."

"I'm glad of that. Next time you go, let me know and I'll go with you. Then you can tell me everything about the baby."

"Chris, what you are saying, it's taken my breath away."

"Get used to it, Jenna. I'm not going anywhere."

Outside the doorway, they both heard Mary shuffle back and forth. It was obvious she was hovering nearby in case Jenna needed her.

"It's cold and rainy out, but I thought maybe we could go for a drive. Or go out for ice cream or hot chocolate. What do you think?"

Going for a drive with Chris meant going around in his heated truck. Since the temperature was hovering around thirty degrees, Jenna thought it sounded like heaven. "I'd like that," she said with a hesitant smile.

"I was hoping you would. I want to be alone with you." As his words hovered between them, he blushed. "I'm sorry, I didn't mean that how it sounded. I just meant I want to talk to you without anyone else around. And then, if you don't mind, I want to take you to my house."

"Why?"

"I want us to talk to my parents together."

"So soon?"

"I think we've waited long enough. Don't you?"

"Perhaps."

"Don't worry, Jenna. You aren't alone anymore," he murmured. "I promise you that. I just want to make everything right. That is, if you want to be with me. If you want to be with a man who isn't Amish."

He hadn't needed to explain himself, because Jenna felt the same way. She was tired of constantly being on edge. Of feeling as if the biggest load imaginable had just been lifted from her shoulders, she smiled at Chris.

She knew what he was asking. She was either going to have to join his world or he was going to have to join hers. But she was so tired of the secrets and lies and worries that she was more than happy to drop them all and just enjoy being by his side.

"Let me get my cloak and tell Mary what we're doing. Then we can go."

"Take your time." He stood up when she did. "I'll wait right here," he said.

And she knew why he said the words, too. Chris meant that he wasn't going anywhere. Not ever.

Or at least, not anytime soon.

Chapter Twenty-Seven

"That weather radio is going nuts," Frank said after signaling John over for a refill. "You should close up shop soon."

As if on cue, the weather radio squawked again. Following the high-pitched noise, a tinny voice announced the latest storm warnings in the surrounding counties.

Earlier, customers had come into the shop and reported the latest weather predictions on the TV. Though John had listened intently, he thought the stories all seemed rather overblown. He figured the news anchors were making things seem as catastrophic as possible so no one would turn off their television sets. Keeping everyone in a panic were the news organizations' ways of getting people to keep listening. "Frank, they're talking about a couple of storms rolling through. That's nothing to be concerned about."

"John, the storms are just west of here. They're coming our way."

"Not necessarily."

But Frank wasn't backing down from his dire warnings. "They're mentioning tornadoes, too."

"It's November."

"Early November. It could happen."

It could, but it wasn't likely. After living in Indianapolis for the majority of his adult life, he'd been through all these warnings before. He'd even gotten shaken up a time or two.

But after sitting in the basement for hours, nothing had ever happened. All he'd done was get himself worried for nothing.

But since he was mindful of Frank's obvious fear, John kept the rest of his skepticism to himself. He didn't want to offend the old guy, but he thought Frank's nerves were starting to get the best of him. Must be what happened when a man had more time to listen to all the news outlets.

Pointing to the TV Amos had installed on the wall just a few days ago, Frank said, "Turn on the news again, John. We need to see the latest tracking reports."

John had just picked up the remote control when Amos darted in through the back door. When he saw three of the tables full and John and Frank on either side of the counter, he scowled.

"Sorry, everyone, but it's time to get on home. Storm's coming."

"Amos, really?"

But Amos wasn't even having a little of John's sarcasm. "I'm serious. They've spotted twisters in the area."

"It's just a tornado watch. Not a warning."

"All the same, we've got to button down the hatches here. Frank, get on now. You've got a ways to travel."

Frank got off his stool and slipped on his hat. "Don't forget about water and lots of extra batteries," he said in parting.

"I've got my things ready. You be careful, too," Amos said.

To John's dismay, the four regulars pulled on their coats and started pulling out car keys. When Amos went right over and turned the open sign to Closed, John had had enough.

"Amos, you're going to turn everyone into nervous wrecks."

"Good. Better that than bumps on a log."

"Is that what you think I'm doing?"

"Pretty much. Otherwise, you'd have already closed up shop."

"If you're that worried, go on home. I'll make sure everything's in order."

"You can't stay here, John. There's no basement. Part of why I stopped by was so I could take you to my house. I've got a good solid basement." Clapping his hands, he nodded. "Yep, what you need to do is pour some of that coffee in a carafe, grab your coat, and come with me."

He'd been in Amos's basement. Filled with too much dusty memories, it was the absolute last place John wanted to spend the next few hours. "I'll be fine. You're worrying about everything too much, Amos. You shouldn't listen to the news like you are."

"I don't need any fancy weather reporters to tell me what the sky looks like."

"Sky?"

Amos's brows snapped together. "Honestly, John. Have you not looked at the sky? It looks bad."

Opening up a cupboard, he pulled out a large stainless steel carafe and emptied the rest of the coffee into it. "I just brewed this, so it should taste fine for a while."

"John, put that down and get yourself together."

John was now pretty much beyond exasperated. Amos definitely had adopted the habit of watching too much overblown weather news and had gotten himself in a bit of a state. "Amos, it's only a little rain. Maybe you should stop getting yourself so worked up. You're going to hurt yourself or something."

Amos's eyes narrowed as he looked John up and down, just like he was no better than an obstinate four-year-old. "*No*, it looks like a *tornado's* coming," he said with an exaggerated tone.

When the radio behind them squawked, sending out another report, Amos pointed to it with a satisfied look. "*See?*"

John finally took the time to listen. As he did, the gravity of the situation slowly became apparent. Outside, the wind was whipping into a frenzy, and a faint, glowing, greenish cast now tinted the sky. His ears popped—his body telling him what his mind was refusing to acknowledge. The pressure in the air was changing, and not for the better.

Then, like the stubborn child Amos had taken him for, John finally said the obvious. "Bad weather is coming . . ."

Amos's hand slapped the counter. "That's what I've been trying to tell you for far too long, young man! Hail has been reported. Twisters have been sighted. This isn't a bunch of old people getting riled up. Take it seriously. Now's the time to take care of yourself and the people you care about."

"I will." He smiled as Amos marched out of the shop, pure irritation evident in his every step.

John shook his head. Then unable to stop himself, he looked up at the television and finally looked at the map they were showing.

And realized they really were in the storm's path. Unable to help himself, he thought about Mary. Her basement was fit, but he also knew she would probably be struggling to take care of the animals. And Abel.

And be worrying about getting Jenna to a safe place.

And she wouldn't have been listening to any of the reports, because she didn't even own a battery-operated radio.

Making a sudden decision, John grabbed his coat and ran to the garage. For a split second, he thought about taking his truck. He hadn't technically joined the church yet. Maybe it would still be okay if he drove . . .

But that wasn't what he'd promised himself. When he had finally made the decision to leave Indianapolis for good and court Mary, he knew he would also become Amish. He'd even met with the bishop and church elders and planned to become baptized in just a few weeks.

It was time. So, though it was raining and the newscasters warned of approaching storms, he bypassed his keys. Instead, he grabbed his hat and heavy coat, and let himself outside. If he hurried, he could probably make it to her house in fifteen minutes.

Tucking his chin to his chest, he started on his way. His heart was telling him he was out of choices. They'd already been made. He'd fallen in love with Mary and Abel. Nothing was going to keep him away. It was time to tell her the truth.

Chapter Twenty-Eight

The minute she realized John had walked to her house in the storm, Mary flung open the door and ran out to him. "John, I can't believe you came all this way on foot!"

His eyes lit up as he reached for her hand. Then, with a wary eye toward the sky, he wrapped an arm around her shoulders and guided her back inside. "You shouldn't have come out here. You're going to get soaked to the skin."

"No worse than you," she said as they headed toward the house. The wind was blowing so hard now that the rain seemed to be falling sideways. Tiny flecks of ice were interspersed with rain, making each drop feel like a pinch when it swiped her cheeks. "I hope you won't catch cold."

"I'm fine," John said as he helped her scramble up the three steps leading to her door.

She held on to him with one hand, and closed her other

hand over the icy railing. With two more steps, they were safely inside.

After closing the door behind them, John looked down on her. For a moment, she thought he was going to lean close and brush his lips against hers, but of course he straightened.

"Mary, I started worrying about you the minute I realized just how bad the storms are. How are you? Are you frightened? Do you need anything?"

She'd been scared to death. This afternoon proved to be another one of those times when she missed her husband terribly. Not only would he have comforted her through the crisis, but he would have taken care of everything, too. In the years since his death, there had been many a time when she'd come to realize just how much she'd taken William for granted.

He'd handled the hard, physical labor on the farm. That was true.

But he'd also had such a steady, confident nature that she'd come to depend on his advice and support. "I've been afraid, but I've been strong," she said. She didn't want John to think she was helpless.

Looking at her, pure pride shown in his eyes. "You're incredible, Mary. Most women I know would be wringing their hands."

"I'm not most women," she teased. Of course, John didn't have to know that she wasn't near as courageous as he imagined. In fact, she would've gladly spent the last hour wringing her hands in worry—if she'd thought it would help. But of course in the years since William had passed, she'd learned that hand-wringing didn't do much of anything besides create sore hand muscles.

She was just considering how much to admit to John when the wind blew hard against the front windows, making them rattle.

Looking at the panes of glass with concern, John threw a question over his shoulder. "Where's Abel? We need to get to a better place fast."

"He's back in his bedroom. I had him gather a few things for the storm cellar."

"Mamm?" Abel called from the hallway as he bounded in. "Mamm, we should go, don'tcha think?"

"Certainly. Especially now that John is here. Abel, he walked all the way over here in the rain. Isn't that something?"

A moment of distrust flashed through the boy's eyes before he contained himself and nodded. "Mr. Weaver."

"I know you two probably have everything under control, but I thought I'd try to lend a hand. If I could." There. He was asking permission, though he really didn't know how he could physically make himself leave if Abel didn't want him there.

As the wind knocked the windows around them, Abel glanced at the windows and then back at John. "I . . . I'm glad you're here. For Mom."

"I am a lucky woman," Mary said, further smoothing things between them. "Now I have two men looking after me." With another awkward smile, she said, "Well, are you two ready to go down to the storm cellar? It's cramped and dark, but we'll all be safer there. You know, just in case the winds get worse."

"That sounds like the perfect plan. What can I carry?"

Mary strode to the kitchen counter. "We have a battery-operated flashlight and a Coleman lantern, too. If you carry these, I'll get the box of food and blankets."

John grabbed both from the counter. "Anything else?"

"Abel, can you think of anything I've missed?"

"*Nee*, Mamm. We just need to go. Now."

"All right, then."

After tossing the two lights in another box, he grabbed one of the blankets she'd been holding and held out a hand to her. "Ready?"

Oh, his voice was so dear. Right then and there, she knew she'd been right to trust him. Right to trust him with her son's behavior, their welfare, and her heart. "I am now."

After helping her grab a few more blankets and the basket full of neatly packed goods, he ushered Mary and Abel outside, holding her arm securely.

"Abel, stay near me!" he called out over the wind.

"I'm trying, but the wind is strong."

"Indeed it is. But we'll be better in your cellar." After they opened the heavy wooden door, he shined the flashlight down into the dark cavity. "Are you ready for this?"

As the wind and rain blew against her face and cheeks, almost stinging her skin, she nodded. "Definitely."

"Can you go first? I'll follow with Abel."

"*Jah*. I can do that," she replied. And amazingly, she could! Everything seemed easier by his side.

After helping her get settled on the wooden bench and giving Abel a reassuring look, John positioned himself right in front of the door—as if he was doing everything he could to ensure their safety.

To Mary's eye, he looked stronger than ever. And he seemed more determined to be a part of their lives. She wondered what had brought about the change. She knew he'd gone back to Indianapolis to not only revisit the past, but to also discover what the future had in store for him.

As the wind howled outside, a look of alarm entered his eyes. "Where's Jenna?"

"She's all right. She's with Chris."

"And who is Chris?"

Mary bit her lip to keep from smiling. Their situation wasn't the least bit amusing, but his reaction was—a true combination of horror and embarrassment . . . and possessiveness. Like he truly cared about Jenna and was anxious to protect her, too.

"Chris is an *Englischer* who she's friends with."

He raised an eyebrow. "Friends?"

With an embarrassed look, she gestured toward Abel. "*Jah.*"

Abel rolled his eyes. "Chris is her boyfriend. He's who got her pregnant."

Mary was beyond embarrassed. "Abel!"

"It's true."

To her relief, John just smiled. "Well, now I understand. So you feel she's in safe hands? He'll look out for her?"

"I think so. I believe they were off to talk to his parents."

As the wind howled again, Abel shivered, betraying

that he really wasn't as brave and fearless as he was hoping to appear. The wind bristled against the door.

Truly, it looked as if it might not be any match for the fierce winds.

What if it wasn't?

"John, there's room on the bench with Abel and me," she said, attempting to sound far more calm than she felt. "Please, come over here and sit with us."

"I think it's best if I stay here by the door. If something happens, I want to be here."

"But you could get hurt," Abel blurted out.

"And we would feel horrible if you were hurt," she added. More quietly, she said, "We would feel horrible if *anything* bad happened to you."

"Nothing's going to happen. I promise. I'll move next to you if the winds get worse." As if on cue, the winds outside gusted and blew, making the cracks in the shelter whistle.

Seeking to reassure them both, he added, "It's also important to me to protect you."

After another flash of worry, Mary nodded. But Abel looked at him. "Why?"

"Why? Because I care about you, of course."

Confusion clouded Abel's eyes. But he said nothing.

John realized it was time to speak from his heart. "Listen, just in case something happens . . . I just want you both to know that you've become my family. You two have become the most important people to me in the world. I went to Indianapolis last week to be sure of some things. See, I started worrying about my feelings for the two of you."

"What was worrying you?" Abel asked.

"My past. Back when I was eighteen, when I left here, I had to make a lot of sacrifices. Turning against my faith and family wasn't easy. In fact, it was the hardest thing I've ever had to do. While I was considering returning to the church, to the Plain way of life, I was beating myself up. Part of me was starting to think that maybe it would be wrong to go back. To go back to everything I had given up."

Mary's face seemed to fill with hope and doubt and kindness. "You wanted to be sure," she whispered.

"That's right." He couldn't help but look at her in wonder. She understood him, even when he struggled to put all his jumbled thoughts in order.

No matter what, she was looking for the best in him.

In that moment, he realized that that was how she would always be. Kind. Giving. Wanting to respect his point of view.

She had survived the loss of her husband and now was ready to move on again. He had never felt more humbled.

"Are you sure now?" she asked.

John looked at her, looked at Abel sitting next to her—silent and waiting, too.

"I'm positive," he said. Just as a terrible noise roared through their valley.

Chapter Twenty-Nine

For Jenna, the last two hours had felt like one of her old daydreams—the kind she used to have when she was sure the rest of her life was going to be sunny and perfect. Of course, she'd long since learned that such things could never happen.

But things had certainly come close. After she and Chris had left Mary's house in his car, they'd driven around the outskirts of Jacob's Crossing. At first, their conversation had been stilted, then things between them had smoothed and Jenna started remembering everything she'd liked about him.

Chris was the type of guy who seemed to actually try to *hear* her when she talked. He didn't interrupt, or try to top her story with one of his. Instead, he simply listened and asked questions. Just as if everything she had to say was important.

He asked about the baby, too. Lots of questions about how she felt and how being with child felt. At first she'd been embarrassed, but then, little by little, she began to enjoy sharing the details with him. She'd been keeping so many things to herself, that it was a relief to share her excitement and apprehensions with him.

Then, after stopping for ice cream, they heard about the storm coming in. Though he offered to drive her the four extra blocks to Mary's, Jenna declined the offer. For reasons Jenna didn't care to contemplate—she wasn't quite ready to leave his side.

Both his parents were in the kitchen when they arrived. Preparing for the onslaught of bad weather, they were searching through drawers for flashlights and batteries.

His mother looked at Jenna in confusion when they'd entered. "Hello?"

"This is Jenna," Chris had said. Just as if he'd told them about her before. As if she mattered to him.

While Jenna had digested that, Mrs. Henderson shot her a somewhat distracted smile. "Jenna, it's nice to meet you. It's good you're here and not out and about. The weather service just announced a storm warning and a tornado watch."

"Yeah, we were driving around and heard about it," Chris said. "I thought it would be safest to come right home." Looking around, he asked, "Where's Elizabeth?"

"She's over at a girlfriend's. They had a sleepover and

with the weather like it is, we decided to let her stay there." His mother looked at Jenna kindly. "I hope you won't want to leave until things get better. I know you can't call home. Will your family be worried if you aren't there?"

"No," she said, not eager to tell them that her parents didn't even care where she was.

Chris opened his mouth, looking like he wanted to blurt out her condition. But to Jenna's relief, he'd said nothing. Just offered to help carry a blanket and flashlights down to the basement.

They'd gotten downstairs just as the house's electricity flickered, then suddenly shut down, covering everything in a cloak of darkness.

Chris quickly clicked on a flashlight. As a circle of light beamed in front of them, a beautiful golden retriever came off of her dog bed and stood next to them, tail wagging. "This is Goldie," he said, looking slightly sheepish. "Pretty original name, huh?"

"I think she's beautiful." Jenna petted her with pleasure. Goldie stepped closer, obviously enjoying Jenna's attention.

Crouching down, Chris knelt in front of the dog and petted her, too. "Goldie's five. She's a great dog." Looking up at Jenna, he said, "I really am glad you're here."

Jenna was attempting to think of something to say when footsteps pounded down the wooden stairs, bringing Chris back to his feet.

"I have a bad feeling about this storm," his mom said as she hurried down the stairs. "I think things are going to get worse before they get better."

"Mom, don't get all excited," Chris blurted. "There's no need to make everyone nervous."

"No, your mom's right. Sirens are going off outside. People are preparing for the worst," his dad said as he stepped out of the stairwell holding a battery-operated lantern.

Jenna felt her stomach clench as fear for her family settled in. Though they didn't want her anymore, she still cared for them, especially her brothers and sisters. Quickly, she closed her eyes and said a prayer for their safety.

When she opened them again, she was calmed by the way the lantern's light cast a warm glow around the four of them and Goldie.

Chris patted her shoulder. "It's okay, Jenna. I won't let anything happen to you."

"No, we won't," his mother added with a smile. "Especially since we finally are getting to meet you. Chris speaks of you all the time."

Jenna tensed, uncertain she believed the words. She was becoming used to no one being eager to see her, and being aware that what they told her to her face was far different than what they said behind her back.

"It's true," Chris said as he reached for her hand.

Immediately, his touch reassured her, though her feelings were at war once again. She knew better than to trust anyone.

Above them, thunder rumbled and the rain poured down so hard it sounded as if rocks were being thrown at the windows. Jenna looked above her head worriedly as, beside them, Goldie whimpered and paced.

Though she'd never been one to be frightened of bad weather, everything about this situation felt different and scary. Maybe it was because she was in an *Englischer's* home? Or, perhaps it was because of the baby she was carrying?

Still staying near, Chris rubbed his thumb along her knuckles. "It's okay. Just hail. We'll be safe here in the basement."

"Oh. *Jah*. To be sure," she muttered, feeling somewhat embarrassed by her skittishness.

Looking around, Mr. Henderson snapped his fingers. "Let's move over this direction," he said. Obediently, the three of them followed, walking across the large expanse of the basement, finally coming to a stop in front of a large walk-in closet. "This is the most stable part of the house," he explained. "Overhead are most of the support beams. We'll be safe here, even if a tornado comes."

Jenna shuddered at the thought.

Chris's mom must have noticed, because she rushed over to one of the padded chairs folded against a wall. "Jenna, dear, why don't you sit down?"

She felt silly, being the only one to sit while the others were standing in the rest of the space. "*Nee*. I'll be fine standing with the rest of you."

To her dismay, his mother apologized. "I know it's not much, it's just a fold-up chair from a game table, but it should be more comfortable for you."

"*Danke*, the chair is fine," she protested as she finally did sit down. "I didn't mean for you to think I wasn't grateful . . . I just don't want to take up too much space."

"You don't," his father said.

Feeling terribly self-conscious, she bit her lip and folded her hands on her lap. Maybe the storm wasn't going to be near as bad as they were predicting. Maybe it would blow over soon and she could go back home.

Well, to Mary's home. Once again, she thought of her parents and her brothers and sisters. Oh, she hoped they were somewhere safe, too.

Chris kneeled at her feet. With deliberate care, he reached for her hands and enfolded them into his own far larger, far warmer ones. "Jenna, I know you're scared, but please let us take care of you," he said softly. "After all, it's my baby, too."

Her heart practically stopped beating as his words pierced the air. Immediately, she darted a look at his parents, practically ready for them to start yelling at her or Chris.

Past experiences told her to pull her hands away and to try to escape. But Chris's hands held firm. And the look in his eyes told so much more. He was showing her that no matter what, he wasn't leaving her side.

A moment passed as Jenna felt his parents exchange glances.

But instead of shouting or acting shocked, his father merely raised a brow as he looked down at the pair of them. "So you finally decided to tell us, Chris?"

"You knew?"

After a moment, Mrs. Henderson spoke. "I heard some rumors the other day, about a very pretty Amish girl named Jenna and how her baby's father was a mystery."

She paused. "Since you had told us all about Jenna, then said nothing, I wondered if maybe this Jenna was the one people were talking about."

Jenna wrapped her arms around her stomach as Chris turned bashful. "I meant to tell you before now. I was just looking for the right time."

"It's my fault," Jenna said. "I didn't tell Chris until recently. I was too embarrassed."

"You had enough to deal with, Jenna. Don't apologize," Chris said. He squeezed her hand softly before getting to his feet.

Jenna attempted to rise, too. But Chris stopped that with a brief look. "It's okay," he whispered, his lips close to her ear. "Please don't worry so much. I promise, we'll have plenty of time to work things out."

She sat back down. As she did, she became aware of the interest his parents had taken in watching their exchange.

"You two really do care about each other, don't you?" his mother said.

"Of course I care about her," Chris replied.

"Have you both decided what you're going to do?"

Jenna tucked her chin. This whole situation was throwing her for a loop.

Never had she imagined she'd even have a relationship with Chris, let alone be sitting with him and his parents, discussing things!

Until Chris had forced answers from her and refused to let her gloss over their relationship as a simple mistake, she'd truly thought they'd never have anything to do with each other again.

But now, here he was, supporting her in front of his parents, protecting her from the storm, and being so loving and tender. So much so, she still wasn't quite sure how to respond to his gestures . . .

When she felt Chris's gaze on her, silently asking for her to participate in the exchange, Jenna shrugged. "I don't know what we're going to do. To be honest, until I told Chris, I had been sure he would be upset with me."

"Upset?" His mom darted a look Chris's way. "I hope not—"

Above them, the wind picked up. Sounds of fallen branches rang through the air. Jenna flinched as several scraped at the windows above them.

Reality set in again, reminding them all that while things might be turbulent in their lives, they were also mighty turbulent in nature, too.

"Let's table this discussion for another day," his dad said sharply. "Nothing discussed now is going to mean much if things get worse."

Jenna shivered at the not-so-subtle reminder that if the tornadoes really did come, the house and their lives would be in danger and might never look the same again.

Chris noticed, and immediately wrapped his arms around her. "Way to frighten Jenna, Dad," Chris said.

"I'm merely telling the truth. Sometimes that's all we can do, right?"

"You're right," Mrs. Henderson replied. "And you're also right about the timing. We need to stand together and hold each other tight. Not worry about what-ifs at the moment."

Jenna relaxed. Chris's warm embrace helped her calm her nerves. As did his parents' no-nonsense acceptance of not only the baby, but their relationship. Truly, it was like night and day from her parents' reaction.

She shivered again as she silently relived her parents' anger and extreme disappointment. Oh, but she'd felt so desperate when she'd shown up at Graham's house. She'd really thought she had no one, and nowhere to go.

She started when she felt Mrs. Henderson's hand on her shoulder. "Please don't worry, Jenna. We'll all get through this. I promise. The timing could have been a bit better, but the news about the baby is good."

Jenna couldn't hold back her shock any longer. "You really think that, don't you?"

"Of course I do. Listen, I've been a pastor's wife for a very long time. Every time I think I've seen or heard it all, God shows me differently. I promise, I've learned that there isn't much that can't be dealt with, as long as people communicate and pray," she added, just as another burst of wind shook the house. A look of alarm flashed in her eyes as she gripped one of the thick columns that supported the main structure of the house. "Craig, I'm starting to get worried. It feels like the whole house is shaking."

"Let's all sit down. Chris, you take care of Jenna, and I'll take care of your mother," Mr. Henderson said.

Seeming more than glad to follow his father's orders, Chris pulled up a chair and nestled beside her, pulling her even closer. Just as he did, the pressure in the air shifted.

Soon, it felt as if all the oxygen was being sucked out of the room.

Jenna clutched Chris's hand and closed her eyes tightly, praying with all her might.

And then an upstairs window broke.

Chapter Thirty

A roar, as loud as a train, reverberated through the valley. And just like a locomotive was near, the ground shook with the storm's vibrations. In the storm cellar, some of the paneling that lined the walls creaked and groaned, making their haven feel even more precarious. Above their heads, the lamp swung wildly back and forth, casting flashes of light into the shadows.

John eyed it worriedly. He momentarily considered standing up and lifting it off the hook, but ultimately decided against it. Though he was trying hard to act unflustered, the deafening roar above them was scaring him something awful.

Beside him, Mary flinched as they heard a crash.

"Do you think that was the house?" Abel asked. "Do you think that was our house coming apart?"

Though John ached to tell the boy what he wanted to hear, he was even less willing to give him false hope. Only God knew what was happening above them.

"I don't know. Perhaps it was just some shingles." As more debris thumped above them, and the ground continued to shake, John added more loudly, "Abel, Mary, I'm afraid this sounds bad. You might want to prepare yourselves for the worst."

The noise got louder. Tears filled Abel's eyes as he curled into a ball, hugging his pillow to his chest. Holding Mary's hand, with his other, John reached for Abel's. To his relief, Abel unclenched his fist enough to take John's hand.

Then they sat in silence as the world seemed to destruct above them.

Minutes later—or perhaps it had only been seconds—the dizzying shriek quieted, replaced by the sound of pounding rain.

Slowly Mary pulled away. "Do you think it's over?"

"I hope so."

Tense, the three of them raised their heads. John got to his feet and stood closer to the storm door. Sounds of branches ripping from trees, then crashing to the ground, reverberated around them. John felt the hair on the back of his neck rise.

"Come back, John," Mary pleaded.

"I'm okay. I won't open the door. I'm trying to listen to see if anything's changed."

But of course, it was a futile proposition. The rain continued to pound and the winds still shrieked. As debris scratched against the shelter's door, John looked at it with worry. More than anything, he hoped no trees or boards from the house or barn would fall directly on the door. If they were trapped, they'd have to rely on being found, and that scared him half to death.

Now pings of hail clanked above them. Mary winced in response. "John, please come back."

As he glanced in her direction, guilt besieged him. He should have put Mary's needs first and held tight to her hand instead of giving into curiosity.

"Of course. I'm sorry," he said. But now simply holding her hand didn't seem enough. Unable to stop himself, John wrapped an arm around her back, holding her close. He looked at Abel. The boy was holding his pillow tight against his chest again and was staring into space.

In the flickering light, Mary looked at her son worriedly. After a moment, she said, "Abel, John, right at this moment, our future seems to be in the Lord's hands. Because of that, there's only one thing to do. We must pray."

"Do you think it will even help?" Abel asked.

"It can only help, *jah*?" Mary countered. "We must pray for our safety and the safety of others."

Immediately, Abel's head tucked. John bowed his head, too. Mary's words rang true. At the moment, he'd never felt more helpless in his life. All he was able to do was hold on to these two people and ask the Lord to watch over them.

"God, please be with us," he said out loud. "Please watch over us and the animals and our family."

"And watch over our friends," Abel added.

"I know you are always with us," Mary finished. "Please protect us now."

Above them, it sounded like the rain was lessening. Perhaps the worst was over.

While Mary and Abel sat in silence, John spoke to God silently. *"I know there's not much to me, Lord. But I finally feel like I've found the right place for myself. Please don't let me lose it now."*

Just then, the air stilled. John gasped, half expecting another rush of wind to blast through the valley. Half expecting the frightful roar of another tornado to come barreling forward.

But instead of loud noise, there was only sudden silence.

Mary loosened her hand from John's grasp and straightened her back with a faint groan. Tilting her head to one side, she listened. Finally, she looked at Abel and smiled. "It sounds like the high winds are gone. The storm has passed."

Abel lifted his head. "Maybe we'll be okay after all."

Abel's voice was so full of wonder, Mary exchanged a smile with John. "Yes, son. I think so."

John stood up. "Your mother's right. We made it."

Mary beamed. "Our prayers were answered."

Abel got to his feet, too. Staring at the storm cellar's thick oak door, he said, "I wonder what it looks like outside."

John motioned the boy forward. "Let's go check, Abel."

Mary scrambled to her feet. "*Nee.* Not yet. Maybe we should wait a bit?"

He knew Mary was nervous and feared for Abel's safety.

John didn't blame her. But he also knew that staying underground like an ostrich wouldn't help things, either. He wanted to see how the animals were doing, and check for the possibility of fire as well.

But because he didn't want to scare her, he kept his thoughts to himself. "We'll only take a peek," he said, carefully. "If things look bad, we'll stay here a bit longer. If not, it will be nice to stretch our legs, don't you think, Abel?"

Abel nodded.

Slowly, John unhooked the latch and then pushed up on the wood.

It didn't budge.

Fear coursed through him. If they were trapped, it could be hours or even days before they were rescued. His pulse racing, he motioned for Abel to stand beside him. "I'm going to need your help to push. Okay?"

"I'm strong." He made a muscle. "I can help."

"All right then." John shifted a bit more so that the boy was more fully situated under the lowest part of the door. "On my count of three, we're going to push. Got it?"

"*Jah.*"

"One . . . two . . . three!"

Arms strained as together the two of them pushed upward with all their might. At first, nothing happened, not even a smidge of movement.

But then something did. The door opened half an inch. Relief coursing through him, John raised his voice. "Abel, that's great! Now, let's push harder. Let's push and get this door open."

Rearranging their hands, Abel looked at him again. "On three?"

"On three." After another count, John pushed with all his might. The muscles in his back screamed in protest. Drops of sweat formed on his brow.

Then, with a creak and a groan and a snap, they pushed the door open.

Before John could warn him, Abel scampered forward, going up the ladder with ease.

When he disappeared from view, Mary leapt to her feet. "Abel! Be careful!"

"I'll go after him," John said, already halfway up the rungs.

But just then, Abel crouched down. And pointed. "Look at this branch. It was blocking us in."

John noticed the branch was freshly split in two. "We broke that getting out."

"We did it together."

John understood what the boy meant. This boy—this boy who struggled in school and had fought the idea of his mother finding new love—had finally realized that he was terribly important and needed. In addition, he'd also learned that John valued him, too.

It was going to take all three of them to make their future a success, and there was room in all their lives for another person to love.

"We did do this together," John said. "Abel, I couldn't have lifted the door without you. You gave me the added strength I needed. Abel, your mother and I couldn't have gotten out without you."

After a brief pause, Abel stared at him with a new resolve—and acceptance—in his eyes. "And, Mamm and I wouldn't have been all right without you, John," he said.

They were still staring at each other when Mary climbed up the ladder and stood by their side.

"Let's go see what the storm brought us," she said.

He smiled at her, then grinned when he saw that her house was intact, all except for a few pieces of missing siding and shingles.

But when he turned toward the barn, he felt himself sway.

And literally could think of nothing to say. Because there was a gaping hole in the side of the barn.

Chapter Thirty-One

"I think it's over," Mary Weaver stated as she lifted her hands off Katie's shoulders. "Praise God for that." With a shaking hand, she pushed back the few strands of hair that had come loose from the bun at the back of her neck. "I don't know when I've ever been more afraid in my life."

"I was scared," Katie said, her usual cheery voice sadly deflated.

When the eerie light of the lantern flickered, illuminating Katie's tearstained cheeks for a brief moment, Mattie looked at her with a reassuring smile. "You were mighty brave today, Katie. We were all proud of you."

Pride flickered in Katie's expression before worry replaced it again. "I tried to be brave, but I wasn't. Not really," she said. "Mamm, I don't want any more tornadoes to come. Ever."

The plaintive command was just what everyone needed to dispel some of the tension in the shelter.

"I know you don't," her mother said with a chuckle. "I, for one, hope the Lord doesn't send us anymore for a while, either."

"I'll pray for that as well," Lucy said lightly from her spot in the very back. "Now may I please get up?"

They'd placed her next to the wall, a warm quilt wrapped on her lap.

Mattie noticed Lucy was only asking out of politeness. In fact, she was already standing up and deftly folding the blue quilt into quarters.

But Graham, obviously unable to resist teasing his brother, said, "Calvin, what do you think? Is it safe for Lucy to move?"

Calvin scowled at him. "I wasn't *ordering* her to sit there, Graham. I just wanted her and the baby to be safe . . ."

Lucy grinned. "I know you wanted me there because you were worried, husband. Don't worry. I'm not upset."

"Now that everything's all good, let's get out of here," Graham said. "What do you think, Calvin?"

Mattie breathed deeply as she looked at Graham. He was standing by the door to the storm cellar and was looking for direction from Calvin.

Mattie admired that. Just as she admired most everything about him. As usual, he was standing stoically, being strong but not showy.

Like he always was.

Graham relied on his easy humor and place in the

family to usually stay in the background, or to support his brothers.

But though he didn't claim the spotlight, it was always apparent that he was definitely as capable and responsible as either of his brothers.

He just didn't have the need to be recognized.

She thought only a person of strong character could do that. It was sometimes hard to let others shine. With some surprise, she realized that time and again, he'd done that for her.

After glancing up at the ceiling again and visibly straining his hearing, Calvin at last looked toward Graham and nodded. "I think the twister has passed. Let's open the door and see what damage has been done."

"Nothing that can't be fixed," Graham said with a reassuring smile toward his sister before stepping closer to the door. With a grunt, Graham loosened the bolt and with the help of his shoulder and Calvin's support, pushed open the heavy door. With a clunk, it flapped open and crashed against the ground.

Immediately, rain flew in, along with only a narrow beam of faint light. The storm clouds had chased away the early evening sunset and left the sky gray as smoke.

With Mary by her side and Katie at their heels, Mattie stepped forward and peered into the opening, not even caring that the cold November rain was splattering against her cheeks and forehead. The wind was still strong, but it came in gusts, not with the heavy, all-encompassing pull and scream from just moments before.

Altogether, they breathed a sigh of relief. The tornado had indeed passed.

"Praise the Lord," Mary said again.

"Yes, our God is good, indeed," Calvin murmured as he stepped aside so Graham could lead the way. As Graham climbed forward, Calvin walked to where Lucy stood and took her hand.

Mattie stood at the opening and waited for Graham to signal her forward. Rain splattered against her skin, soaking the edges of her *kapp*. But instead of backing away into the shelter, she kept her chin tilted. The fresh air was so welcome, Mattie didn't even mind getting her cheeks soaked.

Graham stepped up two rungs and carefully poked his head farther out.

Mattie had to force herself to continue to breathe, she was so on edge. For a moment, no one said a word as they all waited expectantly for news.

But when Graham stayed silent, not conveying any reports, the tension in the storm cellar intensified. Mattie felt warm tears mix with the cold raindrops as fear of the news gripped her.

"Well, son. What do you see?" his mother called out. "Is it safe to come out of here?"

"It's safe," Graham muttered. "You won't be hurt by the storm any longer. I, uh, I see it on the horizon. It's passed."

His words were like a soothing balm, so smooth and calm that Mattie was reminded of how he'd held her when she'd been so sick.

And now, just as when she'd been racked by sickness,

Graham's voice was exactly the voice she needed to hear.

Almost.

Little by little, she realized Graham's tone was off. It was becoming painfully obvious that something was wrong.

Bracing herself for the worst, Mattie called out, "Graham, what is it? What do you see?"

A long moment passed before he spoke. "Oh, quite a bit . . ."

"No real damage?" Calvin rubbed Lucy's back as he smiled broadly.

"*Nee.* I mean I see quite a bit of destruction." Speaking faster, Graham added, "Parts of the house . . . the barn are gone." Each word sounded like it was being choked from his throat. "Mamm, I'm so sorry, but I'm afraid we've lost almost everything."

As Mary stared at the opening in confusion and Lucy gasped behind her, Mattie's heart felt like it stopped. "Surely not?" she asked. "Graham, I bet things aren't that bad . . ."

Graham knelt down so they could see his head. "I wouldn't tease about this. You all ought to come see . . ." He paused, obviously struggling to keep his composure. The muscles in his throat working, he tried again. "I mean . . . I mean, you all need to see this for yourselves."

In the dim light, they were all silent as they watched his feet disappear. Mattie felt frozen. From the stillness around her, she figured Calvin, Lucy, and Mary felt the same.

Only Katie had wiggled forward. With one hand on the well-worn ladder, she looked at her *mamm* curiously.

"Mamm, are we going to go up, too? I want to see what Graham meant."

With a shaky sigh, Mary nodded. "In a moment, dear." She looked toward Calvin. "Son, do you want to go next?"

"All right." Looking to Lucy, he said, "Do you want to come up with me or wait here? You can wait if you're not ready."

"I don't need to wait." With a hint of steel in her voice—reminding them all she was far stronger than she looked—Lucy said, "I'm ready for just about anything."

His mother put an arm on Lucy's back. "Maybe you should wait, Lucy. Just to be sure everything's safe?"

"My place is with Calvin."

"But—"

"I'll be fine. I want to be by his side."

Calvin's smile grew as she stepped forward. Mattie watched Calvin help Lucy up onto the rungs of the ladder, then followed from behind.

Lucy's gasp echoed down the shaft, giving Mattie a chill.

Katie hopped from one foot to the next. "Now, Mamm?"

"*Jah*, daughter. I suppose we'll go next," Mary Weaver said reluctantly. "I mean, if that's all right with you, Mattie?"

"It's fine. Go ahead."

At long last, Mary and Katie climbed the ladder, Katie in front of her *mamm*.

After Katie had disappeared through the opening, Mary looked toward Mattie. "Would you like me to wait for you here? To help you up?"

"*Nee.* I'll be fine. I need a moment, I'm afraid."

"All right." Mary's voice was hesitant. "If you're sure?"

"I'll be fine. I just need a moment with the Lord."

After Mary disappeared, Mattie leaned back against the hard rock that lined the walls and closed her eyes. "Thank you for protecting us, Lord," she said. "And Lord, thank you for helping me now understand why I've had to overcome so many obstacles." As understanding dawned, she continued. "Now I realize that I needed to learn to be strong, and to remember what was important in my life.

"Long ago, I would have said I needed security. I would have protested how I needed things to stay the same so I would feel safe. But now I know that isn't the case at all. Now I know that we can survive anything, as long as we have each other. It is our health and our loved ones that should be treasured. And you, Lord! You. Not everything else."

The faint glow of knowing that she'd said the right words penetrated her right then and there.

With a new resolve, she walked to the ladder. Now she was prepared for anything she faced.

The fresh air brought a fresh beginning, and the unwelcome reminder of what had just passed. By her side, Graham whistled low as he surveyed the land that had been in his family for generations. Debris and torn branches littered the fields. What was left of their barn stood precariously— the wood seemed to shift and sway in a dance, threatening to fall at any moment. In addition, a gaping hole was now where the west wall used to be.

To Mattie's amazement, when she peered inside, there were still some bridles and saddles hanging neatly. The other three walls shook slightly, looking as if all they needed was a soft breeze to encourage them to come tumbling down.

Behind them, the Weavers' home lay in shambles. The tornado had clipped the house, removing part of the roof and upsetting most everything in the living room. Miraculously, other parts of the building seemed completely untouched.

How a tornado could do so much damage to some parts of a home while completely bypassing others was surely one of the Lord's mysteries, Mattie decided.

Of course, she'd long given up trying to figure out or predict God's will. What happened, happened. And He would be by their sides to help and give strength . . . if they wanted it. With that in mind, she closed her eyes and gave thanks again. All of them were fine, not even sporting bruises or cuts. And God had saved the animals in the barn, too. It was a miracle that the wall that had been lifted by the storm had been next to the tool shed and workroom.

But Graham, on the other hand, didn't seem to be counting his blessings or holding out the slightest bit of hope. Instead, he looked as sad and tired as she'd ever seen him—and thoroughly dejected. His shoulders slumped and his face was haggard.

"Graham?" she said. "Are you all right?"

"I don't know." After another long moment of stunned silence, he turned to Mattie. "What am I going to do? Everything's gone."

Things were in disarray, it was true. But all wasn't lost. She could see that now. "That's not true."

He turned to her. "You really think so?"

"I know so. Graham, everything can be rebuilt. And we'll build it better and stronger."

Though he nodded, Graham didn't look as if he believed a word of what she said. "My father built so much of this. He'd be devastated to see that it's ruined."

Mattie had known Mr. Weaver. And she knew something about being in the brink of ill health. After all, her battle with cancer had led her to a terribly dark place. A place where most everything had seemed insurmountable. Almost too hard to bear.

But months of care from friends like Lucy, and seeing how much Ella had wanted to overcome the obstacles in her life, had strengthened Mattie. So had the unfailing support of Graham.

Perhaps he would never realize the impact he had on her life. Perhaps he would never understand how hard it had been for her to move forward.

But maybe that was why God had given them each other. "I disagree," she finally said. "I don't think your father would have been fazed by this at all."

"And why is that? Because he was a much better man?"

"Because he knew what was important in his life," she countered. "Just as I think you know, too, Graham. It's the people who surround us that matter. Not the things. It's our health and our friends and family who can surround us when things are the toughest. Those are the things that count."

"Of course you're right." Running a hand through his hair, he attempted to smile. "It's just a lot to take in right now. That's all."

Of course it was. Anyone would feel at a loss. She knew he was just stunned. Overwhelmed. Playfully, she sought to brighten his mood. "We still have each other."

"Of course we do." He smiled weakly. Then, seemingly oblivious to the wet ground, he sat on an overturned barrel. "But Mattie, I have to tell ya, I'm having a hard time taking all this in. All my life, I've tried to measure up to my *daed*, measure up to my brothers. I never felt like I was ever going to be as good as them. Everything with Jenna truly upset me. I've already lost so much. Lots of people will hardly look at me the same way. And those that do? They look at me differently."

He sighed. "Now I wonder if I'll ever even be as good as I once was."

"Graham, you are a wonderful-*gut* man. You are. And as for the gossips? They'll come around. People always do."

"You haven't heard what people have been saying about me."

Mattie figured the opposite was true. Most likely, he hadn't heard everything everyone had said about him. "You know better than to let the gossips be your guide." Smiling softly, she slipped one of her wool-covered hands in his. "Graham, don'tcha remember what all the gossips had been saying about me?"

"You were either supposed to die, at death's door, or were going to be permanently disfigured." He grinned. "I'd forgotten about all that."

"Because I'm so much better now. Why, just the other day, someone commented on my hair—asked me how it was growing. Things get better, Graham Weaver. They always do. I mean, you've talked to Jenna, yes?"

"Yes . . ."

"And the job at the factory? That's a good thing, too." Moving closer, she set her hand on his shoulder. "And this destruction? It's bad, but it's not the end of the world. Look around you, Graham. Everything can be made right again."

"Maybe. I just don't understand why all of this is happening."

She'd thought those same words so many times, she almost smiled. "You don't have to know."

"So I'm just supposed to bear it all the best I can?"

"I think so. Maybe right now. Right this minute, our Lord is reminding us that we are all survivors. Each of us, every day, has struggles we must overcome. Some are difficult and seemingly unsurpassable. Such as my cancer, or your house. Or your reputation.

"But other things count, too. All the bad things that surface even just dealing with family life. Bad days. Bad relationships. Each of us must overcome and move forward. Into the aftermath. Even if we're scarred. Even if we're damaged. Even if we'll never be the same."

"You really believe that, don't you?"

"I have to. Otherwise, I couldn't go on."

"Do you think you'll be able to move on with me? By my side?"

"What are you saying?"

"I'm asking you to be my girl."

Mattie was amused. Oh, but life was never going to be dull or boring with Graham by her side! "Graham Weaver, this is how you finally decide to court me? In the rain, after a tornado, with everything falling down on us?"

"You're the one who seems to think it's a perfect time," he said, pure amusement making his blue eyes sparkle.

"I didn't say *perfect*."

"You came pretty close to saying that. So, yes, Mattie Lapp. I'm proposing to you, right now. Right here."

"I suppose it's as good a place as any."

"I think it's the best place on earth," he countered. "Here we are, living proof that wonders never cease, and that there're good things to be found most anywhere."

"Well, *that is true* . . ."

His voice softened as he stepped forward. "That is true. I'm a believer, you see."

"A believer?"

"Uh-huh. In miracles. You're the one who taught me to believe in miracles."

"Because I survived cancer?"

"Because you survived losing your faith. And cancer. And instead of folding or getting weaker, you only got stronger. Mattie, you've proven your strength and the Lord's goodness in all of us time and again."

She'd surely never done anything like that! "Graham, I was just trying—"

He cut her off. "Mattie, I need you. I always have, you

know that. I want to court you. I want us to spend as much time together as possible."

She did know. Because Graham's love and friendship had also been an enormous part of her life. "I need you, too. And I want to be with you, too."

"So will you finally stop fussing and tell me your answer? Here in the rain? Here, when I have so little to give you?"

That was where he was wrong. For longer than she could remember, he'd always had so much more for her than she could have ever expected. A little lump formed in her throat when she recalled all the times he'd been there for her, from when they'd been in grade school and he'd shared his sandwich because she'd forgotten her lunch at home, to most recently, when he'd promised her on the elevator that he'd help her find a sweetheart.

But of course that special person she'd needed had been him. It had always been him.

"Mattie Lapp?" His voice cut through her memories like a knife. "Are you ever going to tell me yes?"

"Oh. Yes. Of course." She laughed, amazed that he would ever imagine a different response from her. "Yes, I would love for us to court."

He looked so relieved Mattie couldn't help but tease him. With a laugh, she lifted her head and looked into his eyes. "Did you really think I wouldn't say yes?"

"I've learned to never guess what's going on in your head, Mattie."

Leaning against him, she cuddled close, positioning her

body closer to his when he leaned forward and kissed her brow. With one hand, she traced the lines of his shirt, liking the way the soft cotton felt against her skin. And how the fine muscles of his chest felt underneath the fabric.

Finally relaxing, Graham sighed. "We're going to have quite a story to tell our *kinner*, won't we, Mattie?" he murmured after a few moments.

"Indeed," she replied with a smile. "We finally started courting right after we survived a string of tornadoes touching down right near us. Matter of fact, I can't think of another man who would be thinking of love and marriage right now. It would be more the thing to concentrate on the land and house."

"Oh, I don't think so. I think this is the best time of all to think of the future. After all, it could have just been taken away from us."

She felt his lips kiss her brow. "That is true."

Still imagining how they would tell their children about this special day, Mattie added, "Of course, we'll have to remind our *kinner* that we didn't rush into anything."

"We certainly didn't do that," he said drily.

Ignoring his quip, she added, "I'll tell them how we've been friends forever. And that you helped me with cancer, too."

"And that you believed in me when so few other people did."

Mattie knew he was thinking of Jenna and her lies. "I didn't have a choice. I know the kind of man you are."

"Well, I don't see the need to tell our sons and daughters all that. I'm just going to say that the Lord must have meant for us to be together. After all, we must have survived all this for a reason."

"I couldn't agree with you more," Mattie said, thinking that Graham's words were very true.

Yes, she was a cancer survivor, but now that she thought about it, Mattie reckoned that each person that they knew most likely had a story to tell. Everyone was a survivor of something—whether it was a sickness or an injury. Or a survivor of a difficult relationship like Lucy's. Or an unhappy home like Jenna's, or a failed marriage like the Weavers' uncle John.

Other obstacles came to mind. Friends she knew who'd had a difficult time in school. Or who'd had terrible financial burdens. Or who fought depression.

Over and over, God seemed to be telling her, reminding her, that it wasn't what tragedies a person had to go through that was important. It was how a person overcame them.

Because even scarred and damaged, they were all worthwhile and worthy . . . and so deserving of His love.

And sometimes, Mattie realized, a person could even get something special, indeed. The wondrous love of a very best friend. The kind of love worth waiting for.

Rubbing her arm gently, Graham whispered in her ear. "Mattie, are you happy?"

She was wrapped in Graham's arms—in her fiancé's embrace. She had his love. Finally, she felt at peace with both her disease and her faith.

At that moment, Mattie didn't think it was possible to be happier. "Yes," she said simply. "Right now, right this minute, I am very happy, indeed."

Then she turned her head to his and kissed him. Because truly, there was really nothing more to say.

Epilogue

One month later

"Hurry now, Mattie," Katie urged as she pulled on her hand a little harder. "You're gonna make us late."

Mattie let herself be tugged down the snow-covered path she knew almost as well as the back of her hand. But though she didn't mind being led, she couldn't resist teasing her young sister-in-law a little bit. "Do you really think they'll start without us?"

"They might," Katie replied, her eyes solemn.

"Watch your tongue, child," Mrs. Weaver warned. "It's not your place to be telling Mattie what to do."

"I know, but—"

"Daughter. Settle down, now. And don't pull Mattie so

hard. She could slip and fall and we'd be very sad about that, *jah?*"

Her mouth now tightly shut, Katie nodded.

Mattie watched in amusement as Katie swallowed and tried not to talk . . . until it looked as though she was about to burst. "It's all right," she said, squeezing Katie's hand. "I'm excited, too."

"Promise?"

"I promise."

Katie exhaled. Then, with a satisfied smile, dropped Mattie's hand and scampered a few feet ahead.

"Oh, I tell you, Mattie. Sometimes I think the Lord gave me Katie just to give me exercise."

Mattie chuckled as she noticed that Mary Weaver—her new mother-in-law—wasn't cross as much as exasperated. "Katie is a bundle of energy. All morning, I've been trying to figure out who she takes after the most. Who do you think? Calvin, Loyal, or Graham?"

As they continued down the path toward Mattie's old home, Mary pondered. "That would be hard to say. None of the boys were as rambunctious as this one tiny girl. She seems to have more energy than the three of them combined. But if I had to choose, I would say she's closest to Calvin."

"Calvin?" That surprised Mattie. "I always thought of Calvin as being so fatherly."

"He wasn't fatherly and so responsible until his father went up to heaven. But, see, Calvin is my confident one. He was never afraid to go out in the world and explore. Katie is like that."

Mattie supposed Mary's reflections held merit. Calvin was confident—and Katie had that in spades. As they approached the halfway spot between her home and the Weavers', she tapped the fence. "It's always a good thing when I see this point. There have been times when I've been either too cold or hot, or so plain tired that I was sure I couldn't take much more of the walk."

Mrs. Weaver chuckled. "I've felt that a time or two." Her eyes narrowed as she saw Katie scamper off to the left, where there was enough of a gap that it was possible to see the road.

Mattie jumped when Katie whistled and waved merrily to a passing buggy.

"Hiya Mr. Yoder!"

"*Gut matin*, Katie!" he called back. "We'll see you soon, *jah*?"

"Uh-huh!"

After they directed Katie back to the path, Mary clucked her tongue. "Actually, perhaps I was wrong. Our Katie has a good amount of Loyal's characteristics, too. All his life, Loyal never met a stranger."

Thinking of Loyal's easy smile, and the way he always had a kind word for most everyone, Mattie agreed. "I don't think Katie's ever met a stranger, either. Ella says Katie now knows more people at the library than she does."

"I wouldn't doubt that. Seeing how Katie scampers about, I've always been thankful that we live in a place like Jacob's Crossing. Here, no one is a stranger for long."

That was true. Jacob's Crossing was a town filled with friends, not strangers. Everyone knew each other and their past, too, which was for better or worse, Mattie decided.

Boy, but the gossips had given Graham a time of it. For a while there, he'd hardly done anything but go to work and stay at home, he was so disappointed by their censure.

However, the community also did much for its members, too. When she thought of the hundreds of fried pies the town's ladies had made to help with her medical bills, selling them at fairs and auctions and at charity shows, it truly boggled Mattie's mind.

In the distance, they could see her house now. Ever since she and Graham had announced their engagement, her father, Calvin, Loyal, and Graham had been busy adding on another wing to the house. In no time, her parents would move to the new section.

"Jacob's Crossing is certainly a special place. I can't imagine living anywhere else," Mattie said. "I've never, ever even thought about moving away."

"Neither have I. But, perhaps for people like my brother-in-law John, it is good some people do go for a time. He appreciates things here so much now."

"Most especially Mary and Abel," Mattie said with a smile.

John had married Mary in a quiet ceremony soon after the storm. Though none of them had ever said much about what had happened, it was obvious to all that something momentous had occurred during the storm. Now it was becoming a common thing to see the family of three together. Almost every morning, Mary would be at the donut house with John, working by his side to keep things neat and clean.

"It's still strange to see John dressed Plain," she murmured.

"I never thought he would actually become Amish, if you want to know the truth. I'm amazed he gets around in his buggy as well as he does."

"John told me Amos likes his old truck very much."

"He should. He got it for practically nothing. All he had to do was promise to take John back and forth to work."

"Oh, no!" Katie cried out, interrupting their discussion.

Dismayed, Mattie watched the little girl dart forward and crouch down on her knees.

Mary ran to Katie's side. "What did you find, child?"

"A rabbit. Its leg is hurt."

"*Jah.* That is a shame." Mary shook her head. "The poor hare."

When Mattie saw the animal, she felt her heart constrict. "It's just a baby. I hope it doesn't suffer too much longer."

"It won't," Katie said, scooping it up and gingerly cradling it in her apron. "We need to try and help it, don'tcha think?"

Mary looked at it warily. "I suppose so, though I have no idea how to help it, child."

Katie looked at her mom, her blue eyes wide and tear-filled. "But we can try?"

"Of course."

Seeing the little animal scared and shivering in Katie's

arms made Mattie's heart break. She felt sorry for the rabbit, and sorry for Katie, too. It was never easy to see something so sweet get hurt or pass on to heaven.

Staring down at the bunny, Katie said, "Mamm, we're almost there. Can I hurry and go find Graham? He'll know what to do."

"Of course," Mary said with a bemused smile. When they could only see the faint outline of Katie's skirts, Mary said, "Well, I stand corrected. Perhaps she's most like her brother Graham."

"Truly? I've never seen him rescue rabbits."

"You might not remember, but Graham did when he was small." Looking satisfied, Mary nodded. "Yes, Graham has always had a tender heart. That boy of mine has always cared about others, and yearned to make them better."

Just like he'd done with her, Mattie realized. Time and again, he'd been there for her. He'd been someone she could count on.

And when he wasn't sure if his efforts were doing any good, he'd reached out and tried harder. Yes, Graham was always trying to do the right thing, even when it was hard. "He's a good man. I'm lucky."

"He is a good one. But he's lucky to have you, too," Mary said. "Don't forget that it takes two of you to make something special. And that's what you have, Mattie. A love that is special and true."

Two more steps brought them to the clearing. And there, in the cold January air, were all their family and friends. The moment she and Mary stepped into Graham's line of vision, his eyes lit up.

"Finally," he teased. "I told Katie either my new wife has very slow feet or she has very fast ones."

"Katie is fast. I am certainly not slow."

With a grin, he pulled her close and kissed her brow. "Of course not. Let it never be said that Mattie Weaver can't hold her own."

"How's the rabbit?"

He shrugged. "Katie and I put it in a box filled with a quilt Ella found. There's not much we can do for it besides keep it comfortable."

"Poor Katie."

Graham kissed her brow again. "Oh, she'll be all right. I told her that it might be the hare's time for heaven. She seemed okay with that notion."

"Come on, you two," Calvin called out. "Stop your kissing and come to the front porch. It's cold out, and getting colder! I'm ready to go inside."

"Please, take your time," Lucy countered, with a sweet smile. "We are all fine."

"Speak for yourself," Loyal teased.

Mary clapped her hands. "I suppose it is up to me, once again, to get everyone on track. Gather round, everyone."

When Mattie's parents opened the door, they waved to her and Graham. "Mattie and Graham, welcome home. I tell you, I never thought this day would come."

"That we'd be moving in here?"

"That you'd finally see what had been right before our eyes for many years. That you two were always meant to be together."

Surrounded by the warm comfort of her family and

friends, Mattie turned to Graham. "What do you think, husband? Were we always meant to be together?"

Taking her hands, he squeezed them lightly. "Of course," he said. "I, for one, never had a doubt."

And with that, Graham Weaver guided his wife of one week into the house she grew up in, but would now be in charge of. Where she would have her children, and sip coffee with her sisters-in-law, and give thanks.

And at night, after the sun was set and the world around them was quiet, she knew she'd look at him and smile.

And know that everything was truly right in her world. Right there, in her little town of Jacob's Crossing. Thanks be to God.

Dear Readers,

When I began this series, I wanted to push myself a little bit. The Sugarcreek books felt like warm hugs to me. I loved writing about two close families and their relationships. But I missed writing about edgier topics . . . and edgier people. I wanted to write about people who might look like they've got everything figured out and are doing just fine . . . but inside they really aren't.

I wanted to write about people like Mattie Lapp.

From the moment I wrote the scene in *The Caregiver* where Mattie first greets Lucy in her living room, I knew Mattie had my heart. I loved her friendship with Graham. I loved how she struggled with her faith. And I loved how very strong she became. She's a true survivor to me.

Now Jenna was another story! When I decided to make her lie to Graham, I just didn't know if she was ever going to be worthy. But then I started remembering some of the mistakes I've made over the years. I've made plenty! That's when I decided, for me, Jenna was certainly what God's Grace is all about. He nurtures and embraces all of us, even when we don't always deserve it. Without fail, our Lord finds good in us all.

Once again, another series is complete! I sincerely hope you enjoyed the Families of Honor series. I truly loved writing about Calvin, Loyal, Graham, and their uncle John. And Katie, and their Wal-Mart–loving mother. I enjoyed the Kaffi Haus, with its never-ending supply of donuts, and the tree-lined sidewalks of Jacob's Crossing. I hope you, too, found a character or a place in the series that you liked just as much.

At the end of this book is an excerpt from *Christmas in Sugarcreek*. Oh, this novel is a joy to write! I'm having a lot of fun checking in with Lilly and Robert and Caleb and Anson . . . and I have to say that Judith's romance with Ben just might be one of the most romantic stories I've ever written.

Please look for the book's release in October 2011.

Finally, no reader letter would be complete without conveying my thanks. Thanks to all the folks at HarperCollins for doing *so much*. Thank you for your edits and your advice. For your enthusiasm and your expertise. Thanks for setting up interviews and making the most beautiful covers! I feel so very lucky to be a part of such a wonderful publishing company.

Thank you to my agent, Mary Sue Seymour, for being everything she is. As always, I'm so thankful for my husband Tom, who drives me to research trips, waits patiently while I look at Amish quilts . . . and hardly ever complains when I forget to do the laundry. And most especially, thank you to all of you who read my books. You're the reason I get up in the morning. I'm so grateful for you all.

With God's blessings and my thanks,

Shelley Shepard Gray

10663 Loveland-Madeira Rd. #167
Loveland, Ohio 45140

Questions for Discussion

1. When I read the following verse from 2 Corinthians, I knew it was the perfect verse to guide me while writing this book. I liked how honest the verse was— that even long ago people still struggled with such emotions and actions. Is there a sin or a flaw in your life that keeps you from being the way God wants you to be?

I'm afraid that maybe when I come that you will be different from the way I want you to be, and that I'll be different from the way you want me to be. I'm afraid that there might be fighting, obsession, losing your temper, competitive opposition, back-stabbing, gossip, conceit, and disorderly conduct.

—2 Corinthians 12:20

2. I particularly loved the character of Mattie Lapp. I appreciated how her journey through cancer had ups

and downs . . . as well as moments of joy and true heart-ache. Have you, or anyone you know, gone through a cancer battle? What were some of the emotions that you or they went through?

3. Graham's faith and honor were tested in this novel. He realizes that until Jenna spread a lie about him, his faith had really never been tested. Do you think this is a fair assessment? Does everyone need to go through a difficult time in order to feel strong in his or her faith?

4 Jenna Yoder was a difficult character for me at first. However, I grew to like and even respect her. To me, she personified God's grace. She repented and asked forgiveness from both Graham and Chris, and therefore had her own happy ending. Was this enough?

5. Mary Zehr had her hands full with her son, Abel. Her struggles with her child reminded me a bit of some of the challenges I faced with my kids when they were twelve and thirteen. How do you think Abel's relation-ship with John will help both of them heal?

6. In *The Protector*, John must choose whether Jayne or Mary is right for him. In *The Survivor*, he must come to terms with his choice and change his life. Do you think he did things in the right order, or should he have decided whether or not to become Amish first?

7. Surviving was the obvious theme for this book. Not only did Mattie survive cancer, but Graham survived having his reputation stained, Jenna survived facing the truth—and its consequences—and all of them survived a storm. I believe we are all "survivors" of something. . . . What have you survived?

8. This Amish proverb seemed to fit this novel perfectly:

We value the light more fully after we've come through the darkness.

What "light" do you now value more fully than you used to?

Turn the page for an exciting preview of
Shelley Shepard Gray's next book,

Christmas in Sugarcreek

On sale October 2011

Ten days until Christmas
5:45 P.M.

"Judith, are you sure you don't mind locking up tonight?" Joshua asked, guilt heavy in his tone. "I feel bad letting you close the store two nights in a row."

"You shouldn't. I don't mind staying late at all. That's what sisters are for, *jah*?"

When Josh continued to look doubtful, Judith Graber lifted her chin and forced a smile she didn't feel inside. "Come now, Gretta needs you. As does Will. Go on, or you're going to be late. You two have plans, don'tcha?"

"Nothing much. We're just getting together for supper with some other couples. You know, before things get too busy."

She knew Joshua was talking about Christmas get-togethers and other holiday parties. Every *frau* she knew was busy baking and cooking for the planned activities.

Being single, she was not. "Go now, Joshua. I'll be fine."

"I promise I'll close the rest of the week," he said as he shrugged on his coat.

Judith crossed her arms over her chest. "You better," she teased with a mock frown.

However, she doubted her *bruder* had even noticed her

expression. He'd already opened the wreath-decorated door and let it close behind him with a jingling of bells.

Through the store's large picture windows, Judith watched her brother weave in between two parked cars, almost knock into a woman carrying a wrapped package on the sidewalk, and then practically race toward his home.

His new home.

Just two months ago, he and Gretta had told the whole family that they were moving into a small house two blocks from the store. Living above their family's shop no longer made sense, especially with Gretta in a family way again.

Not a member of the Graber family disagreed with their decision.

But, of course, none of them had been prepared for the adjustments that would have to be made because Joshua was no longer on the premises at all times. Now they each had to take turns opening and closing the shop. Well . . . she, Joshua, and her father. *Mamm* was still too busy at home with the little ones to come in much, and Caleb had recently started at the brick factory. Anson was still a little too young to be of any real help.

So it fell on Judith to do the majority of the work. As always.

Because she was the steady one.

The reliable one.

More like the one who had no life, Judith thought wryly. While Joshua had been falling in love, and her brother Caleb had been struggling with his future, and even as

Anson wrestled with his own growing pains, she had held steady and had quietly done what was expected of her.

Everyone was appreciative, to be sure. But that didn't ease the restless ache that seemed to be growing inside.

Wistfully, Judith looked out the window at the gently falling snow, the wheel ruts in the lane, the road beyond that led . . . somewhere else.

She wished she, like Joshua, had somewhere to run to. Wished she had someone who was counting the minutes until they saw her again.

If only . . .

Realizing she'd been standing there in a daze, Judith slapped her hands on the counter. "If you're going to be so dreamy, you might as well be truthful about it," she said out loud. "You don't wish just for *someone*. You wish you had *a man, a sweetheart,* counting the minutes until he saw you again."

Her hollow laugh echoed through the empty store. A store that surely needed tending—and she knew from experience that wishes and dreams surely didn't get things done.

Since there were only five more minutes until closing time, she left her spot behind the counter and began her usual walk through the store. As she did so, she organized stock and picked up stray pieces of trash people had left behind. A child's toy, a gum wrapper. Grocery list.

The bells on the door jingled merrily, causing her to straighten.

"Hello?" a deep voice called out.

Well, of course, someone decided to come in. Now that

it was mere minutes before closing time. Irritation flowed through her as she straightened and, with her hands full of trash and a metal toy car, darted toward the front. "May I help you?" she called out.

Then skidded to a stop. Because right there in front of her was Benjamin Knox.

Recognition flashed in his eyes as he glanced her way. And then a long, slow smile spread. Knowing and too personal. "Judith Graber. Hi."

"Ben." She lifted her chin, pretending that she wasn't shocked to her core. Two years ago, Ben Knox had left Sugarcreek under a haze of disapproval. Gossips reported that he'd gone to Missouri to help some cousins on their dairy farm, but had, in truth, done little besides flirt with the girls.

She needed to remember that. Keeping her voice cool and even, she asked, "May I help you?"

Under his black hat's thick felt brim, his hazel eyes seemed to take in every inch of her. She felt his gaze's sweep as surely as if he'd run a hand right down her periwinkle dress, down her black apron, along her black stockings.

"*Nee,*" he said.

She couldn't remember what she'd asked him. "*Nee?*"

"No, I don't need your help," he said with an almost-smirk. "I'm not here for anything special. Just thought I'd look around for a few minutes."

Judith went cold. Not here for anything special? Was he purposely being rude, or was she being too sensitive?

Probably a bit of both.

Keenly aware of the tension she felt around Ben—that bit of unease she'd always felt around him—she cleared her throat. "Just to let you know, we're closing in one minute."

An eyebrow rose. "In exactly one minute? Then what happens? All customers get locked in?"

"Of course not!" Oh, but, of course, he was teasing her. "What I meant to say is that you should probably leave."

"Right now?" He turned around and stared at the clock above the door. The ridiculous clock with birds on the face instead of numbers. The clock that chirped on the hour, much to the amusement of her mother . . . and to her extreme annoyance.

Before she could answer, the clock struck six and chirped. When he grinned, she felt her cheeks heat. Wished she was absolutely anywhere else but here. With him. Alone in the store.

Ben Knox bit the inside of his cheek to keep from bursting out laughing.

It wasn't because of the clock—his aunt Becca had a large collection of handpainted birdhouses on a shelf in her kitchen. He was used to such silly items.

No, what had him tempted to laugh was the girl standing across from him. Standing as stiff and looking as ruffled as the fierce mother sparrow painted on the clock's face.

Though, of course, Judith Graber was far from being just a girl, and she was not drab at all. No, her bright blue eyes and lovely light brown hair with its streaks of auburn caught his eye like little else.

He found her exasperation with him amusing. And very

little had amused him in a long time. "I guess the cardinal's trill is my signal to leave?"

Her gaze seemed to give off sparks. *"Jah."*

He turned away, but a nagging question turned him back around. "Why are you working here so late, and all alone? I would've thought your husband would want you home by now."

"I work here because it's my family's store, of course." After a pause, she looked down at her hands clasping the countertop. "Besides, I'm not married."

"Are you courting?" It was rude of him to ask, but he couldn't help himself.

Raising her chin, Judith's lips pursed, just as if she was searching the air for the right words. At last, she sighed. *"Nee* . . . though it surely isn't any of your business."

Now it was his turn to be surprised. All his life, he'd thought of Judith Graber as being the ideal girl. She was lovely and kind and a hard worker—nothing like himself.

And she was loyal. Vividly, he recalled her standing up for her brothers any time someone ever threatened them, or put one of them down.

In short, she was the type of girl men like him never spent time with. She was too fine for Benjamin Knox, and everyone knew it.

For the first time, though, the thought made him sad. Like he'd missed his ride and was going to be reduced to waiting on a street corner for another person to pick him up—but no one was approaching.

"Why did you come back to Sugarcreek, Ben Knox?"

"Because it was time," he said, though it really told her

nothing. And told himself nothing, too. He'd come back because he was tired of Missouri and wanted to see his house before he put it on the market, even if the place where he'd grown up was full of hurt and bad memories.

When Judith still stared, all bright and beautiful, he forced himself to tell her the truth. Just this once.

"I wanted to come back and have Christmas in Sugarcreek. Just one last time." Because he'd told her too much, he winked. "Not that it's any of your business."

With that, he forced himself to turn. Opened the door. Walked right under the chirping bird clock, and away from the temptation that was Judith Graber.

The bitter cold felt like heaven.

In spite of her best efforts, she still was a terrible cook, Lilly Miller decided as she pulled the roast chicken out of the oven and set it on the counter. Grimacing, she examined it closely. Hoping, that under closer scrutiny, things were better than she thought.

However, they weren't. Without a doubt, she'd burned dinner. Again.

With a sigh, Lilly tugged on a wing. Instead of staying put, it pulled right off, just like it was relieved to be free of the burnt carcass. "I don't blame you, wing," she said out loud. "I'd escape this meal if I could, too. I've managed to ruin yet another meal. Now what am I going to feed Robert?"

For a moment, she stared at their house phone. It would be so easy to call her mom and ask for cooking help. But her mom was busy with baby Beth and certainly didn't need Lilly bugging her again.

With a wince, Lilly knew she'd asked her mother for help more times during the last two months than she had for the first eighteen years of her life.

Being married was not for sissies! Though she and Robert had been married for two months now, Lilly was still finding it challenging. First there were the adjustments to be made, living as a Mennonite. Then there were all the challenges of being newlyweds. And being married to a man who'd been married before—to the perfect woman.

More than any of that, she was finding it difficult to be worthy of a man like Robert. A man who'd given up practically everything for her. After all, she couldn't even roast a chicken properly. Or make decent mashed potatoes.

Or bake his favorite cake.

The fact of the matter was that sometimes when he left for work, Lilly wondered if he was glad to be away from her. She was young and impulsive and sometimes—okay, most of the time—spoke without thinking first.

Feeling even more depressed and annoyed with herself, she left the burnt offering and sat down at the kitchen table. Here it was, ten days before Christmas, and she'd promised him that she wouldn't buy him a gift. Instead, she was going to make him something—just like he'd promised he was going to make something for her. But the problem was, she wasn't crafty. She couldn't sew. Or cook all that well.

Okay. She couldn't cook at all.

As time marched closer to Christmas Day, a small knot of worry in her stomach seemed to grow bigger each day. She needed to make something wonderful for Robert for

Christmas—or face the horrible truth: Sooner or later, Robert Miller was going to regret marrying her.

Caleb Graber rolled his neck as he walked along the snowy sidewalk, half attempting to get the stiffness out of it from lifting dozens of palates of bricks at the factory, half in an effort to get mentally prepared to see Rebecca.

It was pretty much a fact—he was completely infatuated with Rebecca Yoder.

Of course, there was no way he was going to act too eager to see her. Even he knew that girls didn't like pushy, clingy men. But that's how he'd felt. Like there wasn't a moment during his day that he didn't want to be with her.

Which took him completely by surprise.

From the first moment he saw her at Mrs. Miller's, Caleb had been eager to see her again. After the year he'd had, constantly feeling a part of two worlds but never being a good match in either, the comfort he felt from being near Rebecca was a peace he couldn't deny. She always looked at him with acceptance. As if seeing him made her day.

Which was how he felt. However, he was afraid he'd scare her off if she knew just how much he was starting to realize he needed her. If she realized that he was thinking about scary things whenever he was around her. Things like courting and marriage.

Marriage! At seventeen!

Even thinking about that made him woozy. No, he was just going to have to play it cool.

With that in mind, he stomped up the snow-covered

stairs leading to the library and carefully schooled his features to look cool. Almost bored.

Before he could even open the front door and step inside, Rebecca walked right out. "Hi, Caleb."

Her eyes were shining, her wheat-colored hair as shiny and glossy as ever. And, just like that, he gave in and grinned as well. Being "cool" was overrated anyway. "Hi, Rebecca."

She already had on her black cloak and bonnet. "I didn't want you to have to wait long, so I'm all ready," she said by way of explanation.

"I wouldn't have minded waiting. I wouldn't have minded getting you at your house, either."

Her smile dimmed. "There was no need for you to go there. This was closer to your work."

Her words were true, but still Caleb felt awkward. So far, whenever he'd seen her, she had always insisted on meeting him someplace. It was almost like she never wanted him to see her house.

Or maybe it was that she didn't want him to meet her family?

"Rebecca, next time I'll come get you at your house, okay? I don't want your parents to think I have no manners."

"There's no need for you to do that."

"But—"

"I promise. They think you're fine," she said hurriedly. Leaning a little bit closer, her smile turned brighter. "Caleb, have I told you that I think it's so sweet of you to help me work on Christmas baskets?"

That was him, Mr. Sweet. Fact was, he would have helped her pick up snakes and spiders if that's what she wanted. "You have," he said, taking care to sound like he couldn't care less. "Besides, you need some help carrying everything."

"I do." When she paused at the top of the steps, Caleb reached out and held her elbow. Just to steady her. So she wouldn't trip or fall, of course.

When they reached the sidewalk, he still had his hand cupped around her elbow. Actually, his hand had crept up and was carefully holding her arm. When she looked into his eyes and blushed, he dropped his hand.

"Danke," she murmured. "The steps were a bit slick."

They paused, standing close together. Close enough for him to notice the little flecks of silver in her blue eyes. To see that there were five freckles, not six, that dusted her nose.

Close enough that if he leaned down just a little bit, he could brush his lips against her forehead. Or maybe even her cheek. Or maybe even . . .

Clearing his throat, he stepped back. "We better get going," he said. "It's too cold to just stand here."

"All right, Caleb," she said with a hint of a smile.

As they started walking—side by side but not touching—Caleb wondered how much longer he could go before he made a complete fool of himself and told her that he really liked her.

Before he leaned in and actually did kiss her.

Before he risked getting his heart stomped on while she laughed at him.

Hopefully none of that would happen until well past Christmas Day.

BOOKS BY
SHELLEY SHEPARD GRAY

FAMILIES OF HONOR

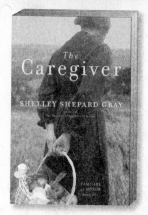

THE CAREGIVER
978-0-06-202061-1 (paperback)

A chance encounter changes the lives of a young widow and a broken-hearted man. While they try to forget each other, neither can disregard the bond they briefly shared.

THE PROTECTOR
978-0-06-202062-8 (paperback)

Ella Troyer feels bitterness towards the man who bought her family's farm once her father passes away. What she does not know is that he secretly hopes Ella will occupy this house again . . . as his wife.

THE SURVIVOR
978-0-06-202063-5 (paperback)

In the final book in the Families of Honor series, young Amish woman Mattie Troyer has healed from the cancer that nearly took her life . . . but can she find the man who can mend her lonely heart?